Pulphouse

FICTION MAGAZINE

Issue Zero, November 2017

Edited by
Dean Wesley Smith

A WMG Publishing Inc. Magazine

Pulphouse

FICTION MAGAZINE

TABLE OF CONTENTS

SHORT STORIES

Pulphouse Fiction Magazine

A WMG Publishing Inc. Magazine

Publisher
Allyson Longueira

Associate Publisher
Gwyneth Gibby

Director of Sales
Billy Reese

Executive Editor
Kristine Kathryn Rusch

Editor
Dean Wesley Smith

Managing Editor
Josh Frase

Pulphouse Fiction Magazine Issue #0

Published by WMG Publishing Inc.
Cover and interior design copyright © 2017 WMG Publishing Inc.
Cover art copyright © by Raycan/Dreamstime

From the Editor's Desk

Dean Wesley Smith

BACK HOME AGAIN

"Knock knock. Anyone home?"

Silence.

"Hello? Anyone here?"

The hinges squeaked and complained as I pushed open the old front door to what had once been a fun place full of stories and art.

Pulphouse.

The big party room looked sort of the same, yet different with most everything covered in dust from the twenty-one years of waiting. The light was low. Everything felt gray and old.

Would it be possible to bring the fun and attitude back?

It didn't feel possible to me.

I remembered the parties, the fun, the excitement, the great stories from all those years before, now mostly forgotten memories packed away in boxes and haunted by old dead friends. It seemed suddenly that twenty-one years might just be too many to overcome.

I stood in the center of the big room that had been Pulphouse, doubting the very idea of trying to bring life back to the place.

Then, from hidden corners and side doors, hundreds of people jumped forth shouting "Welcome Back!"

Suddenly the dust was gone, the light filled the space and the party had started all over again.

Pulphouse had returned, not dead, not even dusty, ready for a second life.

Who knew that it had just been sleeping?

That is what it felt like deciding to bring back *Pulphouse Fiction Magazine* and then having the Kickstarter campaign for the magazine be such a success.

Wow! Just wow!

The party has started again and more than anything I want to thank everyone holding this Issue Zero right now for deciding to join the fun and craziness.

So what is Pulphouse actually about?

Quality fiction, first and foremost. Fiction that feels strange, a little off, a little attitude. Sometimes a lot of attitude.

Just read the stories in this Issue Zero to see what I mean.

The magazine, starting with Issue One, will have both original stories and reprint stories. This Issue Zero only has reprint stories, but I will wager you will have not read most of them.

Back all those decades ago, Pulphouse Publishing always did an Issue Zero to test out new book lines or magazines. The original incarnation of this magazine had an Issue Zero. I knew we needed to do another to test out the layout, and discover where problems in this new world of publishing might be.

What a difference a few decades make.

Let me lay out a comparison between the world of publishing of the original run and this world now. The differences are amazing.

In 1991 when this magazine started, we printed off Pagemaker files from a MacPlus with a whopping 20k storage. We then cut and hand-pasted the pages onto master sheets and delivered the master sheets to a web-based printer sixty miles away (in the snow, uphill both ways).

The covers were printed by a different printer and the two were combined and stapled (saddle-stitched).

We would load up huge boxes full of magazines to take them to the Pulphouse building and then many people would pack them into envelopes and do all the postage-stuff required at that point to ship magazines.

We did that process for 20 issues if you count Issue Zero.

Now, with the new incarnation, everything is laid out on the computer, sent directly to the printer electronically, and that's it. The electronic subscriptions are laid out and sent directly to subscribers.

For the first run in 1991, we sent copies to newsstands just in the US to sell. Today the paper and electronic copies of this magazine will be available for sale in most online bookstores all over the world.

In the old days, the copies vanished after a month or so. In this new world you can buy a copy of any issue long after it has come out.

In other words, this new world is so much better and easier.

Who is behind Pulphouse Fiction Magazine?

No magazine of this scale could ever be done by one person. Not possible. And certainly not me.

I am the editor, the guy who picked the stories way back in 1991 for the first incarnation and I am still picking them today. I am the voice of the magazine.

Back in 1987, Kristine Kathryn Rusch and I decided to start Pulphouse Publishing with an anthology series called *Pulphouse: A Hardback Magazine* that Kris edited. That got us many award nominations and we even won the World Fantasy Award at one point.

That original idea grew into a good-sized company with Debra Gray Cook, now Debra De Noux, as a major center figure. At one point, Pulphouse filled a two-story office building with employees and, except for this magazine, we pioneered "on-demand" printing for our books.

Pulphouse Publishing Inc. shut down and dissolved in 1996.

Years went by.

In 2010, Kris and I decided it was time for us to jump back into our own publishing company again. We started

WMG Publishing, which became a full corporation in 2012.

Now WMG Publishing employs nine people, has three brick-and-mortar stores, and has over 700 titles in print.

WMG Publishing is run completely by Allyson Longueira, the CEO and publisher. Besides being a brilliant publisher, she is also a great editor and a brilliant cover designer. Allyson is the heart and soul of WMG Publishing.

Josh Frase gets to step into the role of managing editor of this magazine. He will not only help on the subscription side, but be in charge of the website we hope to bring up into an interactive and fun place as time goes along.

Plus Billy Reese, as director of sales for WMG Publishing, and Gwyneth Gibby, associate publisher, will help keep the magazine headed in the right direction.

So for this magazine, this incarnation, I am the editor and voice and Kris uses a firm hand to keep me on track. Kris and I weren't sure we should start this party again. But now we are glad we took the chance and opened the doors back up.

It really wouldn't be possible without the wonderful support your readers and subscribers have shown already. That old dusty memory of a project long buried in the past now feels fresh and alive and ready to go.

I hope you enjoy all the wonderful stories in this test issue as much as I did remembering them and putting them all together.

Onward. It's going to be fun.

Kent Patterson was a polio survivor and one of the nicest and smartest men I have ever had the pleasure to meet. Those of you lucky enough to be young enough to not remember the polio epidemic and the vaccine that saved us, do go look it up. A nasty disease.

Kent's body was ravaged by his days with polio, yet it never seemed to slow him down. As one of the longest-lived survivors, Kent decided to take up fiction writing and he did it with his usual charm and wit and incredible drive.

Everyone who has read a Kent Patterson story has a different favorite. This is mine. I published it in issue #17 of the original Pulphouse Magazine *in 1994 and a short time later Kent finally lost his lifetime fight with polio. But during his short stint writing fiction, he had sold to* F&SF, Analog, Pulphouse, *and many other magazines.*

And thanks go to Jerry Oltion for doing the fantastic work of keeping Kent's wonderful stories in print and available after two decades.

Spud Wrangler
Kent Patterson

WITH THE SUDDENNESS OF A RIFLE SHOT, a desert thunderclap rumbled and rolled across the Idaho plains. Here and there scattered rain drops fell, kicking up tiny puffs of dust where they hit the dry ground.

"That there were a close 'un," drawled old Parley McKonky. Clucking gently, he reined in his horse. "Now, now, there, there," he said, patting the horse's neck. "Just a little desert storm, and it ain't agoin' to eat you." The horse trembled, its nostrils flared and its eyes wide with fear.

Brig Clark's horse stood placidly as a cardboard cow. Couldn't even hear it thunder, Brig thought with disgust. Of course they always gave the oldest horse to the newest wrangler. A fourteen-year-old boy got treated nothing better than a baby when wranglers were concerned. He glanced at Parley. The old man's face was as wrinkled as a outcropping of lava. Hat off, head raised, he sniffed the air. So did his horse.

"Boy, there's trouble brewing." He looked at Brig. "You're going to earn a wrangler's pay today. That lightning hit close. Real close. Somewhere around Twin Missionaries Springs. Now tell me what you smell."

Brig sniffed. He smelled mostly horse, sage brush, and maybe a touch of grungy underwear. He took off his hat and tried again. There was something else. The musty scent of desert rain. And something else yet, a faint aroma which reminded him of his mother's kitchen.

"That's the smell a spud wrangler fears most, son." Parley gave him a keen glance. "That smell, son, is baked potato." He raised his hand for silence. "Put your ear to the ground, boy, and listen."

Brig climbed down from his horse. Holding the reins in one hand, he lay flat. Raindrops speckled the dirt with little brown craters. Brig placed his ear on the ground and strained to hear. He heard leather reins creaking, the hoarse breathing of his horse. A hoarse horse, he thought wildly.

Then he heard it. Not a sound, really, but a trembling in the ground.

"That's a stampede, son, and it's coming our way." Parley lit a cigarette, the smell of tobacco permeating the air. "They're coming our way, and they're coming hard. And there ain't one damned thing between them and Snake River Canyon but you and me."

An image of Snake River Canyon flashed through Brig's mind. You popped over a little ridge and there it was, a sheer cliff of black lava dropping four hundred feet straight down. He'd seen a horse fall off it once. Ants had eaten the remains. There wasn't a piece big enough to interest anything else.

"That herd's the entire year's crop." Parley looked at Brig. "If the panic spreads to the main herd, which it will if we don't stop it—," his voice dropped off. "Well, it'll be a mighty long, hungry winter in Idaho. We got maybe two hours."

"But I don't have a watch."

"Take a look at where the sun is," said Parley, pointing to the sun which just now burst out from behind the storm cloud. "See where it's going to hit Hanged Man Spike?" Brig looked. Hanged Man Spike was a lava outcropping that stabbed into the Western sky like a broken tooth. "By the time the sun hits the Spike, the herd will hit the Canyon."

"What we going to do?" Brig asked, ashamed at the quaver in his voice.

"We got us a few minutes to spare. I'm finishing my smoke. You, well, boy, if you got to go, you better go now. You might not get a better chance all day."

Brig looked around for a rest room, or even a tall bush. Nothing for miles except tumbleweeds, scanty patches of cheat grass, and knee high sage brush stretching off in all directions in rows as neatly as if it had been planted. He took a deep breath, unzipped, and peed standing in the open desert like a man, leaving a miniature Snake River Canyon in the dust.

He remounted his horse, pulled an Idaho Spud candy bar from his saddle bag, split the wrapper with a single thrust of his thumbnail like his daddy had taught him, and began to eat. The rich, chocolate marshmallow taste mixed with the flavor of horse and desert dust.

Now the air reeked with the smell of baked potato.

The ground trembled. Brig munched his candy bar. Control yourself, he told himself. Real wranglers don't sweat. He stole a glance at Parley, puffing his smoke calmly as if the stampede were a radio show on a station he couldn't get.

Now the trembling in the ground shook the air. Parley's horse pranced back and forth, rolling the whites of its eyes and sawing its mouth against the bit. Even Brig's horse lifted its head and whinnied, staring off to the north where a low ridge of lava blocked the view. "Finally something woke you up," Brig whispered to the horse. "I thought you was dead."

The rumbling became a roar. Now even Parley stared at the giant clouds

Don't Miss Issue One...
Coming In January.

www.pulphousemagazine.com
All Issues Also Available at Your Favorite Bookstore

of dust billowing up in the North. He glanced at Brig. "You ready, son?" he shouted over the roar.

Not trusting himself to speak, Brig nodded.

"Remember, boy. We're all there is between the herd and the canyon. We don't turn 'em, you know the only thing we'll need?"

A brown tidal wave of potatoes burst over the low lava ridge. A flood of Idaho Number One Bakers the size of bread loaves, tumbling end over end, eyes white with panic.

Parley's last few words died in the thunder of the stampede. But the joke was ancient, and Brig knew it well. If the herd went over the canyon wall, all a spud wrangler needed was five hundred tank cars of gravy.

"Ki yi yee yee, roll you bakers roll!" Parley shouted the traditional cry of the spud wrangler. His horse shot forward like a cannonball. Through the last of his candy bar, Brig tried shouting too, but his mouth was so dry he only succeeded in spraying himself with chocolate marsh-mallow and bits of coconut. He glanced at the hordes of potatoes now streaming through every gap in the lava ridge and rolling down the plain as irresistibly as Noah's flood. His horse whinnied in fear and, in spite of Brig tightening the reins, it shied backwards, away from the thun-der of the onrushing spuds. "You're mak-ing a coward of me, horse," Brig said.

But it was him making a coward of himself. He whose sweaty hands slipped

> *If the herd went over the canyon wall, all a spud wrangler needed was five hundred tank cars of gravy.*

on the reins, whose breath came short, whose pulse pounded like Satan's own trip hammer in his brain. He tried to yell a "Ki yi yi" but the sound turned to dust and chocolate in his mouth.

Spur your horse, spur you coward, he screamed in his mind. But try as he might, his spurs seemed to have a will of their own. Unbidden, tears sprang to his eyes. Bless the Lord that Parley was half-way across the flat and couldn't see.

Turn back. Get out of here.

For a second he decided to give the horse its head, race away from that implacable, thundering mass of spuds, get away and live.

But, even as his horse turned, an im-age flashed through his mind. The wran-glers gathered around the chuck wagon after a hard day's work. Tired, aching, maybe hurt, but each knowing he'd done his share, that he'd never let a partner down. The Idaho sunset, turning the des-ert purple and pink, with maybe a single puff of cloud flaring gold in an empty sky. Night slipping across the desert plain, the camp fire crackling, smelling of sage. A couple of prime Idaho Number Ones turning on a spit, the comforting sound of male voices laughing, joking about big spuds and beautiful women.

If he turned away now, he would nev-er be one of them. Oh, no one would say a thing. Not by a whisper, not by a hint, would anyone breathe the word "cow-ard." No one would have to.

But in the morning when he woke up he'd find a potato peeler by his bed. There was nothing written down, but the rule was iron. Men herded spuds. Cowards were only fit for making french fries.

Brig closed his eyes. "Ki yi yee yee," he squeaked. He opened his eyes and shouted louder. "Ki yi yee yee." Louder yet! He spurred his horse. It shied. He spurred harder. "Ki yi yee yee!" he screamed at the top of his voice. "Roll on, you bakers." Hooves drummed on the dry desert dust as his horse headed for the rampaging herd of potatoes.

Minutes turned into hours, days, as Brig charged down the long lines of the potato herd. Screaming, shouting, waving his arms and brandishing his long black spud masher, he and Parley drove the huge lead spuds back. If these turned, the herd followed, rumbling along like a freight train. But sometimes the lead spuds resisted even the masher, and then Brig would resort to the spud wrangler's greatest and most ancient weapon, holding his arms overhead in the mystical half circle that for reasons unknown drove terror into the very starch of even the toughest tuber. That always worked, though no spud wrangler knew why.

Dust billowed high into the sky, the few sprinkles of rain long since dried out in the blazing summer sun. Brig pulled his bandanna over his nose and mouth. Dust covered him until he and his horse looked like some grey monster out of the past.

But the herd turned. Gradually, the lead spuds circled, sweeping their followers into a gigantic spud whirlpool. Hoarse with shouting, his face caked with dust, Brig felt like a hero, a genuine spud wrangler at last.

In the distance, he saw Parley riding up fast, waving his arms and yelling words lost in the thunder of the spud herds.

So what now, Brig thought. The work's nearly over. He couldn't make out what Parley was saying. "How we doing?" he shouted as Parley came up.

"Run for your life!" Parley shouted.

Only then did Brig notice the rumbling of the spud herds had taken on a deeper, throbbing, more menacing sound. He looked to the north. Over the ridge came a solid wall of bakers which blotted out the sky. Brig had never seen spuds panicked like that, climbing on top of each other to get away. He knew this could only be the main herd, the livelihood of half the state. It was a spud avalanche, a city of spuds set up on edge and stampeding across the Idaho plains. Parley streaked towards the high ground of Mormon Butte. Brig followed.

He didn't have to urge his horse to run. However old and tired, she was a spud horse and knew all too well what that ground-shaking roar meant.

Brig didn't look back. He could sense that towering mass looming over him.

A shadow slipped over his head. The potato herd blocked out the sun. Now he was on the welcome slopes of Mormon Butte. Higher! He had to get higher up the slope to be safe, "Come on, old gal," he urged on his horse. "Just a few more steps." He glanced back as the great wave of potatoes crested high over his head. "Jump for your life!" he shouted, driving in his spurs. With one great convulsive heave, his horse leaped just as truckloads of spuds smashed down.

"Good horse, great horse!" She stood shivering, foam spuming down her flanks. High on Mormon Butte, they were safe for the moment. Brig watched the masses of spuds surging by. Thousands had been broken or mashed. The air reeked with hot starch. The horse's flanks rose and fell.

"Parley!" Brig shouted. Parley lay flat on the ground on his back. One hand held his horse's reins. Brig dismounted, leading his horse, and ran up to Parley.

Parley stared at the blank sky. One arm jutted out at an impossible angle. A trickle of blood ran from his mouth.

"Parley, you're hurt."

"Don't mind me, kid. Mind the herd."

"But there's too many of them."

Parley coughed, and stared at the sky. Then he spoke.

"They're scared, son. Just plain blind panicked. And a scared spud can't see beyond the sprouts of its eyes. It's barely an hour now till they hit Snake River Canyon. Take my horse. It's faster. You've got to stop them. Everything's up to you now." Parley turned his head.

"What do I do, Parley? How can I get them to turn?" He looked down at the ocean of spuds. Nothing could turn that herd.

"Only one way to turn a herd of scared spuds, son," Parley said. "Get there first and find something to scare them worse than the lightning did. Now git. Go."

Without a word, Brig mounted Parley's horse and spurred along Mormon Ridge. The ridge, he knew, ran southeast a couple of miles, then petered out. He had to flank the spuds, run along the ridge until he could get in front of them, then drop down to the plain. He glanced over his shoulder at the sun. Hanged Man's Spike nearly touched the round red disk.

He could get ahead of the spuds, but then what? How could a lone boy turn a herd that skunked even real wranglers? The horse's hoofbeats drummed in his head like some mocking song. You got to find something to scare them worse than the lightning did.

But what? Certainly not a lone boy on a horse. They'd trample him to pink gravy. What scared a spud? What could possibly be worse for a spud than being baked in a lightning bolt? It had to be something big, something terrible.

Brig tried to remember the stories his daddy had told him, stories handed down by spud wranglers since the earliest days. Many of the legends predated the arrival of the white man, and more often than not made no sense in the modern world. Stories about how the Quetzal flew the spirit of the potato northward from South America, or how an ancient tuber tribe went mad in the canyonlands of what was now Utah. Brig had never been interested in his father's stories, but now he wished he had paid more attention. There might have been a tidbit of wisdom in there that could help him now.

He could barely hear himself think over the roar of the stampede and the hoofbeats of Parley's horse, but he noticed with grim satisfaction that he was gaining on the herd. He could beat them to the canyon, but what could he do once he got there?

There was one thing that always scared a potato: the half-circle of arms over the head. No one knew why it struck such fear into the hearts of spuds, but its effect was undeniable. It was such a primal image to a spud that any kind of half-circle would make them skittish. Something as simple as an arched gateway could keep a ranch house's yard free of even the boldest spud.

Yes, the half-circle would scare a spud, but this herd was so vast that most of the spuds would never see him making the sign. He needed something bigger, and in the failing evening light, he needed something that would shine out like a beacon to the advancing herd.

There was only one chance. Joe Handy's construction crew. Brig had seen him working at the new Big Falls market just yesterday. He'd be working today. Brig glanced back at Hanged Man's Spike. If there were only more time!

He had managed to flank the herd. Coming down on to the plain, Brig knew what he had to do. The herd would follow the plain to hit Snake River Canyon about three miles from Big Falls City. He had to get to the City first, grab Joe Handy, then get there before them. There wasn't a second to waste.

His mouth set, Brig spurred towards Big Falls City.

***

"MAN, YOU'RE PLUM LOCO!" Under the dust, Joe's face showed white as a sheet. Actually whiter than a spud wrangler's sheets. Standing on the bed of his ancient Ford pickup, Joe tightened the connections to a portable generator. "I'm on duty, and I ain't supposed to leave my place. And this," he pointed to the contents of the truck, "is supposed to run 24 hours a day."

"Yeah, well, get it running now," Brig snapped. In the west, Hanged Man's Spike speared the bottom of the sun.

"I ain't staying here. Them spuds'll push you right over the edge of the canyon."

The air shook with the rumble of the advancing spuds. A column of dust marked the herd. In maybe five minutes they'd be here. But the herd was tiring. That was good.

"You just get that equipment working. I'll be the one throwing the switch." Brig wiped his brow. Involuntarily, he glanced over the canyon edge. Four hundred feet straight down to a black rock floor. Far below he could see buzzards wheeling in

"You rustled my spuds. I can smell baker on your breath."

the updraft. From here, they looked no bigger than gnats.

This had better work. If it didn't, mashed potato city, with Brig on the bottom. Bring on the gravy.

He looked back up just as the electrician's broad back disappeared over a lava outcropping to the east.

Damn! What a coward. For a second, Brig considered joining him. Then he jumped into the bed of the pickup and slapped Parley's horse on its rump. "Run for your life, boy." The horse bolted after the electrician. Brig hated to see it go, but if this didn't work and he went over the side of the canyon, the boss would resent losing a good horse.

Suddenly the spud herd burst into view. Not as tired as Brig had hoped. In front of them, frightened jackrabbits and a lone coyote scampered.

Brig pressed the start button on the generator motor. Damn. Nothing. The wall of spuds came nearer. Now Brig could smell the starch.

Forcing himself to stay calm, Brig tested each wire on the generator. Now the thundering spuds drowned all other sounds. Running at full speed, a jackrabbit thudded into the side of the pickup. It dropped to lie quivering in the dust.

A wire came loose in Brig's hand. Bad connection. He glanced up, and gasped. All he could see was a wall of spuds. His sweaty fingers shoved the wire into place, and he jabbed the starter button.

The generator motor whirred, coughed, and quit.

The reek of hot starch and potato peels clogged Brig's nostrils. The first few spuds splattered against the side of the pickup.

Brig jabbed the start button again.

The motor whirred, coughed, then roared into life. Quickly Brig flipped the light switch to "on."

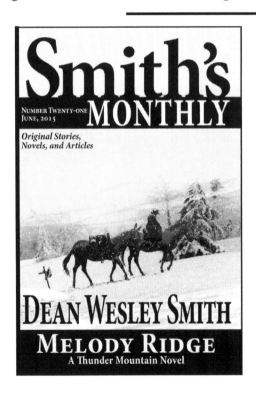

From the very edge of Snake River Canyon, two gigantic golden arches lit up the Idaho sky. They were just yellow marquee lights on a wire frame, but they stood out stark and bold against the blackness beyond.

The oncoming herd recoiled. In a twisting, seething mass of brown, spuds bounded backwards, piling on top of the herds still streaming in from the plain. A mountain of spuds reared into the sky, looming over the low plain like some new volcanic cone. Then, gradually, the mass turned on itself, the herd streaming back north, northeast, northwest—any direction to escape those terrible glittering golden arches.

Exhausted, Brig stepped down off the pickup and lay down in the warm starch-smelling dust. He closed his eyes, wondering if spud wranglers would ever learn why the occult and archetypal symbol struck such fear into the hearts of spuds.

"Brig. Ya OK, son?"

Brig opened his eyes. Parley stood over him, bandages covering his chest. His arm lay in a sling.

"Parley. I thought you was dead."

"Not hardly, son."

"How are the..."

"The spuds? Well, I reckon they're about ten miles out in the desert by now, and a tireder and more docile pack of tubers you ain't never going to see in your life." Parley grinned. "Let the tenderfeet and the little boys round 'em up." He pulled a silver flask and an Idaho Spud candy bar from his saddle bag. "We wranglers got some serious resting to do."

~

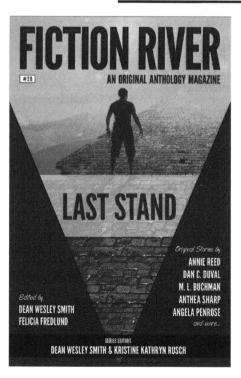

I have been a fan of Nina Kiriki Hoffman's fiction since the day we challenged each other back when we were first starting out as young writers.

This story had become legend by the time Kris bought it for Pulphouse: The Hardback Magazine *back in the late 1980s. Nina had read it aloud at a few conventions, never being able to keep a straight face, which caused the audience to react and it went from there. (Nina has an infectious giggle so that when she laughs, it is impossible to not laugh with her.)*

Nina has written hundreds and hundreds of wonderful short stories over the decades as well as many highly acclaimed fantasy and young adult novels. You can't go wrong when picking up a Nina Kiriki Hoffman story or novel.

Savage Breasts
Nina Kiriki Hoffman

I WAS ONLY A LONELY LEFTOVER ON THE TABLE OF LIFE. No one seemed interested in sampling me.

I was alone that day in the company cafeteria when I made the fateful decision which changed my life. If Gladys, the other secretary in my boss's office and my usual lunch companion, had been there, it might never have happened, but she had a dentist appointment. Alone with the day's entree, Spaghetti-O's, I sought company in a comic book I found on the table.

In the first blazing burst of inspiration I ever experienced, I cut out an ad on the back of the *Wonder Woman* comic book. "The Insult that Made a Woman Out of Wilma," it read. It showed a hipless, flat-chested girl being buried in the sand and abandoned by her date, who left her alone with the crabs as he followed a bosomy blonde off the page. Wilma eventually excavated herself, went home, kicked a chair, and sent away for Charlotte Atlas's pamphlet, "From Beanpole to Buxom in 20 days or your money back." Wilma read the pamphlet and developed breasts the size of breadboxes. She retrieved her boyfriend and rendered him acutely jealous by picking up a few hundred other men.

I emulated Wilma's example and sent away for the pamphlet and the equipment that came with it.

When my pamphlet and my powder-pink exerciser arrived, I felt a vague sense of unease. Some of the ink in the pamphlet was blurry. A few pages were repeated. Others were missing. Sensing that my uncharacteristic spurt of enthusiasm would dry up if I took the time to send for a replacement, I plunged into the exercises in the book (those I could decipher) and performed them faithfully for the requisite twenty days. My breasts blossomed. Men on the streets whistled. Guys at the office looked up when I jiggled past.

I felt like a palm tree hand-pollinated for the first time. I began to have clusters of dates. I was pawed, pleasured, and played with. I experienced lots of stuff I had only read about before, and I mostly loved it after the first few times. The desert I'd spent my life in vanished; everything I touched here in the center of the mirage seemed real, intense, throbbing with life. I exercised harder, hoping to make the reality realler.

Then parts of me began to fight back.

I reclined on Maxwell's couch, my hands behind my head, as he unbuttoned my shirt, unhooked my new, enormous, front-hook bra, and opened both wide. He kissed my stomach. He feathered kisses up my body. Suddenly my left breast flexed and punched him in the face. He was surprised. He looked at me suspiciously. I was surprised myself. I studied my left breast. It lay there gently bobbing like a Japanese glass float on a quiet sea. Innocent. Waiting.

Maxwell stared at my face. Then he shook his head. He eyed my breasts. Slowly he leaned closer. His lips drew back in a pucker. I waited, tingling, for them to flutter on my abdomen again. No such luck. Both breasts surged up and gave him a double whammy.

It took me an hour to wake him up. Once I got him conscious, he told me to get out! Out! And take my unnatural equipment with me. I collected my purse and coat and, with a last look at him as he lay there on the floor by the couch, I left.

In the elevator my breasts punched a man who was smoking a cigar. He coughed, choked, and called me unladylike. A woman told me I had done the right thing.

When I got home I took off my clothes and looked at myself in the mirror. What beautiful breasts. Pendulous. Centerfold quality. Heavy as water balloons. Firm as paperweights. I would be sorry to say goodbye to them. I sighed, and they bobbled. "Well, guys, no more exercise for you," I said. I would have to let them go. I couldn't let my breasts become a Menace to Mankind. I would rather be noble and suffer a bunch.

I took a shower and went to bed.

That night I had wild dreams. Something was chasing me, and I was chasing something else. I thought maybe I was chasing myself, and that scared me silly. I kept trying to wake up, but to no avail. When I finally woke, exhausted and sweaty, in the morning, I discovered my sheets twisted around my legs. My powder-pink exerciser lay beside me in the bed. My upper arms ached the way they did after a good workout.

At work, my breasts interfered with my typing. The minute I looked away from my typewriter keyboard to glance at my steno pad, my breasts pushed between my hands, monopolized the keys, and drove my Selectric to distraction.

After an hour of trying to cope with this I told my boss I had a sick headache. He didn't want me to go home. "Mae June, you're quite an ornament to the office these days," he said. "Can't you just sit out there and look pretty and suffering? More and more of my clients have remarked on how you spruce up the decor. If that clackety-clacking bothers your pretty little head, why, I'll get Gladys to take your work and hers and type in the closet."

"Thank you, sir," I said. I went back out in the front room and sat far away from everything my breasts could knock over. Gladys sent me vicious looks as she flat-chestedly crouched over her early-model IBM and worked twice as hard as usual.

For a while I was happy just to rest. After all that nocturnal exertion, I was tired. My chair wasn't comfortable, but my body didn't care. Then I started feeling rotten. I watched Gladys. She had scruffy hair that kept falling out of its bobby pins and into her face. She kept her fingernails short and unpolished and she didn't seem to care how carelessly she chose her clothes. She reminded me of the way I had looked two months earlier, before men started getting interested in me and giving me advice on what to wear and what to do with my hair. Gladys and I no longer went to lunch together. These days I usually took the boss's clients to lunch.

"Why don't you tell the boss you have a sick headache too?" I asked. "There's nothing here that can't wait 'til tomorrow."

"He'd fire me, you fool. I can't waggle my femininity in his face like you can. Mae June, you're a cheater."

"I didn't mean to cheat," I said. "I can't help it." I looked at her face to see if she remembered how we used to talk at lunch. "Watch this, Gladys." I turned back to my typewriter and pulled off the cover. The instant I inserted paper, my breasts reached up and parked on the typewriter keys. I leaned back, straightening up, then tried to type the date in the upper

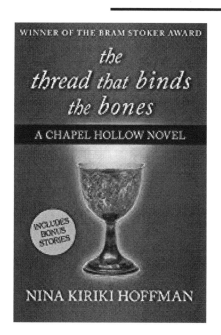

right-hand corner of the page. Plomp plomp. No dice. I looked at Gladys. She had that kind of look that says *eyoo, ick, that's creepy, show it to me again.*

I opened my mouth to explain about Wilma's insult and Charlotte Atlas when my breasts firmed up. I found myself leaning back to display me at an advantage. One of the boss's clients had walked in.

"Mae June, my nymphlet," said this guy, Burl Weaver. I had been to lunch with him before. I kind of liked him.

Gladys touched the intercom. "Sir, Mr. Weaver is here."

"Aw, Gladys," said Burl, one of the few men who had learned her name as well as mine, "why'd you haveta spoil it? I didn't come here for business."

"Burl?" the boss asked over the intercom. "What does he want?"

Burl strode over to my desk and pushed my transmit button. "I'd like to borrow your secretary for the afternoon, Otis. Any objections?"

"Why no, Burl, none at all." Burl is one of our biggest accounts. We produce the plastic for the records his company produces. "Mae June, you be good to Burl now."

Burl pressed my transmit button for me. I leaned as near to my speaker as I could get. "Yes, sir," I said. With tons of trepidation, I rose to my feet. My previous acquaintance with Burl had gone further than my acquaintance with Maxwell yesterday. Now that my breasts were seceding from my body, how could I be sure I'd be nice to Burl? What if I lost the company our biggest account?

With my breasts thrust out before me like dogs hot on a scent, I followed Burl out of the office, giving Gladys a misery-laden glance as I closed the door

behind me. She gave me a suffering nod in return. At least there was somebody on my side, I thought, as Burl and I got on the elevator. I tried to cross my arms over my breasts but they pushed my arms away. A familiar feeling of helplessness, one I knew well from before I sent away for that pamphlet, washed over me. Except this time I didn't feel my fate lay on the knees of the gods. No. My life was in the hands of my breasts, and they seemed determined to throw it away.

Burl waited until the elevator got midway between floors, then hit the stop button. "Just think, Mae June, here we are, suspended in midair," he said. "Think we can hump hard enough to make this thing drop? Wanna try? Think we'll even notice when she hits bottom?" With each sentence he got closer to me, until at last he was pulling the zip down the back of my dress.

I smiled at Burl and wondered what would happen next. I felt like an interested spectator at a sports event. Burl pulled my dress down around my waist.

"You sure look nice today, Mae June, " he said, staring at my front, then at my lips. My breasts bobbled obligingly, and he looked down at them again. "Like you got little joy machines inside," he said, gently unhooking my bra.

Joy buzzers, I thought. Jolt city.

"You like me, don't you, Mae June? I can be real nice." He stroked me.

"Sure I like you, Burl."

"Would you like to work for me? I sure like you, Mae June. I'd like to put you in a nice little apartment on the top story of a real tall building with an elevator in it." As he talked, he kneaded at me like a kitten. "An express elevator. It would only stop at your floor and the basement. We could lock it from the inside. We could ride it. Up. Down. Up. Down. Hell, we could put a double bed in it. You'd like that, wouldn't you, Mae June?"

"Yes, Burl." When would my mammaries make their move?

He bent his head forward to pull down his own zipper, and they conked him. "Wha?" he said as he recoiled and collapsed gracefully to the floor. "How the heck did you do that, Mae June?"

I decided Burl had a harder head than Maxwell.

"Your hands are all snarled up in your dress. You been taking aikido or something?"

"No, Burl."

"Jeepers, if you didn't like me, you shoulda said something. I woulda left you alone."

"But I do like you, Burl. It's my breasts. They make their own decisions."

He lay on the floor and looked up at me. 'That's the dumbest-assed thing I ever heard," he said. He rolled over and got to his feet. Then he came over, leaned toward me, and glared at my breasts. The left one flexed. He jumped back just in time. "Mae June, are you possessed?"

"Yes!" That must be it. The devil was in my breasts. I wondered what I had done to deserve such a fate. I wasn't even religious.

Burl made the sign of the cross over my breasts. Nothing happened. "That's not it," he said. "Maybe it's your subconscious. You hate men. Something like that. So how come this didn't happen last time, huh?" He began pacing.

"They were waiting to get strong enough. Oh, Burl, what am I going to do?"

"Get dressed. I think you better see a doctor, Mae June. Maybe we can get 'em

tranquilized or something. I don't like the way they're sitting there, watching me."

I managed to hook my bra without too much trouble. Burl zipped me up and turned the elevator operational again. "Do you hate me?" I asked him on the way down.

"Course I don't hate you," he said, shifting a step away from me. "You're real pretty, Mae June. Just as soon as you get yourself under control, you're gonna make somebody a real nice little something. I just don't want to take too many chances. Suppose what you've got is contagious? Suppose some of my body parts decide they don't like women? Let's be rational about this, huh?"

"I mean—you won't drop the contract with IPP, will you?"

"Shoot no. You worried about job security? I like that in a woman. You got sense. I won't complain. But I hope you got Blue Cross. You may have to get those knockers psychoanalyzed or something."

He offered to drive me to a doctor or the hospital. I told him I'd take the bus. He tried to get me to change my mind. He failed. I watched him drive away. Then I went home.

I picked up the powder-pink exerciser and took it to the window. My apartment was on the tenth floor. I was just going to drop the exerciser out the window when I looked down and saw Gladys's red coat wrapped around Gladys. My doorbell rang. I buzzed her into the building.

By the time she arrived at my front door I had collapsed on the couch, still holding the exerciser. "It's open," I called when she knocked. My arms were pumping the exerciser as I lay there. I thought about trying to stop exercising, but decided it was too much effort. "How'd you know I'd be home?" I asked Gladys as she came in and took off her coat.

"Burl stopped by the office."

"Did he say what happened?"

"No. He said he was worried about you. What did happen?"

They punched him." I pumped the exerciser harder. "What am I going to do? I can't type, and now I can't even do lunch." I glared at my breasts. "You want us to starve?"

They were doing push-ups and didn't answer.

Gladys sat on a chair across from me and leaned forward, her gaze fixed on my new features. Her mouth was open.

My arms stopped pumping without me having anything to say about it. My left arm handed the exerciser to her. Her gaze still locked on my breasts, Gladys gripped the powder-pink exerciser and went to work.

"Don't," I said, sitting up. Startled, she fell against the chair back. "Do you want this to happen to you?"

"I—I—" She gulped and dropped the exerciser.

"I don't know what they want!" I stared at them with loathing. "It won't be long before the boss realizes I'm not an asset. Then what am I going to do?"

"You...you have a lot of career choices," said Gladys. "Like—have you ever considered mud wrestling?"

"What?"

"Exotic dancing?" She blinked. She licked her upper lip. "You could join the FBI, I bet. 'My breasts punched out spies for God and country.' You could sell your story to the *Enquirer*. 'Double-breasted Death.' Sounds like a slick detective movie from the Thirties. You could—"

"Stop," I said, "I don't want to hear any more."

"I'm sorry," she said after a minute. She got up and made tea.

We were sitting there sipping it when she had another brainstorm. "What do they want? You've been asking that yourself. What are breasts for, anyway?"

"Sex and babies," I said.

We looked at each other. We looked away. All those lunches, and we had never talked about it. I bet she only knew what she read in books too.

She stared at the braided rug on the floor. "Were you...protected?"

I stared at the floor too. "I don't think so."

"They have tests you can do at home."

***

I THOUGHT IT WAS BURL'S, so my breasts and I went to visit him. "You talk to them," I said. "If they think you're the father, maybe they won't beat you up anymore. Maybe they're just fending off all other comers."

Between the three of them they reached an arrangement. I moved into that penthouse apartment.

I shudder to think what they'll do when the baby comes.

～

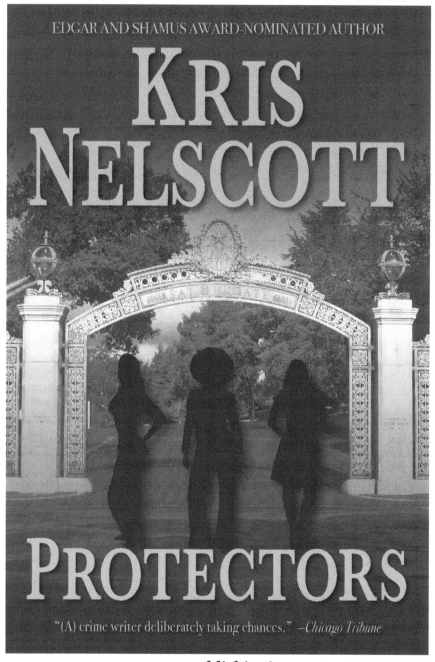

Annie Reed is considered by many to be one of the best new writers appearing in fiction. Her stories appear regulary in many varied places and I am proud to say she is a regular in Fiction River. *I hope to have an Annie Reed story in just about every issue of this magazine as well. (An editor can hope, can't he?)*

For example her story "The Color of Guilt" was selected for The Best Crime and Mystery Stories 2016. *She is also one of the founding members of the innovative* Uncollected Anthology, *where this story first appeared.*

So welcome to the strange and wonderful worlds of Annie Reed. I think you'll love them as much as I do.

The Library
of Orphaned Hearts
Annie Reed

GRETTA FOUND A HEART ON MISSION.

Red and beating and lonely, tucked into the narrow breezeway between two boarded up buildings, the heart lay on the filthy concrete next to the remains of a shattered six string guitar.

She picked up the heart and tucked it inside herself, safe next to her own beating heart, and its sweet melody filled her head and lightened the weight of the backpack on her shoulders.

She bent to adjust the straps of her sandals, old friends comfortably molded to the shape of her feet by the long miles and years they had walked together. The sounds of the city, people and cars and seagulls chasing each other inland from the bay, harmonized with the heart's timid song and energized her old bones. She straightened her spine and let her feet carry her toward Haight and the library nestled in its eclectic midst.

She side-stepped the boisterous patrons of an open-air sports bar on Duboce, the celebration of their team's victory spilling over like strong whiskey to the sidewalk and adding fuel to the trash can fires at the curb. She kept the tender heart safe from the crowds on Market, so intent on their destinations they failed to notice her fragile cargo. She walked past the meat markets and the taquerias on Haight, and the colorful murals that camouflaged buildings long past their prime with joyous art celebrating life and death and rebirth, and all the time she felt the heart she sheltered growing stronger.

Her sandaled feet came to rest at the base of a staircase, the cracked concrete steps leading up to a wooden door warped by damp air and nighttime fog. Gilded letters on door's windowpane, faded over time, looked as new and fresh to her as the day she'd painted them.

She climbed the stairs, her joints creaking, and produced an old-fashioned iron key from her backpack. Bent, arthritic fingers slid the key in an equally old-fashioned lock.

"We're home," she whispered to the heart, and it trembled as all hearts did when faced with the unknown.

The old wooden door protested the intrusion as she nudged it open, taking her time. Hearts and doors and all things battered by the world deserved gentle treatment, and Gretta was in no great hurry.

She breathed in the welcoming smell of well-used books, rows upon rows of them packed on narrow shelves, and her own heart smiled. Dust motes floated in the air like notes freed from the constraints of staff and clef and beat, performing for a cherished audience of one. Gretta rewarded them by humming a tune she'd learned from the timid heart inside her.

"It's time," she murmured to the new heart inside herself. It fluttered, but Gretta soothed it as she would a frightened kitten facing an uncertain future. She turned the little sign in the door's window to "Open" and gave herself and her precious charge over to the comforting world of her library.

* * *

GRETTA HAD COME to the city in her youth, a wild child drawn, like all wild children of her time, by the promise of love and joy and freedom.

She had music of her own then. Vibrant, living music that filled her head and flowed from her fingertips to whatever instrument she had at hand, and there had been instruments too numerous to count.

Exotic instruments, like sitars and tambura and dilruba, baglama and kemence and ud. Guitars that spoke of a heritage of fine craftsmanship and loving creation when she touched them, and violins whose weeping strings made her cry.

She'd let her own heart soar free to sail over the whitecaps on the bay and past the Golden Gate and out to the vast ocean beyond. In the evening it always came back to her, riding on the fog that blanketed the city, and it shared with her all that it had seen and heard and experienced.

She slept with others like herself in parks and along sharply slanted streets where shopkeepers appreciated the crowds drawn by the music, and she ate rich food steeped in the ethnicity of the city's culinary artisans. She imagined that life on Olympus in the days of myth and legend could not have been quite so perfect, and her wild heart celebrated each dawn and dusk as a new adventure.

But adventures, like days made of perfection, eventually end.

A new hardness settled over the city. Gretta felt it in her bones, and her fingers twisted and faltered on the strings. Other street musicians felt it, and they took their fine instruments and their fragile hearts and turned away in search of a place more welcoming of their songs. The culinary artisans felt it as well, no longer sharing their creations freely, and the food lost its richness and unique flavor.

Gretta stayed even as the city changed around her. She sang the songs her fingers could no longer play, but her voice had never been her finest instrument. Her heart grew despondent and weary, and one night when she sent it soaring out over the bay to the vast ocean beyond, it failed to ride the fog back home to her.

Bereft, she wandered the streets looking for that part of herself she feared she would never see again. She slept in strange doorways and ate scraps of leftovers that had no taste and little aroma. Her body aged and her hair grew unkempt and gray, and even though she sang the songs she knew well, the melodies grew rough and unfocused without her heart's influence.

She thought herself lost forever until one night a stranger placed an old-fashioned iron key in her upturned hat next to the quarter she had placed there herself.

"What's this for?" she asked.

The stranger, who looked less like a man and more like a piece of air made of shadows upon shadows, held out a book, battered and worn, the dust jacket ripped and faded.

Gretta took the book with crooked, trembling fingers, unable to read the language of the words on the spine.

Turning the book over, she expected to see more unreadable words describing a story she could never know. Instead, a plain back greeted her. The words "The Library" had been written in a spidery hand in the middle of all that blank plainness, and below an address on Haight.

The book pulsed beneath her fingertips, and she felt a familiar longing for strings and hollow wood and the whitecaps on the bay.

Could it be?

"Is it mine?" she asked.

"No," the stranger said, voice neither male nor female but kind. "It's only a loan."

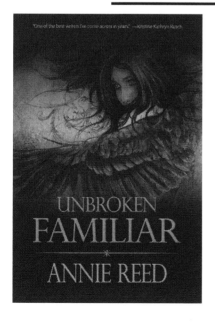

UNBROKEN FAMILIAR

Nothing can break the bond
between a familiar and a wizard.
Except death.

Nothing can break the spirit
of a bonded familiar.
Except the murder of her wizard.

For this book and other
Annie Reed stories and novels
go to:
https://anniereed.wordpress.com/

Trembling for a different reason, Gretta felt like holding her breath, but she asked a question that became more familiar to her over the years than her own name.

"How long?"

The stranger smiled a smile she didn't need to see in order to know it existed.

"As long as you need."

* * *

THE LIBRARY DOOR squealed in protest, the old wood complaining, as a new patron entered the library.

Thin and blonde and dwarfed by the guitar case strapped on her back, the girl's shoulders hunched as if the weight of the world rested on her fragile bones. Her age was hard to judge. Gretta would have thought her young, but the ashy emptiness she brought in with her like winter fog made her seem ancient.

Ancient and lost, as lost as Gretta herself had been.

"I don't know why I'm here," the girl said in greeting. "I've never been in this part of the city, and I..."

She shrugged, the gesture expressing a feeling Gretta knew well but hadn't been able to put into words herself when she'd first been handed a book from the library.

Gretta hadn't meant to take responsibility for the library, hadn't meant to become the guardian of the well-used books and their precious cargo. She'd only meant to return the book she'd been given, but the iron key implied otherwise. When she'd unlocked the protesting wooden door and stepped into the shadowy depths between the shelves for the first time, the books had welcomed her with an unabashed enthusiasm that made

her own heart swell, and she knew her new purpose in life.

"Perhaps you'd like a book," Gretta said.

The girl shrugged again. "I don't read much." Her eyes wandered the dusty shelves. "I really don't know why I'm here."

The girl's hand fluttered in frustration, and Gretta saw the calluses on the tips of her fingers, new ridges carved deep into old scars, and she knew the girl still chased the songs known only to her absent heart.

It was the reason her wandering feet had found the library. Her heart wasn't broken or discarded like the heart Gretta had found on Mission. This girl's heart only needed a little help to find its way home. If the girl hadn't found her way here, in time Gretta would have found her on the street the same way the man made of shadows had found Gretta so many years ago.

"Let me make a suggestion," Gretta said.

She turned toward the shelves, asking the same silent question she always asked the books when a new patron entered the library: *Which one of you will help her?*

Gretta's hands traced along the broken spines and tattered dust jackets until she received a timid answer, and she smiled in return.

She held out the book and the heart it contained, the heart Gretta had sheltered inside herself, to the girl.

"This one," she said, still smiling.

The book had been written in a language Gretta didn't understand, and the girl looked dubious.

And frightened.

Gretta's heart sank, its hopeful song tinged now with the mournful tones of a chance abandoned.

Not all those who came to the library took one of Gretta's books. Only a rare few were brave enough to welcome a heart not their own, even for a little while.

The girl's thin lips narrowed and her mouth set in a firm line of determination, and she took the book from Gretta with a nod to herself.

Gretta felt the happiness of the hearts in her library warm her back like a sudden ray of sunshine.

The girl's eyes grew wide, and Gretta knew she'd sensed the song of the timid heart within. The girl's fingertips formed the chords of a song she'd never played before, and she laughed, a sound of absolute joy.

"Is it mine?" the girl asked, hugging the book to her chest like a long-lost lover. "Can I keep it?"

"It is only a loan."

The girl's smile dimmed, as the smiles of all patrons dimmed when they learned their new joy was fleeting. Gretta wanted to tell them greater happiness awaited, that they would no longer need the books when their own hearts returned, richer and fuller for the time spent away, but each patron needed to discover that on their own.

Just like she had.

Fingertips still sketching chords on the plain back cover of the book, the girl asked the question Gretta knew she would.

"For how long?"

Still smiling, Gretta thought of the timid heart she had found on Mission leaving the library for the first time in the care of someone who appreciated its music, who would play and sing the songs the little heart knew as a way to help her own weary heart find its way home. A journey like that could not be quantified in time but only in terms of accomplishment, a good deed done well.

"As long as you need," Gretta said. "Take as long as you need."

* * *

GRETTA FOUND a joyful heart in a music club on Mission.

She paid no entrance fee at the door, her purpose known well to the musician who collected the money, his own mended heart having found its way home after the loan of a book from Gretta's library. Instead he gave her a hug and handed her an empty book in a language she might have known once in her youth.

"In case you need it," he said.

She always needed books for the hearts she collected, a sad fact of life in a city still hard on fragile hearts, and she thanked him for the new addition.

She shrugged off her backpack and slipped the empty book inside next to the rest of the books she carried when she walked the streets of the city. Veteran hearts beat within their pages. Strong, capable hearts that had made many journeys since Gretta had found them hurt and lonely and in need of the comfort offered by the heart beating within Gretta's own chest.

"Thank you," she said to the musician whose eyes didn't quite focus on her face, and she wondered if he saw a wizened old woman in well-worn sandals, or shadows upon shadows in the vague shape of a woman who smiled on him from time to time.

No matter. She had not come here for him, but to give her own heart the reward it so richly deserved.

A young woman stood in the spotlight on a stage barely large enough to hold her and her band. A tall man who played bass like his fingers were part of the strings crowded next to the drummer, an exuberant man of indeterminate age with fuzzy hair as dark as a coal black dandelion. On the other side of the drummer a dark-haired boy no more than eighteen with handsome, striking features played guitar, and his heart was so strong it made Gretta's leap for joy in her chest.

But that wasn't the only source of her joy.

The young woman on center stage, blonde and thin and dwarfed by the acoustic guitar she played, sang with a radiant smile on her face, her fingers coaxing soaring melodies from the strings like seabirds racing sailboats across the bay.

She'd returned the book and its borrowed heart to Gretta's library the day before, shyly inviting her to come to the show.

"I owe it all to you," she'd said, but Gretta knew that wasn't true.

The precious hearts she found, the orphans she nurtured within herself until they gained strength enough to coax other wounded hearts to return to their homes, they deserved the praise. Gretta was merely their guardian, a grateful recipient of the kind of magic the cold, hard world refused to believe existed.

Gretta had always believed magic existed. Magic had drawn her to the city and given her the ability to play instruments she'd never seen before like she'd been born for no other purpose. When her heart had fled, she'd believed the magic was gone for good, but the stranger with the old-fashioned iron key and a tattered library book had changed all that.

Just like Gretta and the books had changed it for the musician who manned the door.

And the girl on center stage.

Gretta stayed until the girl and her band finished playing. She stayed while the audience filed out, their own hearts briefly lifted by the joy and energy and music flowing from the stage.

She stayed until she felt a familiar tug at her own heart, and realized that her sandals had led her here for another purpose as well.

In a dark corner of the club, in a spot as far from the stage as possible, a young man sat at a deserted table, his eyes downcast and his arms folded around himself as if he could fix the empty space in his chest just by holding himself tight.

Gretta approached him, and he raised his dull eyes upwards, not looking at her but at the spot at center stage where the young woman had stood. A tattoo graced the dark skin at the corner of one eye, not a teardrop but a single musical note unfettered by staff or clef or beat.

Gretta held out a book from her library. "I think you need this," she said.

He shook his head, still not looking at her. "Books aren't my thing."

"Try."

He looked at her then, and she knew he saw a wizened old woman, not shadows upon shadows. "I said no."

The musician from the door came over to stand next to Gretta. "Dude, take it," he said. "She doesn't give them to just anybody, fool."

The young man with the vacant space where his heart had been took the book from Gretta's hand with a rough, resentful motion, and then his eyes widened. His fingers started tapping out a beat on the spine, and Gretta realized he hadn't been watching the young girl as she sang but the drummer with the black dandelion fluff hair who'd stood behind her.

"What the..." He gathered the book to his chest as if he could press it inside himself, and his eyes turned shiny bright. "How?"

Gretta only smiled in response.

"You givin' me this?" he asked.

"It's only a loan."

He looked at the musician from the door and then back to Gretta, but his gaze didn't stay on her face. She had become shadows upon shadows to him, as it should be.

He asked the same question all the patrons of her library asked, the question Gretta herself had asked when she'd been given a book and a second chance.

"How long?"

Gretta gave the answer she always did, the one that kept the magic alive.

"As long as you need," she said. "Take as long as you need."

~

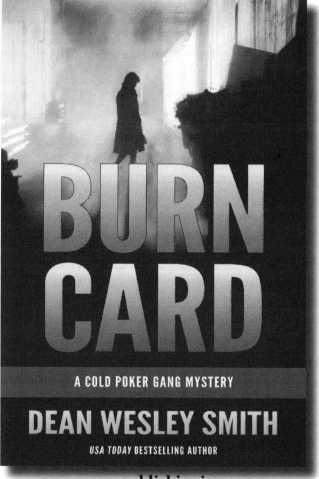

J. Steven York tends to write Pulphouse *type stories that sometimes I'm even afraid to publish. And that's going some.*

Steve is the author of well over twenty novels and in the last three decades has written in various aspects of the writing world, from Star Trek novels to Conan novels to gaming books, not even counting his original work. He pretty much has done it all. On top of that, he lives with another writer, Chris York, who is known under two different pen names as a cozy mystery writer.

Back in the early Pulphouse *days, Chris and Steve did* The Report Magazine *for* Pulphouse, *a really fun magazine for writers. I published this story first back in Issue #9 in 1992.*

Steve is also doing a really fun and off-the-wall internet comic, one of which he has allowed me to put in each issue on the back page. Between this story and that comic, you can get an idea of the fun and wonderful stuff coming up in these pages from J. Steven York.

Cooties
J. Steven York

I KNEW IT WAS TROUBLE as soon as I saw Erik emerge from the shadows under the playground slide.

"Girls got cooties," he announced with the kind of confidence that comes only from supporting an idea that cannot easily be tested. Eight-year-old boys have their own particular form of scientific method. Anything which cannot be disproven is probably true. Truth is power, and eight-year-old boys are power mad.

"They do not," said Billy. Billy is me. Was me. They called me Billy then, and I hated it. I had two reasons for saying "They do not;" to challenge Erik, the dominant male in our little social group and because I had a terrible crush on Noel Thomas, and could not stand the idea of her having cooties, whatever they were.

Erik recognized the challenge at once. He planted his sneakers solidly in the good playground dirt, rose to his full four foot three, threw out his chest and said, "They do too." The weapons of verbal bantering used by small boys are not sophisticated, but the rules under which they are employed are as sophisticated as anything ever employed in the history of human warfare. Erik was a master of those rules, so he did not merely answer my challenge, but brilliantly countered it with one of his own. "How would you know anyway, useless you've been check'n it out with Noel?"

This was entirely true, which put me at a tremendous disadvantage. To any adult, the answer to this dilemma would seem simple. I would only have to answer, "Yes,

I have checked thoroughly, and Noel Thomas is entirely free of cooties," and the contest would not be won. But of course, it was more complex than that. Such was the tactical brilliance of one Erik L. Patterson, school yard tough and master of the entire territory between the jungle-gym and the merry-go-round. For such an announcement by me would be social suicide. I would be branded forever as a "lover-boy," a sissy by association. I would win the battle, only to have lost the war completely and utterly.

While I then lacked the strategic brilliance of Erik, I was also no fool. I recognized my dangerous position, and sought a speedy retreat. "Aw," I said, spinning on my heels, "who cares about girls anyway." Then I ran off and away from confrontational disaster.

Yet echoes of that epic exchange followed me, through the rest of recess, and through the rest of that day. In the world of eight-year-old boys, the lead male does, to an extent, define the reality of those around him. If he says that there was once a terrible murder in the old house on Seller Street or that the principal sometimes takes kids down to a dungeon off the furnace room for punishment, then it is so. If I could not publicly challenge Erik's statement or his status as lead male, then I could not privately deny it either. It sat heavy on my mind, like a lump of undigested oatmeal.

At two forty five and thirty-eight seconds, I sat at my desk, ignoring my math book and attempting instead to speed the second hand on its course through sheer force of will. As I stared at the big clock on the wall, I could see Noel, just at the edge of my field of vision. I tried to ignore her just as I did the book. But books do not smile. Despite myself, I found I was admiring the soft curve of her cheek, her bright blue eyes, the way delicate strands of sunlight-colored hair framed her face.

Quite deliberately, I opened the rings of my notebook, placed my left index finger in the waiting maw, and snapped the rings shut. I suppressed a cry, and freeing my finger instantly became the single most important task in the near universe. In the course of the struggle, my gaze swept the room. Quickly I fixed my stare on the pencil sharpener in the far corner, the spell broken. I carefully avoided looking at the clock again, lest I see Noel again and forfeit my free will.

Some interminable period of time later the bell rang, and I scrambled for the door, so as not to be cornered. Outside, I dashed for the bike rack, jumped onto my hand-me-down Huffy, and pumped off down the street.

But I did not go home. The day's events still troubled me. For a time I traveled without destination, hoping that the physical exertion and the solitude of near-flight would drive away my personal demons. When this failed to work, I was forced to consider a more direct plan of action. I steered right at the next corner and pulled into the parking lot of the 7-11. I jumped the curb and slid to a stop in front of the pay phone. Legs spread wide to balance the bike, I searched my pockets for my "emergency quarter". I found it wadded inside a spelling test (grade: C-).

I dialed home. Mom answered. I told her that I didn't have any homework (which was a lie) and that I wanted to meet some friends at the park for a game of softball (which was also a lie). She agreed, but I could detect the suspicion in her voice. I hung up the phone knowing I had not heard the end of the matter.

I knew every inch of Noel's route home. I had memorized it, along with a million other once-unimportant details about her, since I had succumbed to her charms. Not only did I know where she would walk, but how long it took her to travel each portion of that route. Applying mathematical skills I would not demonstrate in the classroom for years, I determined how far along that route she would be by this time.

In a moment I was out of the parking lot onto Summit Street, and picking up speed down the hill. I veered off of Summit and cut a diagonal through a vacant lot, then made my best speed down Maple Avenue. I turned left at the next intersection, and pedaled along Main until I reached the library. I coasted my bike across the lawn and into the shade of an ancient oak tree. I jumped off the bike and let it fall to the ground. Young boys have no idea what a kickstand is for, and it's a mystery why boy's bikes are equipped with them at all.

The grass was soft, and the oak offered a comforting solidity to support my back as I settled in to wait. Comfort was of paramount importance, as patience is not an eight-year- old's strong suit. Even so, it was fortunate that I did not have to wait long. I soon spotted Noel at the end of the block, headed my way. I pretended not to notice her until she was close enough to touch, and then only because she spoke to me.

"Hello, Billy." Her voice startled me, though I was expecting it.

I felt the familiar tightness in my chest as I tried to speak. The physical effects of young girls on young boys are well documented, but I felt as though I could add a few volumes of my own just then. "Oh, hi Noel. I was just hanging around. I forgot this was how you walked home."

She smiled, seemingly not at all offended that I did not stand in her presence. Eight-year-old girls know better than to expect that eight-year-old boys be polite. They realize the significance it shows when one of them goes so far as to avoid being rude.

"You go'n home?" I asked.

"Yeah, I've got to get my homework

done." She studied me for a minute, my freckled face and tousled brown hair. "You want to come over to my house and help me with it?"

I found myself laughing, despite my nervousness. "Me help you with homework? You're the best student in every subject. My mom grounds me for a week every time I get a report card." There was no shame in my admitting this. In a boy's world, there were many barometers of status, and academic achievement was near the bottom of the list.

"Then I'll help you. How about it?"

I considered carefully. I had never been in Noel's house, though I knew where it was. I knew too that, like many of my friends, Noel was a latch key kid. Her mom worked until early evening and we would be unsupervised. My mom had expressly forbidden me to go into other kids' houses without an adult home. But I had already lied to my mom about what I was doing. Breaking one more rule wouldn't make much difference, would it?

"Sure," I said, "why not?"

I unhooked the elastic cord that held my books onto the back of my bicycle, added hers to the stack, then refastened them all into place. I pushed my bike and we walked toward her house.

Noel lived in a large and ancient house located on a dead-end street. I leaned my bike against the rusty iron fence surrounding the yard. I removed our books from the bike and coiled the elastic cord around my hand, thinking I could use it to keep my nervous hands busy and out of other mischief. We started up the weathered concrete steps.

It was the kind of house that I associated with elderly relatives, holidays, and funerals. The inside was uncomfortably clean, and cluttered with interesting, if fragile, antiques and bric-a-brac. As we stepped into the kitchen, a clock somewhere chimed the half hour.

"Would you like some milk and cookies? My mother makes them," she said.

I mumbled yes, and sat down at the kitchen table. Something about the house was adding to my jitters. What did I hope to accomplish here? How could I talk with her about *that?* I had yet to develop the skill of subtlety, and so was forced to be direct. "I was talking with a guy today."

She poured my glass full, and put the carton on the table. The picture of some missing kid stared at me from its back.

"What guy?" she asked.

I shrugged. "Just some guy. He said the craziest thing." She placed a plate with a couple of cookies next to the carton. I took a bite of one, hardly tasting it. "He said that girls have cooties."

She laughed loudly. "Cooties? I wonder how he knows?"

She took a drink of her milk. I chewed a bit of my cookie. Direct was not working. I chose to be even more direct. "It's not true, is it?"

She put down her glass. "Is what true?"

I swallowed the lump in my throat, along with a bit of cookie. "That girls have cooties."

She laughed. "What are cooties anyway?"

Nervously, I laughed back. "I figured that if you had them, you'd know."

"Come on," she said, "we can work upstairs in my room."

I stuck the last cookie in my mouth, picked up the pile of books with the elastic cord sitting on top, and followed her up the dim stairway. I was half way to the

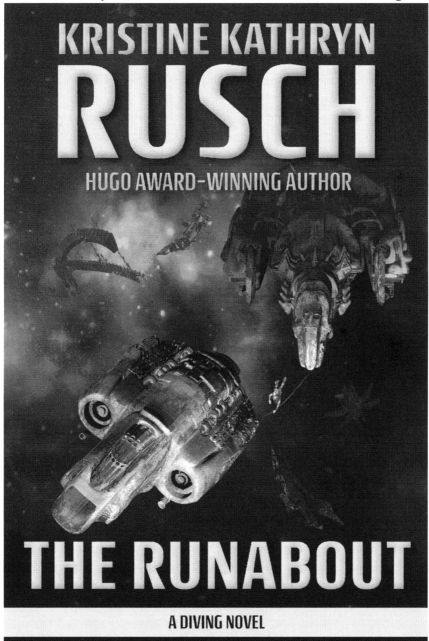

top before I realized she had never answered my question.

Her room was at the end of the hall, which was no brighter than the stairwell. When she opened the door to her room, I had to squint against the relative brightness. The room itself was like some picture in a magazine. I had never seen a kid's room so neat. There was a bed with a canopy and a pink ruffled bedspread. The drapes matched the bedspread, and the dresser and vanity were white, as were the carpets. Dolls and a few stuffed animals were tastefully arranged around the room, staring at me with blind plastic eyes.

I put the books on the vanity, but did not take my hand off the stack. "Nice room," I said.

"My friends and I like it."

I wondered if she meant her dolls. Then I heard a noise, like bugs crawling on crumpled paper. It was gone before I could identify it. "What was that?"

"What?" she said.

"A noise." I waited, mind racing with wild fantasies. What was a cootie anyway? Then I heard the noise again. "It sounds like it's coming from the closet," I said.

Noel smiled, as though that was that she had been waiting for. "The closet?" She looked toward the louvered doors. "Let's see."

As she stepped toward the closet, I felt the terror boiling up in my insides. I clutched at my books and sprinted for the door. The books fell, defiling the floor with their presence, and I found myself holding only the elastic cord. I didn't stop to retrieve the books. I heard the closet door open, and Noel called my name.

I did not look back, but slammed the door to her room, held it shut with all my strength, then wondered what to do next. I could hear that dry rustling sound again, louder now. It sounded like it was coming from right behind the door. The knob jumped in my hand. "Open the door," I heard Noel's sweet voice say, but I also heard the other sounds coming from her room.

What now? If I let go of the door to run, whatever was inside the door could get out. I might trip in the dark hall; on the dark stairs I would certainly have to slow down. Something brushed my shoe. I looked down. In the sliver of light shining under the door I could see *something* trying to reach me, spidery projections (legs, antenna?) slithering through the thin opening.

I had to go *now*.

Then I remembered the cord in my hand. I wrapped it around the knob, ignoring the protests from within. I took the other end, stretched it as far as my strength would allow, and hooked it into the frame of the adjacent door. Then I ran.

We live in a subjective universe, and circumstances can alter our perceptions. It seemed to be miles to the front door, and the streets darker and more empty than I ever remembered them. It took fifteen minutes to get home, but it seemed like a week.

I managed to get myself calmed down before Mom saw me, and nobody asked who won the game. That night I slept with the lights on.

By morning, it all seemed like a foolish fantasy. How would I face Noel? What if she told people how silly I had been? What if her mother called mine? How would I get my books back? Marshaling my courage, I resolved to confront Noel first thing. But Noel avoided me, acted as though I didn't exist. Later, I saw her smiling at Erik. Erik smiled back.

I could not find her at recess, and she gave me the slip in the hall after school. I was about to give up and head for home, but then I remembered the time I had dropped my math book off the bridge into Miller's Creek and the terrible wrath that had followed.

I *had* to talk to Noel. I rode to the library and waited.

When I spotted Noel down the street, she was walking hand in hand with Erik. I quickly pushed my bike around back of the building and stayed out of sight until they were gone.

I went home, via the most direct route possible. I told my mother that I had lost my books at the park, and took my punishment stolidly, taking comfort in the knowledge that there were far worse things in the world.

I never told anyone what *really* happened.

Erik didn't come to school the next day, or the day after. The teacher finally stopped calling his name in roll, though she paused a bit and seemed uncomfortable when she hit the point where his name should have been. It would be months before I saw Erik's picture on the milk carton, and was really sure.

On that day, I sat alone at recess considering what I had learned from this strange experience. Knowledge is truth, and truth is power after all. Then I saw the new kid. What was his name? Allen? He was watching with more than casual interest as a pretty redhead skipped rope.

I strolled over to Allen's side. He noticed me, and tried to pretend that he hadn't been watching the girl.

"Girls got cooties," I said.

~

"Trust me, dear. She knows where the Cooties live."

41

Back in the first incarnation of this craziness, O'Neil De Noux not only wrote great mystery novels, but he worked at Pulphouse Publishing for a year as an editor.

In the last twenty-five years, his production of high-quality fiction has continued. His awards include The United Kingdom Short Story Prize, the Shamus Award (for best private eye fiction), the Derringer Award (for excellence in mystery short fiction) and Police Book of the Year. Two of his stories have appeared in the prestigious Best American Mystery Stories *annual anthology.*

Not only is O'Neil a great writer and former homicide detective, he's also a really nice guy. You can't go wrong finding and reading any of this stories.

Don't Make Me Take Off My Sunglasses
O'Neil De Noux

EVER SINCE I BOUGHT THESE extra-dark Ray Ban *Balorama* sunglasses, two weeks ago, I won't take them off during the day. It annoys people, especially my sergeant and lieutenant. I like that. I like the way the thick black frame almost wraps around my face, the way the curved lenses give me that predatory, bug-eyed look, the way they hide my eyes, especially while I'm sitting in bumper-to-bumper rush hour traffic on a steamy, New Orleans Friday afternoon.

Thankfully, my AC's working fine as I inch my unmarked Chevy Caprice into the right lane of I-610 to creep up to the Canal Boulevard exit. Don't want to be late for another date with Angie.

A man in a black pickup leans on his horn next to me as if that'll do any good. Just as I reach for my PA mike to tell him to lay off, my portable police radio blares, "Headquarters—3124."

This can't be good news. Not at four-thirty. I'm about to get nailed just before knocking off. Picking up my radio I answer, "3124—go ahead."

"The subject at Charity just expired."

There it is. Another evening ruined. No way I can punt this to the evening watch. Son-of-a-bitch!

Slapping my blue light up on the roof of my car, I tap the siren and take to the shoulder.

"3124—10-4?"

"I'm in route," I tell headquarters.

My sergeant cuts in—if I need help, let him know.

Yeah. Yeah.

Now what had Officer Cruz told me when she called an hour ago from Charity Hospital's Emergency Room? She had a robbery victim shot in the upper leg. He'd lost a lot of blood and might not make it. I told her to call back if he dies, giving her the old cliché—"It's not *almost* Homicide. It's Homicide Division."

It takes me a good half hour of creative driving before I park my car in the *Police Only* zone behind the hospital. I climb out and stretch my 6'2" frame, brushing my hair out of my eyes. I need another haircut.

Leaving my suit coat in the car, my gold star-and-crescent badge is clipped to the front of my black belt holding up my dress gray pants. My charcoal tie is loosened. My stainless-steel, nine millimeter Beretta 92F rides in its canvas holster on my right hip, my portable police radio in my back pocket.

With a homicide detective's most important weapons in hand, notebook and ball point pen, I walk up the ramp into one of America's busiest emergency rooms. The air inside is cool and damp and smells of antiseptic, sweat and faintly of blood. I ease around rows of folding chairs filled with people patiently waiting their turn.

Two women in the far corner of the room are crying. The man standing next to them wears a pink shirt streaked in blood. He eyeballs me as I pass, heading straight for the pay phones in the hall outside the ER.

I call Angie but get her answering machine.

"Sorry, Babe, but I just got nailed *again*. I'm at Charity. I'll call you in a little bit."

Stepping back into the ER, I come face-to-face with Officer Cruz. Thick-bodied, standing on the short side of 5'5", she's pretty with hair as dark brown as mine. She wears hers in a bun at the back of her neck. She focuses her chocolate-brown Latino eyes at my sunglasses and holds out her right hand. She's young, in her early twenties. I'm pushing thirty-one.

"Juanita Cruz," she says.

"Beau. Homicide." We shake hands and that familiar look comes to her eyes as she realizes —

"As in John Raven Beau?"

"Yeah." I pull my hand away and let her take a long look at this half-Sioux, half-Cajun detective the newspapers love to describe as a one-man-judge-and-jury-killer-cop. Thankfully the Grand Juries didn't agree, declaring all five shootings justifiable homicides. Still, I'm a killer.

"So what we do we have?"

Cruz clears her throat and explains how one Charlie Langford was brought in by his friend after Charlie was shot by an armed robber.

"They were in a car on France Road when a 'big black man' tried to rob them, panicked and shot Langford in the upper leg."

She points across the room to the man in the pink shirt and the two crying women. "The friend is Andy Pratt and the big girl is...was...Langford's girlfriend. I have their IDs." Cruz passes me three Louisiana driver's licenses. "The older woman is the girlfriend's mother."

I smile at Cruz and tell her that's good work, getting their IDs before they disappear.

"They taught us that at the Academy."

I'm not rude enough to ask if she's still a rookie, but her eagerness tells me she hasn't been on the street long.

"Where's the victim?"

She leads me back into the hall next to the trauma rooms, stopping at the third room. She opens the curtain for me. The body of the victim, lying naked with tubes in his mouth and arms, is streaked with blood. A nurse with curly red hair pulls the tube from the victim's mouth as I move around to get a better look at the entry wound in the upper leg.

The wound is consistent with a small caliber gun.

"Where are his clothes?" I ask the nurse, who points to a plastic bag attached to her side of the trauma table. I explain they aren't to be touched until the crime lab technician arrives to secure them.

She's tall and thin, this nurse, with a prissy expression on her face as she asks, "Something wrong with your eyes?"

I stare at her eyes. "Ever read the X-Men?"

"The what?"

"Comic books. Fella named Cyclops wore sunglasses like a visor to keep the lasers from shooting out of his eyes."

Cruz chuckles behind me. I like her. The nurse isn't amused and is less amused when she tries to sponge down the body and I tell her it's not to be touched.

"Let the coroner's people bag him."

"Fine by me." She steps back and pulls off her plastic gloves. "We'll just let the coroner's men bag him."

"Thanks. I need the name of the doctor who declared."

She gives me the doctor's name and time he declared death, cause of death listed as exsanguination due to penetrating gunshot wound. I jot it all down, along with her name, which I read from her name tag: A. Jones.

"The bullet's still inside," she volunteers on her way out, "lodged in the hip."

"Ex… what?" Cruz asks.

"Exsanguination. He bled to death."

THE GREAT BEAU

The mysterious death of an elderly man draws NOPD Chief Inspector John Raven Beau into a complex case involving priceless art, stolen Nazi loot, a dead deerhound, a haughty countess, a ruthless killer and featuring the irresistible NUDE IN RED woman.

For this book and other
O'Neil De Noux stories and novels
go to:
http://www.oneildenoux.com/

Stepping through the curtain, I spot the girlfriend hurrying our way. She's pushing six feet, with long brown hair and a reddish, contorted face. She wears a yellow sundress and white high heels.

"Donna Porter," Cruz tells me before the angry girlfriend arrives.

"Where's Charlie!" Donna demands, hands on her hips.

"You can't see him now," I tell her softly. "I'm Detective Beau. We need to talk." I point to the waiting room. She huffs twice, turns and stomps back out.

I lean over and ask Cruz if the doctor's told them he's dead.

"Yes."

"Good."

I follow Donna and catch her before she reaches her mother. I lead her to the other side of the room where we sit away from her mother and the man in the pink shirt. Both give me owly stares, so I nod toward them and Cruz immediately moves their way, giving me time to speak with my victim's girlfriend.

"I knew something was wrong." Donna wrings the bottom of her dress in her hands. "He's never late." She's talking to the floor now. "He was late once. Just one time." She suddenly looks up at me. "And I chewed his ass so much, he's never been late since."

Tears stream down her face and she raises the bottom of her dress to her eyes and cries. It takes me a moment to realize she has her dress up to her waist now. Glancing around, I see two elderly men checking her out. At least she's wearing panties. Pink bikinis.

I wave to Cruz who's quick to see what's up and comes over. I move toward the man in the pink shirt. As I pass Cruz, she reminds me his name is Andy Pratt. I know that but can't help liking her enthusiasm.

Donna's mother passes me, heading for her daughter.

Andy Pratt folds his arms as I arrive and introduce myself. Looking into Pratt's eyes from behind my Ray Bans, I say, "So what happened?"

He tells me quickly how he and Charlie pulled over on France Road and got out to switch positions in their car. Charlie wanted to drive. He was in a hurry to see Donna. Didn't want to be late. Cruz quietly steps next to me.

"And a guy came up and pulled a gun. Said to give up our money. And he shot Charlie for no reason and I think the gun fell into Charlie's pocket."

The gun fell into Charlie's pocket?

"And the guy ran off so fast." Pratt waves his arms. "And Charlie was bleeding man, like unbelievable."

The gun fell into Charlie's pocket?

Pratt folds his arms again and stares at my sunglasses.

"What did the man look like?"

Pratt leans close and says, "Black. Tall and skinny."

"What was he wearing?"

Pratt shrugs.

"Tuxedo? Jock strap?"

"Black T-shirt and jeans and black running shoes."

"What kind of gun?"

> ***"And he shot Charlie for no reason and I think the gun fell into Charlie's pocket."***

"I dunno."

"Silver colored like mine." I twist so he can see my stainless steel Beretta. "Or blue steel?"

"Blue, I think. I think it fell into Charlie's pocket."

Cruz bumps my elbow and I tell Pratt to sit down and relax. I head straight back to the trauma room with Cruz following.

"The gun fell into his pocket?" She whispers as soon as we're out of hearing range.

"I'll be getting back to that."

"He told me the shooter was big and black but never saw what he was wearing."

We step back into the trauma room.

"He's making this up as he goes along," I tell Cruz as I lean over the bag of clothes. Nurse Jones comes in for a blood pressure cup. I ask for a pair of rubber gloves. She points to a box on the other side of the table and watches me pull the gloves on.

"Could there be a gun in the victim's pants pocket?" I ask.

"A gun? No way."

I carefully reach into the bag and fish out a pair of dark blue pants. They're heavy enough and I slip my hand into the left front pocket. I put the small revolver on the foot of the bed and Nurse Jones takes a determined step forward and says, "Son of a bitch."

It's a blue steel Charter Arms .22 revolver with a black plastic grip.

"How the hell did I miss that?" Nurse Jones stammers.

"Don't beat yourself up over it. You're only human."

"No I'm not." She turns to leave. "I'm a nurse!"

Just as I'm explaining to Cruz how Jones was probably pretty excited when she was cutting off the victim's clothes, the crime lab technician steps in. Although he knows the routine, I ask him for photos, fingerprinting the gun, securing the clothes.

I lose the rubber gloves and head back for the wonderful Andy Pratt, who's leaning forward in his chair with his beefy arms around his belly.

When he looks up at me, I ask, "Did you come in contact with the gun?"

"Huh?"

"Did you touch it in any way, try to block it or anything?"

He looks at Cruz and says, "No."

"Where is the car?"

Pratt leads us out to a dark green Honda Accord, parked at the bottom of the ramp, a parking ticket already affixed to its windshield. I pull the ticket off and stuff it into my pocket. It'll have a time on it, for my report.

Blood is streaked outside the front passenger door and the seat is drenched. The steering wheel appears clean. So does the driver's seat.

"Show me how it happened."

Pratt explains how he was driving when Charlie insisted on driving.

"It's his car," Pratt explains, "Like I said he was afraid he was gonna be late. Donna would give him ten shades 'a hell."

I look at my notes as I ask, "Y'all got out and a man approached and tried to rob you?"

"Yeah."

"If y'all got out for Charlie to drive, how come he was shot while in the passenger seat."

"Huh?"

"Twice you said y'all got out and switched positions. For Charlie to drive. But he was shot while in the passenger seat." I point to the bloody seat.

Pratt looks at the seat as if it held the answer, then says, "He was getting out. I was out."

"How'd the gun fall in his pocket?"

"I guess the guy dropped it. He must have."

"And you saw it fall in Charlie's pants pocket."

Pratt nods and wipes perspiration from his brow. He won't look me in the eye. I spot the crime lab tech approaching and ask him to swab Pratt's hands.

"What?" Pratt asks.

"You're part of the crime scene, Mr. Pratt and we need to swab your hands in order to conduct a Neutron Activation Test."

Pratt folds his arms and asks what's that for.

"Did you fire a gun recently?"

"No."

"Then it'll prove you didn't." I point to the tech who already has the vial and swab out of his case. "We're going to swab Charlie's hands too."

As the tech swabs Pratt's hands I tell him, "See. It doesn't hurt."

I point to the car and ask the tech to do his magic there too. He rolls his eyes and nods.

"Any powder burns on the victim's pants?" I ask.

The tech shakes his head.

Turning to Pratt, I ask him to come with me to the Detective Bureau so I can secure his formal statement.

"But I want to stay with Donna and her mother."

"They'll be fine," I assure him firmly as I take his elbow to lead him to my car.

"Can I come along," Cruz asks. "I just got off. I'll turn in my unit and meet you at the Bureau. OK?"

"Sure."

After jotting down the information from the mother's and Donna's driver's licenses, I pass them to Cruz and ask her to return them and get their phone numbers.

"OK."

She sure is eager.

***

I PUT PRATT in one of our small, windowless interview rooms. Sit him behind a small table on a hardback chair whose front legs have been shaved a half inch so he'll have to fight from leaning forward, awkwardly.

Starting a pot of coffee and chicory, I go over to my desk and call Angie. Her answering machine answers and I leave another message. I call home and check my message and she's left one.

"Babe. Got your message. I'm coming over to wait for you." I erase her message and leave one for her to wait there. This shouldn't take long.

Officer Juanita Cruz, still in uniform, walks into the Detective Bureau just as I pour myself a cup of thick coffee. I drop in two sugars and pull out another mug for her.

"Thanks," she says as she passes between the government-issue, gray metal desks.

We move over to my gray metal desk, in the center of the Homicide Division area. She sits at the next desk as we drink our coffee. She gets up immediately to pour in more cream and sugar.

"I like mine strong," I explain.

"Where's Pratt?"

I explain how I'm letting him sweat, letting him try to get comfortable in that hard chair, letting him fester for a good half hour before I go in.

"Can I go in?" Her eyes bounce in anticipation.

"Sure."

Sitting back, she smiles and says, "What's with the sunglasses. Really?"

I pause, as if I'm thinking, before saying, "I look cool, don't I?"

She giggles.

Forty minutes later, we step into the interview room. I put my mini-cassette recorder on the table as Cruz puts a cup of coffee in front of Pratt. She steps back against the door as I take the only other chair in the place, one with small cushions, across from Pratt. I open my ID folder, pull out the laminated Miranda Warning card, turn on the tape recorder and start the introduction.

"The date is … The time is … This is Detective John Raven Beau speaking. This tape will contain the statement of Andrew Pratt." I list his vitals. "Also present in the room is Patrol Officer Juanita Cruz of the Fifth District, first officer at the crime scene."

Then I read Mr. Pratt his rights. "Before we ask you any questions, you must understand your rights. You have the right to remain silent. You understand?"

"What's going on?" Pratt leans far back in his uncomfortable chair.

"Do you understand what I just said?"

"Yeah, but what's happening?" He looks over my shoulder at Cruz, but she's too smart to say anything.

"Anything you say can and will be used against you in court."

Pratt interrupts me again and I tell him he can ask any questions and talk all he wants, as soon as I finish reading him his rights. He lets me finish and asks excitedly, "What's going on?"

"You are a suspect in a crime," I explain calmly.

"What crime?"

"The shooting of your friend Charlie Langford."

"But …" His lower lip quivers and his eyes redden.

Come on. Cry. When they cry, they're usually close to confessing something.

Pratt catches himself and looks at the blank wall.

After a minute, I say, "Staring at the wall isn't going to solve your problem."

He tries staring at me, hard at first, then slowly slipping into a puzzled look.

"Well?" I ask.

He shrugs.

"Tell me how your friend was shot."

Pratt stammers out his explanation in less than thirty seconds, giving us the details, putting in this time how Charlie was sitting in the passenger seat. He finishes in a flurry and tries to lean even further back.

I wait a couple seconds before telling him, "It's time to quit lying, Andy."

"Huh?"

"Don't make me take off my sunglasses!"

He sits up slowly and looks at Cruz again.

"That Neutron Activation Test the crime lab tech did on your hands checks for antimony and barium. Those elements are pretty rare, but common in gunpowder."

Pratt's eyes widen.

"A revolver, like the one from Charlie's pocket, emits gases from its cylinder when fired. Microscopic particles are imbedded in the hand of the person who fired the weapon. What do you think that test will show us about your hands?"

Pratt closes his eyes and shakes his head.

I try another tack. "How long have you worked for NASA?" I have to ask it twice.

"I don't work for NASA."

"That's right. You're no rocket scientist, Andy."

He nods almost imperceptibly.

"And you're not smarter than us. We know you haven't told the truth."

Pratt stares at his hands lying in front of him on the desk. He's breathing heavily now. I wait until he looks up at me.

"You're gonna make me take off my sunglasses, aren't you?"

Even through my glasses I see his eyes are red.

I snatch off my sunglasses. And no, lasers *do not* shoot out of my eyes. But he does recoil from the glare in my light, brown Sioux eyes.

"There's no way on heaven or earth that gun just *fell* into Charlie's pocket."

Tears flow down Pratt's face.

"Did you put it there or did he?"

"He did."

Pratt starts bawling and I tuck my Ray Bans into the top pocket of my shirt and move my chair around to his side of the table. I lean close to Pratt and soften my voice. "Go head. Let it out."

Between sobs, Pratt tells us, "It … was … an *accident*. He … was so … late he didn't … want … Donna … to be mad … at him."

I put my Ray Bans back on.

It takes even longer to get the whole story of how girlfriend-frightened Charlie Langford came up with the bright idea of letting his buddy shoot him in the leg so he'd have a reason to be late and have a reason for his girlfriend to fawn over him.

Why did he have Pratt shoot him? Simple. Charlie knew, from watching cops shows on TV that if he shot himself, there would be powder burns on his leg.

"He wanted me to shoot him."

"I know."

"He wasn't supposed to die. He just didn't want to be late, again."

"I know."

I ask Pratt if there's anything he wishes to add or take away from his statement, before turning off the recorder. Cruz and I go out for fresh cups of coffee.

"What are you booking him with?"

"First Degree Murder," I tell her as I re-fill her mug.

"Technically it isn't …" She starts to tell me.

"Always book 'em with the most serious charge. Keeps him from making bail easily. Let the D.A. negotiate the charge."

I can see she's hesitant.

"What if his story changes tomorrow? What if we find out Donna paid him to kill Charlie? After all, Donna and Pratt are both wearing pink."

It takes her a moment. She nods, a smile returning to her eager face.

After filling out Pratt's arrest report, Cruz and I take him around the corner to parish prison for booking. She beams when she realizes I list her and me as the arresting officers.

"Thanks for letting me hang around," she tells me as we walk out of the booking area.

I tap my Ray Bans down and gleek her over the top of my glasses, telling her no problem. I like smart cops.

***

BUCK HEARS me approaching my houseboat and starts barking before I reach the gate. I have to lift my sunglasses to see well enough in the darkness to unlock the gate. Buck runs in a tight circle, yelping as I step on *Sad Lisa*. He's a Catahoula hound, with the usual mottled coat of black and brown spots on a gray background and those clear water blue eyes. I found him during the great May flood, a puppy lost in the rain.

He jumps up on me and licks my hands.

I see food in his dish as I cross to the cabin door. Angie's fed him.

Buck follows me into the main cabin. The scent of meat sizzling on the gas stove has my stomach grumbling before I put down my briefcase. I step into the kitchen area where Angie stands holding a frying pan with two thick steak-burgers inside. She's in a yellow T-shirt and cut-off jeans. She's given up on me taking her out tonight—again.

She finally turns to me and brushes her long brown hair away from her face and in that moment, I feel it again, that warm flush inside at the sight of this woman. She's twenty-two and stone innocent-gorgeous, doesn't even realize how gorgeous.

Turning down the burner, Angie steps over and pulls off my sunglasses. I look down into those blue-green, aquamarine eyes. Her face is so serious as she stares back, letting out a long breath.

"So what was it this time? A police shooting? Triple murder?" She digs a teasing finger into my side. But I don't pull away. I lift my hand and trace my finger gently over her sculptured lips she's painted with deep crimson lipstick.

"You are so beautiful," I tell her and she sighs again.

"Don't start putting those Cajun moves on this city girl." She's trying to stay angry, but it isn't working.

I lean forward and brush my lips across hers. She pulls back and fights to keep from smiling.

"So, what was it? They need the Sioux tracker to chase down a desperado?"

I step back and tell her, "A guy named Charlie Langford was late for a date with this girlfriend, so he got his buddy Andy Pratt to shoot him in the leg so she wouldn't kick his ass."

Angie closes her eyes.

"Only Charlie bled to death and I had to book his buddy."

Angie turns back to the stove and flips the burgers.

"You can just tell me the truth, you know."

"That is the truth." I reach into the fridge for an icy Abita beer. I show it to Angie and ask if she wants one.

"He was late for a date?" She puts a hand on her hip.

"Seriously," I try to take a swig of beer, but I start laughing instead. "He's dead because he didn't want to be late for a date."

Angie shakes her head and goes back to cooking.

I look down at Buck who twists his head as he looks up at me and I can see in those blue Catahoula eyes, he doesn't believe me either.

❧

Ray Vukcevich has, without a doubt, one of the most unusual voices and minds working in all of fiction. He writes perfect Pulphouse *stories and I started buying his stories almost at once for the magazine back at the start.*

Since the first incarnation of this magazine shut down, Ray kept on selling his stories to many magazines and anthologies over the years, as well as numbers of novels and collections.

I hope to now continue to publish more of Ray's stories once again right here in these pages, so stay tuned.

A Breath Holding Contest
Ray Vukcevich

I'LL BREATHE THROUGH MY EARS and win, or I'll die. I won't give in. I fully expect my ears to save me. It's a faith inherited from my father who, in endless attempts to verify his theory of teleportation, used to lurk in shadows, inside closets, behind bushes and trees, under my bed to pop out screaming like a crack-crazed axe murderer, hoping I'd just go somewhere else. If you're scared enough, he'd say, your mind will move your body, Sonny. I used to think that's the way he got rid of Mom—teleported her and her hardware selling boyfriend to Florida.

I've round-robined my way into the finals, and now I sit lotus fashion on the beach in front of the local champion, a tiny whisper of a woman like a famine victim in a yellow swimsuit. She looks familiar, but after all these years, opponents tend to blur in my mind. Her name is Marcia, and, like me, she wears an orange scuba mask, her mouth sealed shut with adhesive tape. She's beaming evil thoughts at me, her beady blues narrowed but steady. She's got that "I win, you lose" look. People tell me I wear that look, too, meaning it as an insult, but I always take it as a compliment. Contests, any and all kinds of contests, are my meat. Marcia doesn't realize who she's dealing with.

She makes me nervous, though, and I get offensive. I put together a thought and shoot it across the space that separates us.

I can eat more Jalapeno peppers than you can!

She doesn't seem impressed. This could be trouble.

I can stand on my head longer than you can, she fires back.

The spectators crouch like scavenging sea gulls on the slick, black rocks that circle Marcia and me where we sit locked in our combat, noisy as corpses with our weakly bottled up gases. The Pacific washes the rocks, but it doesn't move the onlookers, the fans, in their tennis outfits, their bikinis, their cutoff jeans and dopey hats. They shake away the salt spray and laugh. They won't admit it, but they hope one of us dies today. That's what spectators are for—to look upon the twisted, purple face of defeat and shiver deliciously.

Drops of sea water dot the glass of my mask. I smell wet rubber. I taste hospitals in the tape over my mouth. Huge hands crush my chest. I want to breathe! God, how I want it. Just to gulp in big bites of cool ocean air, smell again the pine forest lining this Oregon beach, taste the fishy sea soup in the breeze. I wouldn't turn my nose up at even the waves of sun screen and sweat wafting from the spectators. I ache. I ache. I mustn't let it show.

I can do more one-armed pushups than you can, I tell Marcia.

I can do more tap dance steps, she rallies.

She's got a point. If I get out of this alive, I'm going to have to bone up on my tap dancing. She knows she's scored a hit. I must work fast. I can feel the membranes that close my ears move back and forth, back and forth, holding fast. Surely they will break soon. I must be ready. When the air streams through my ears and into the back of my throat, I must play it cool, take little breaths, no great chest heaves.

I hit her with another thought. I can chug more beer than you can!

That makes her pause. I can tell a little person such as herself couldn't chug much beer.

I could run circles around your beer belly.

She's good. I decide to try another angle. I can name more vice presidents than you can!

BOARDING INSTRUCTIONS

Ray Vukcevich's new collection includes thirty-three previously uncollected stories, all with his trademark whimsical, skewed look at the world around us. It's a world seemingly not our own, and yet if we look hard enough we'll find that world just out of sight around the corner.

Wonderfully inventive and wildly unpredictable, these stories are sure to entertain you and keep you wondering: "Are we there yet?"

For this book and other
Ray Vukcevich stories and novels go to:
http://www.fairwoodpress.com/

She thinks about it. She doesn't seem worried. I have a wild moment of panic, but I fight it down. I won't give in. I'd die of shame if I lost to this woman. My vision is blurring, and muscles all over my body twitch and jerk. I make fists of my hands and put them under my thighs to hold them down. I can see that Marcia won't quit either. This is like being married again. Women just won't quit, no matter what you do to show them who can do more, who knows more, who should say what's what and when. No, they always have one more last word waiting.

I shouldn't have thought that. She jumps right on it.

I can maintain a relationship longer than you can, she tells me sweetly.

Oh, yeah!

My longest was three months.

Ah ha! Got her. My longest was six months!

I lied. My longest was a year.

I'm stunned. A year!

Marcia's turning an ugly shade of blue, and there are red blotches around her mask and tape, but I don't think I can outlast her. I must look worse. The shame sits heavy in my stomach like too many tacos. It doesn't look like I'm going to be able to breathe through my ears after all.

You didn't last long with me, Sonny. Her thought is all ice.

That's it. She's been playing an unfair advantage. She knows me. I dig in my memory, and find her there in Maine that winter of the lobster eating contest, the night we had after I beat the bib off her and everyone else.

I'm better in bed. I must make up lost ground.

I love better.

Even she must know how weak that is. She hesitates, but before I can fire an-other round, she gets in her best slash so far. I know where my mother is.

That unhinges me. My brain is starving for oxygen. I shoot wild. I own the railroads. I've got Park Place!

Somehow the spectators know I've missed. They know the end is near. Her fan club chants, "Marcia! Marcia!"

Her cheeks are puffed up big, and she looks like a frog or a trumpet player, but I see the cold fire in her eyes as she delivers her coup de grace. My father's not squatting in some doorway drinking shaving lotion and puking on his shoes!

Darts, balls, hoops, scoops, pucks! I cry. No air is ever going to come through my ears. I'm bouncing on my butt in the sand and making little whimpering sounds behind my tape. It can't end like this.

Even when you win, Sonny, you lose.

I'm snatched away like a tablecloth, leaving Marcia, the black rocks, and the spectators trembling in their places on the beach. I appear some two-hundred yards up the beach on the deck of the SeaView Restaurant. I rip the mask from my face, the tape from my mouth. The air I gulp is god-I-died-and-went-to-heaven good. Thank you, Dad. Oh, thank you. Lots of eyes on me—old people in their Sunday best, young couples with wine. I see I'm about as welcome as a little accident Muffy, the pooch, might have left behind. A waiter is moving swiftly my way. He'll tell me to get lost, keep moving. I open my arms to the sky.

"It isn't fear that moves me, Dad," I tell him, wherever he is. "It's chagrin."

~

Esther M. Friesner was a major supporter of the first incarnation of this magazine. Not only did she sell me stories, but she did a wonderfully funny column called "Ask Auntie Esther."

Since this new incarnation will have no regular columns, just fiction, I couldn't ask her to bring back her column, but I most certainly wanted one of her brilliant and funny short stories.

Over the decades, Esther has published close to a hundred novels and hundreds of short stories and edited numbers of anthologies as well. It is a wonderful pleasure for me to have her back in these pages.

Jesus at the Bat
Esther M. Friesner

PHILIP ROTH HAD ALREADY WRITTEN *The Great American Novel*; Victor Harris was screwed. If you're going to be successful with the writing thing you have to write about what you know, and the only thing Victor Harris really knew was baseball. (He thought he knew sex, but that's another story.) The only question remaining was: How much longer would be able to keep up the sweet, unstressful position of sensitive, creative, Aspiring-Author/Househusband (without actually becoming *Published* Author/Househusband) before Barb, his wife, caught wise?

He kept a copy of Steven King's *Playboy* interview prominently displayed in the small basement cubby that was his "office," the better to remind Barb of at least one loyal lady who'd held down a decidedly unfun job (Dunkin' Donuts) while hubby mud-wrestled with the Muse until he hit pay dirt. *Stand by your man*, it seemed to say, *and soon you shall limo beside him. Cast your sugar crullers upon the waters and they shall be returned unto you a hundredfold as caviar.* But the interview was curling with age faster than Victor's first rejection slip (also prominently displayed: it was from the *New Yorker* and had the distinction of sporting an actual, human, handwritten note of comment scrawled in the margin, *viz*.: "Sorry." Whether this referred to the rejecting editor's regrets or the manuscript's quality was best left nebulous.) and Barb was starting to get the hard-bitten, narrow look of a ten-year-old facing off against parents who persist in chirping about Santa. Not good.

So the King interview was a life vest whose kapok molecules were rapidly metamorphosing into cesium. Victor told himself that many a good woman of Barb's generation would be grateful to have a fulfilling multiphase career as aesthetician by day, Amway rep by night, but Barb didn't see it that way. Why didn't she appreciate the stresses of Art? Why must he cringe each time she demanded, "Haven't you sold anything *yet*?" or "Why don't you go down to Four Corners Used Cars and see if Jerry'll give you your old job back?" or "Why in hell did you ever major in *English*? Everyone around here speaks it already."

Useless to attempt explaining the creative nature to such a scrawny soul. Futile to preach the exquisitely painful yet glacial process of inspiration, motivation, and execution in *l'oeuvre* Harris to the heathen. None so blind as they who will not see themselves vacationing in Hawai'i—*again!*—this year and the Millers next door have already gone *four times!*

Of the bricks of such marital differences are the divorce courts of this fair nation built. So, too, the occasional ax-murder-with-P.M.S.-defense case. On the surface it would seem that a miracle

---

"Why in hell did you ever major in English? Everyone around here speaks it already."

---

would be necessary to save Victor Harris' neck from the chop. That was where the Brothers' Meeting Little League came in.

No, really.

And that was why, with luck, there would forever be one less used car salesman at Four Corners and never a moment's peace for the Harris family at the Sharon Valley Regional Elementary School P.T.A. spring picnic.

"Barb, hon, you look just gorgeous!" Sally McClellan swept down on Barb like a tornado on a trailer park.

The McClellans and the Harrises didn't usually move in the same circles. Victor Harris moved in circles pretty constantly, while Phil McClellan moved solely in a steep, straight line of ascent to the windswept heights of financial success whence he might safely piss on the upturned faces of those below.

However, when the first sweet shoots of spring green burst through the hard Sharon Valley earth, Phil McClellan graciously maintained temporary bladder control so far as Victor's face went. As he told The Little Woman, if kissing Victor Harris' skinny ass was called for to achieve your goals, then by God and Ted Turner Industries, Phil McClellan would take a back seat to no one when it came to posterior pucker-ups. The Little Woman conducted herself accordingly as regarded *Mrs.* Victor Harris' more shapely buns, indeed.

Barb was nobody's fool except Victor's and he'd had to marry her for that privilege. She knew just what Sally was after and she sat back on the picnic table bench with all the smirking superiority of a Renaissance prince contemplating where to insert his next dagger. "Sally darling," she purred. Cheeks brushed. Kissy-kissy mwah-mwahs were uttered. "When are you gonna come around to the *La Belle* so I can get my hands on your hair?" (The *La Belle* being the town aesthetorium where Barb currently aestheted.)

Sally gave a nervous little giggle and fluffed her golden pouf of curls with no apparent need. "Oh, I'll be around. I don't think I'm due for a trim just yet."

"Every six weeks." Relentless, that was Barb in the spring. "And I know I haven't seen you since last September." Somewhere a ghostly poniard glittered. "I hear tell you've been going up to Pittsburgh to have it done." *Zzzip-zot*, a slender blade slipped in and out between Sally McClellan's spareribs without The Little Woman feeling anything but a draft tickling her pancreas.

Sally turned bright red. "Who told you that?"

"Marylynn Drummer." Barb's eyes were hooded and inscrutable, but she licked her lips to savor the taste of blood.

"Well, it's just a baldfaced *lie*!" Sally spat. "When did she say so?"

"Mmmm, hard to recall." Barb sucked a few last crimson drops off the tip of her index finger. "I see her so often. Every week she's in the *La Belle* for a shampoo and blow-dry at least. She's got a standing appointment." It was time for the *coup de grâce*, the mercy stroke to end the victim's misery but good. "Sometimes she even brings in little Bobby, and you would be amazed to see how that boy has grown. Why, just the other day Vic was

saying to me, 'Barb, I'd like to see what Bobby Drummer could do if I gave him a chance to pitch, I really would.'"

It was all over except where to ship the body.

Sally McClellan's face sank in on itself like an old helium balloon with a pinhole leak. "Isn't that interesting," she said through a smile so stiff it clattered. "But do you think it's wise? My Jason has always pitched for the Bobcats, and I assumed—"

Barb laughed. "It's not like Vic was breaking up a *winning* team setup, sweetie. Who knows? If Vic gives Bobby a chance to pitch, maybe that'll turn the trick. And you should have seen Bobby's little face light up when I told him what Coach Vic was considering."

"Considering? Then it's not settled?" Sally's eyes flashed. She fingered her hair. "You know, it's so easy to let yourself go over the winter, don't you agree, Barb? Maybe I should take a lesson off Marylynn Drummer. You got room for another standing appointment on your calendar?"

"I'll see what I can do," Barb murmured. "Of course it is harder to fit things in these days. Did I tell you that Pauline Fleck's having me host an Amway party at her family reunion?" Needless to say, Barb went on to rhapsodize over how much dear little Scott Fleck had grown this past winter and didn't Sally agree that the boy deserved a tryout as pitcher for the Bobcats, too?

That night, Victor didn't have to listen to Barb's barbs about where he was on the stairway to success and where he ought to be. Happily swamped with pleas for *La Belle* and Amway appointments (high tips and high sales guaranteed, you betcha), Barb had better things to do with her tongue than rag on the man whose chronic underemployment made his Little League coaching job possible. Yes, baseball season was upon them once more, and so long as Victor owned the power to say whose son played (and whether the boy's field position was somewhere in this time zone), domestic bliss and Barb's own auburn-turfed diamond were his all his.

Nor did it matter a lick that the Brothers' Meeting Bobcats were a team so slack and poorly that a reputable publisher of dictionaries had asked them to pose as an illustration for *pathetic*.

No, it didn't matter to Coach Vic at all, but it mattered very much to Vic Junior.

Vic Junior loved baseball. He was one of those pure souls born with a vision of The Game untainted by the dross and illusion of this sorry world. To him, baseball spoke of Buddha-nature, not Lite Beer. (The *Tao* which can be named is not the *Tao*, but the *Tao* which has its batting stats printed on the back of a trading card is way awesome.) The smell of a newly oiled glove, the clean crack of bat hitting ball, the sight of so many strong, young lads tearing around the bases in those tight-fitting pants, all moved him in ways he could not yet hang a name on. It was a source of spiritual pain to him that his team so seldom won.

It was a pain less spiritual every time Jase McClellan knocked him down in the school yard and taunted him with the fact that he wouldn't be on the Bobcats team at all if not for the fact that his old man was the coach.

Vic Junior could have tattled on Jase, but he was what adults call a *good* child. In other words, there were sponges adorning the ocean floor who had more

backbone than he. He went to church without a fuss and even listened to what his Sunday school teacher had to relate of Hell. He tithed his allowance not because his mother made him but in the sure and simple hope that he was making time payments on one colossal, outsize, super-mega-omniprayer of his own asking being answered some day. He wasn't sure what he was going to request when he finally submitted his sealed bid to Glory, but he knew it would be something *much* better than just asking God to burn Jase McClellan in the fiery pit until his eyeballs melted and his hair frizzled away and the skin on his face blackened and cracked and flaked from the charring bones and his dick fell off.

And then, one day, something happened. Who knows how these things get started? So much depends on serendipity. Pharaoh's daughter might have kept on walking when she heard that wailing in the bulrushes. "Just one of the sacred cats being devoured by one of the sacred crocodiles," she'd say with a shrug of her sweet brown shoulders, and Charlton Heston's resume would have been several pages shorter.

What serendipped in this case was Vic Junior came into *La Belle* to see his Mom and by some karmic radar happened to find the one copy of *Sports Illustrated* in the whole establishment. Like a crow among the lilies it reposed in dog-eared splendor amidst the issues of *Mademoiselle* and *Woman's Day* and *Good Housekeeping*. Last desperate refuge of the male compelled for whatever unholy cause to accompany his woman into the lair of glamor, its well-thumbed antique pages gave moving testimony that a man will submerge himself in last year's sports "news" sooner than he will open a copy of *Cosmopolitan* to read "Impotence: Things Are Looking Up."

"Mom!" Vic Junior cried, bursting in on his hard-working parent, waving the tattered magazine. "Mom, did you *see* this?"

Barb was giving Edna Newburgh a streak job. Mom couldn't see much of anything for all the ammonia fumes peeling her eyeballs raw. "Don't bother Mommy now, sweetheart," she said testily.

"But Mom, *look*! There's an article in here about how the American Little League champions got to go to Japan!" Vic Junior was insistent. Despite the noxious atmosphere he jiggled closer to Edna Newburgh's reeking head and thrust the magazine under his mother's nose.

"So what's that to you? *Champions* means *winners*. I said not *now*!" Barb snapped, flipping the open copy out of Vic Junior's hands with one jab of her elbow. (That she could do this at all was mute testimony to the worthiness of Vic Junior's team nickname, "Wimpgrip Harris.") Like some monstrous mutant butterfly, the magazine took wing and fluttered to the hair-strewn floor.

Giving his mother a cold you'll-be-sorry-when-I-grow-up-to-become-a-crossdresser eye, Vic Junior gathered up his treasure, brushed clots of brown, black, blonde, and red tresses from the slick pages, and retreated to his chair in the waiting area.

He didn't need her to tell him what *champions* meant. It was a fishbone of resentment lodged deep in his throat, proof against all psychological Heimlich maneuvers, that the Bobcats were the losingest team in the history of Little League, baseball, and American sport. The only time a group of kids ended up

with that much public egg on their faces was during the Children's Crusade when hundreds of starry-eyed junior pilgrims to the Holy Land ended up in the slave pens of the East instead. But even some of those guys could hit better than the Bobcats.

For Vic Junior it was his mother's scorn that hurt more than losing *per se*. A man might rale against the sun's rising in the east as easily as against the Bobcats once again playing the part of the walked-on in the league's latest walk-over—such were the dull-eyed Facts of Life—but she didn't have to be so *mean* about it! Of course *she* wouldn't see it that way, *she'd* say she was only being realistic.

In his subconscious, Vic Junior understood as follows: *A man ought to be entitled to hold onto his dreams without some female always yawping at him about reality. Somewhere in the Constitution it should say that any woman apprehended in the act of trying to yank us back down to earth by the seat of our pants will be stood on her head in a pit of hog entrails and left for the buzzards just to see how she likes* that *for reality!*

But a little above the subconscious, in his heart-of-hearts, all that Vic Junior said to the listening dark was: *Please, God, give us the way to win!*

It was a child's simple prayer: sincere, unadorned, pure as a baby dewdrop. On the cosmic scale of values it had clout, pizzazz, and buying power.

It worked.

***

"EXCUSE ME, SIR, but is this where the Little League tryouts are?"

Victor Harris looked down at the brat presumptuous enough to tug at his clipboard-toting arm. "Who are you?" he snapped. His mirrorshades filtered through the picture of a skinny twelve-year-old kid like many others on the team: dark hair, dark eyes, all arms and legs, a little more sunbrowned than most of the specimens currently blundering through warm-ups on the outfield. "Did you sign up at school?"

"No, sir," the kid replied, too respectful to be true. "I just got here." He tapped the brim of his cap so Victor could see the *Angels* logo.

Fine, good, no *problemo*, that explained it. Brothers' Meeting wasn't exactly your hub of suburban commerce, but it was close to Pittsburgh. You did get the occasional corporate family popping in from points unknown to settle down amongst the simple natives to swap beads 'n' trinkets until Daddy's company shipped the poor bastard somewhere else.

"L.A., huh? Nice tan. Okay, kid, what's your name?"

"Yeshua ben Jose."

Was that an accent? Accents made Victor nervous. So did names that sounded like they ought to be stuffed in a pita pocket instead of spread on Wonder Bread.

"Yeshu—what?"

"Yeshua ben Jose, sir." The kid pounded a fist into his glove. "Can I play?"

Victor thumbed back the brim of his cap. "You're not from L.A., are you, son?"

"No, sir." The boy did not volunteer anything more. In another kid, you could put it down to obnoxiousness, but this one's face was empty of anything except a clear-burning eagerness to please. It wasn't natural and it made Victor's teeth curl.

"You wanna tell me where you *are* from?"

"Israel."

A big fat wrinkled *Uh-oh* ticker taped across Victor's face and stayed there until he heard the kid go on to say: "Last thing, I was in Jerusalem, but I was born in Bethlehem and—"

"Bethlehem?" It was like saying *Paris* to someone from Kentucky. Notre Dame and *la Tour Eiffel* just didn't show up in the equation. "Oh, hey, fine, that's all right, then. My mother's people came from Bethlehem," Victor said. He clapped the boy on the shoulder. "So your father worked in the steel mills before or what?"

For the first time, the boy looked doubtful. "My father works just about everywhere."

"No fooling. It's a pain, isn't it?" Victor was starting to feel sorry for the kid. Hard enough row to hoe, coming all the way from Israel where things kept going *kaboom*! Harder when your old man couldn't hold down a job and had to keep switching positions and places to live and even countries just to earn a living. At least the kid had been born in this country, but still, just wait until the other Bobcats found out he was Jewish! (Brothers' Meeting wasn't exactly world famous for its cosmopolitan attitude in matters of religion. Old Mrs. Russell, a devout Presbyterian, had disinherited her daughter for entering into a mixed marriage with a Lutheran.)

Maybe the kindest thing to do would be to send him out onto the field for the tryouts and let him fall on his face. That shouldn't take too long. Everyone knew for a fact—including Victor Harris, who had once owned a Sandy Koufax card—that Jews played even worse baseball than Bobcats.

Of course the kid was dynamite. Prayers for smiting your enemies don't get answered with your enemies just catching mild colds and missing a couple of days' work, oh no! It's the plague or nothing. The same and more goes for a child's prayer that the hand of the Omnipotent yank his Little League team out of the cellar. Yes sir, one look at how little Yeshua ben Jose (simpler to call him "Bennie" and be done with it) hit, pitched, fielded, and ran, and Coach Vic was left slack-jawed, poleaxed, and passionately in love at home plate.

"Porter Rickin'," he declared later that night while Barb cleared the dinner dishes. "That's got to be the only explanation."

"What has?" Barb asked, not really giving a damn.

"That new kid, Bennie. I mean, with a last name like *Jose*? I know he doesn't pronounce it Spanish, but still—I mean, there is no other way to account for how good he is and he's still Jewish. His folks might come from Israel, but somewhere back along the line they must've had a Porter Rickin' in the kibbutz woodpile. Or a Mexican at least. Now *they* can play ball!"

"Uh-huh, uh-huh, uh-huh, uh-huh," said Barb which was her little way of playing ball with her husband without having to endure the drag of actually listening to what he had to say.

"He's pretty good, isn't he, Dad?" Vic Junior asked brightly, proud of himself.

"Good? Why he's a fuckin' mira—!"

"I'd rather be playing Little League fantasy baseball."

"Victor!" Barb's warning tone got drowned out by the shrilling of the telephone. Coach Vic was still going on about how he was going to play Bennie to best advantage when she went to answer it.

She returned a grimmer woman.

"That was Sally McClellan," she said, in the same way a medieval peasant might have returned from a visit to the local witch to announce *The* good *news is I've got the Black Death.* "She says you're not letting her Jason pitch this year."

"You bet your sweet ass, I'm not!" Victor beamed. "With someone like Bennie who can actually get the ball over the center of the plate ten out of ten, I should put in 'Twelve Thumbs' McClellan? What am I, crazy?"

"What you are," Barb said, "is stupid."

"Look, Barb, I know baseball, and I've been coaching this team for five years, ever since Vic Junior was in Pee Wees and didn't know which end of the bat to hold. And five years is exactly how long it's been since I saw a *glimmer* of hope for the Bobcats winning even one damn game. I'm telling you, Bennie is *it!*"

"Is Bennie's mother going to take over the weekly appointment Sally McClellan just cancelled, and pay up all the ass-kissing big tips that went with it?" Barb shot back. "Is she going to buy all the Amway products that Sally McClellan just *happened* to discover were defective and wants to return for a refund? And if she'll do that, will she do the same when all the other mothers come after us with chainsaws because you dumped Jason as pitcher and didn't replace him with one of *their* brats? Oh no! *You* had to pick a newcomer, a foreigner, a *Jew!*" She stomped out of the house. The two Victors could hear her car tires gouging canyons in the gravel driveway as she roared off.

Barb's outburst was so shocking that it left her husband staring off agape into space. "Do you think I did the wrong thing, son?" Victor asked his boy. Normally he never asked Victor Junior anything except *Where did your mother hide the butter?* but these were special circumstances.

"I've got faith in you, Dad." Victor Junior reached across the table to pat his father's arm and got his elbow in the leftover mashed potatoes.

Faith can move mountains even if it's no good at getting mashed potatoes out of the way. In the next few days, Coach Vic had his faith sorely tested in the raging fires of angry mothers. At every practice, he found another of the ladies lurking for him, wearing flinty eyes and a deadly *ninja* combat brassiere that turned perfectly good ornamental boobs into twin symbols of outthrusting nuclear warhead-tipped aggression.

The questions they inevitably shot at him were always the same:

"Who *is* that kid?"

"Why are you letting *him* pitch and not my [insert child's name here]?"

"Is something funny going on?"

"What, did his mother sleep with you or something?"

"Why didn't you tell *me* that was the way to do it?"

Coach Vic just as inevitably replied, "Bennie, because he's good, no, no," and "Well, it's too late for that to change anything *this* year because I've got the roster all set up but I bet by *next* season Bennie's folks will have moved somewhere else so see me then, honey."

Then the Bobcats met their first opponents of the season and it was a whole new ball game.

***

"WE WON."

It was uttered as a whisper, softer than a butterfly's tap-dance routine, on a dozen lips at once. No one dared to say it out loud, at first, for fear that they would wake up and discover it had all been just a Frank Capra movie.

Still, there were the Bobcats, for once getting to *give* the Good Sportsmanship cheer to the losing team. It was a simple "Two-four-six-eight, who do we appreciate?" holler, but there was a slight delay while Coach Vic taught his boys the never-used words they'd long since forgotten.

"We won."

Mothers turned to fathers, eyes meeting eyes in a climax of mutual awe and wonder better than what most of them had been having in the bedroom. Hands clasped hands, bosoms swelled, manly chests inflated, pulses raced. (There were more than a few damp spots left behind on the bleachers, but delicacy prevents any closer investigation of how they got there.)

"We fuck-u-lutely *won!*"

Coach Vic shouted in the confines of his home, and got a dirty look from Barb that quickly melted when she recalled the ecstatic smiles of the other mothers. For once they had seen their man-children taste the thrill of victory, and lo, it was savory to the max. Their maternal fibers exuded endorphins like crazy. They were *happy*. A happy mom is a beauty-shop-going, Amway-buying mom.

"You fuck-u-lutely said it!" Barb shouted back and threw her arms around her hubby's sweaty neck.

Well, there it was: They won. And there it was again the next week, and the next. Bennie's skills on the mound left other teams looking at a steady diet of three-up-three-down while his batting *savoir faire* was—

Hmmm. Honesty's best when speaking of matters pertaining to the divine or the IRS. Bennie could hit, but Bennie was only one skinny little kid. He got a homer every time he was up, then Coach Vic had to plod his hitless way through the team roster until Bennie's number came up again before the Bobcats could get another run on the board. They won, but never by much. It was galling.

Still, since Bennie's pitching disposed of the other team one-two-three and the other team's pitcher could do the same for every Bobcat save Bennie, the local Little League enjoyed a season of the shortest games on record. Parents with limited attention spans and only one six-pack in the cooler were grateful.

Ward Gibbon was not grateful.

***

WARD GIBBON was the father of Jim Gibbon of the Breezy Lake Lions, and up until this Bennie-kid showed up, Jim Gibbon looked fair to cut a major Bennie-like swath through the local opposition, hauling the Lions along with him to the Championship in true and veritable Bennie-style.

Now you've got to understand something about Ward Gibbon: He was a man embittered to the bone. It began when his loving parents named him after their favorite Golden Age television character. Naturally, once he hit school-age, he was dubbed Mental Ward by his juvenile cronies at Breezy Lake Elementary. (A few of the better educated children preferred to seize upon his last name as the means to make his life a living hell, following him around the school making hooting noises and pelting him with bananas.) Worse, creeping nostalgia for Golden Age TV struck his marriage a telling blow when the kittenish Mrs. Gibbon insisted on initiating intimacy by announcing coyly, "Ward, I'm worried about the beaver."

Ward bore his nominal cross grimly, but resolved that no son of his would suffer so. That was why he gave the boy a simple name: *Jim!* So crisp, so clean, so common! Let the infant rabble try to make mock of *that*!

Children love a challenge. Ward Gibbon heard with horror from his son how the other kids at school called him Jungle Jim and Jim-Nastics and Jimbo Bimbo. And there were still some kids around not wholly sunk in the Teenage Mutant Ninja Dorkocracy who knew what a gibbon was. Young Jim Gibbon came home with enough mashed banana in his hair to prove that.

Ward was not a man who gave up easily. If he could not save his son from the horrors of the nyah-nyah mob, he resolved to at least make him proof against all taunts. To this end, there was only one means: Excellence! And for this purpose, diamonds were also a boy's best friend.

Who mocked at Darryl Strawberry's juicy name? Who jeered and jiggled digits at Rollie Fingers? Who had ever been fool enough to make wiggling whisker-signs at Catfish Hunter? Once you climbed the mountain, few *hoi polloi* you left behind had the nerve to toss insults at you, nor the arm to fling bananas to that Olympian height. Let Jim Gibbon triumph on the Little League field, and none would dare sneer at him. So Ward Gibbon commenced to push his son hard-

er than Mrs. Gibbon ever did in all her nineteen-and-a-half hours of hard labor, and do you know what—?

It worked. Isn't life strange? No operating manual accompanies the afterbirth, yet somehow, sometimes, natural-born humans do manage to stumble across one of the Answers To It All. For the Gibbons, *père et fils*, that Answer was baseball.

Or it was until they came up against Bennie.

Ward Gibbon sat on the top rung of the bleachers, his Sans-a-Belt slacks pressed into permanent horizontal ridges across his butt by the hot aluminum slats. With his 'nuff said *I'm With Stupid* cap pulled low over his eyes and his beaky red nose thrusting out from beneath the visor, he glowered over the ball field like an avenging, alcoholic owl. He was pissed.

Most loyal dads will become pissed to a greater or lesser degree when their son's team is losing, but this went beyond mere *pro forma* pissitude. His son's team—his *son,* goddamit!—was losing to the *Bobcats*! Losing scorelessly, what's more. It was like being told you'd come in second to Lizzie Borden for the title of Daddy's Girl.

Ward Gibbon's eyes narrowed. He wouldn't know a gimlet unless you poured it into a cocktail glass, yet for all that he now fixed a steely gimlet eye on the one spectacular, incredible, patently obvious cause of it all: Bennie. There was something about that kid...Ward's mouth screwed up into a hard, bitter nut of sullen wrath that boded no good if cracked.

The Breezy Lake Lions lost the game, and with it all chance to go on to the Regionals. Jim Gibbon flung down his glove and burst into tears. Ward Gibbon descended from the bleachers with hate in his heart and cold-blooded, premeditated research on his mind.

***

"DISQUALIFIED?" Victor Harris bellowed into the telephone. "What the fuck are you talking about?"

There was a pause while the party on the other end of the call explained. From the motel bed, Barb watched her man go whiter than a sheet washed in Amway detergent. He slammed down the receiver hard enough to score several Looney Tunes sight gags by making the furniture jump.

"Honey, what's wrong?" she asked.

"Son of a walleyed *bitch*," he explained. This might have been enough for other wives, but Barb was a Virgo. She wanted details.

Vic strode to the window and gazed out at the inspiring panorama of Williamsport, PA, site of that cosmopolitan Holy Grail, the Little League playoff Finals. The Brothers' Meeting Bobcats had sheared through all intermediate opposition like a hot knife through a mugging victim. Somewhere out there was a Taiwanese team who were about to get their sorry asses kicked (in the spirit of international brotherhood and good sportsmanship). To this peak of glory had Bennie's prowess brought the team, and now—O ironic son of a walleyed bitch!—from this peak of glory was Bennie about to get them booted. Off. Of.

"You don't have any forms turned in for the kid?" Barb skirled. "All this time he's been with the team and you never got his papers in order?"

Vic did not like the way she was so lavishly using the second-person-singular.

Voiced that way, the situation seemed to be all *his* fault. He was quick to pivot the spotlight of blame right back to where it truly belonged.

"Shit, those desk jockeys wouldn't've even noticed Bennie's papers weren't in order if not for some asshole troublemaker coming in, nosing around, and making them get off their butts to look up the kid's records. You think all I've got time for is *paperwork*? The boys need me on the field, not stuck behind some desk shuffling bureaucratic crap. You think they'd have come this far on *paperwork*?"

"No," Barb said. She was a reasonable woman. "But if I know my bureaucrapheads, I'll bet no paperwork for Bennie equals no Finals for the Bobcats. Also disqualifications on all the games that brought them here. Also one hell of a shit storm for my *La Belle* and Amway profits when the team parents find out." She reached for the telephone. "Hello, Information? Brothers' Meeting, please. I'd like the number of Four Corners Used Cars."

Vic burst out of the room, his jawline a white, tight wedge of bone knifing through taut, scarlet skin. He rolled out of the motel and down the street like a storm cloud. His years as a writer had taught him that there was always a way out: an eraser, a bottle of Wite-out, a *delete* command, a hundred last-minute ways to drag the cavalry over the hill to the rescue. He would lay his case before the Little League Powers That Be. He would cajole, he would reason, he would threaten, he would beg, he would cite patriotism and misrepresent the entire Brothers' Meeting Bobcats team composed exclusively of spunky, HIV-positive hemophiliac orphans if he had to, but one thing he would not do:

He would *not* go gentle into that Only-one-owner creampuff good night.

***

THE TAIWANESE TEAM was good, but as Vic Junior told Bennie, they were godless.

Bennie scratched his head and eyed the opposing dugout. "No, they're not."

"Yes, they are," Vic Junior maintained. "They don't believe in *You*, do they?"

"Well, maybe not specifically, but—"

"So that means they're godless, and *that* means they're all going to Hell, and that *really* means they can't win this ball game," he finished with satisfaction.

"Look, Vic, about Hell..."

"Yeah?" A keen, canny look came into Vic Junior's eye. Ever since Bennie had showed up and made his true self known (It's only good manners to inform the petitioner when the Answer to his prayers blows into town), Vic Junior had peppered him with questions about the Afterlife. In particular, Vic Junior wanted to know what sort of gory, painful, humiliating eternal trials and punishments awaited bullies like Jase McClellan. Bennie remained closemouthed under direct inquiry, and even reprimanded Vic Junior quite sternly into matters Man Was Not Meant to Know (i.e. "Mind your own beeswax!"). But as long as Bennie himself had brought up the subject...

"Yeah, what *about* Hell?" Vic Junior demanded. Hey, the back door's better than no door!

Bennie sighed. "Never mind."

"Aw, *c'mon*!" Vic Junior whined. "I won't tell anyone. Is it really full of fire and brimstone and cool shit like that? Our Sunday school teacher told about how

You went down into Hell to yank a whole bunch of guys out, so You oughta know. I mean, how hot *was* it?"

"Suffer the little children, suffer the little children, suffer the little children," Bennie muttered to himself *mantra*-wise, eyes on the blue sky above. It was the perfect day for a ball game, cloudless yet cool and dry. He was jabbed out of his reverie by Vic Junior's bony elbow and nasal bleat:

"Pleeeeeeze?"

Bennie gave Vic Junior a look that would have sent a whole passel of Temple moneychangers scurrying for cover. It was a scowl of righteous wrath fit to turn innocent bystanders into pillars of salt, or fig trees, or divorce lawyers. Just so had artists through the ages portrayed Him enthroned in glory on Doomsday, running sinful Mankind across the celestial price-scanner to separate the metaphysical Brie from the pasteurized American-style-flavored cheese-food product. He opened his mouth to speak and Vic Junior heard a distant rumble of thunder, saw tiny lightnings flash behind Bennie's retainer.

"Aw, skip it," Vic Junior said. He knew when to quit. He was one of the Top Ten quitters of all time, but for once it was a good idea.

"Blessed are the peacemakers," said Bennie with a smile.

"Yeah," Vic Junior agreed. "Now let's kick butt."

The flags were raised, the anthems played, the cry of "Play ball!" rang out, and the teams streamed onto the field to the wild applause and cheers of the spectators. The Brothers' Meeting Bobcats' parents shouted encouragement to their youngsters and hardly any racial slurs worth mentioning at the Taiwanese team.

"Eat *sushi*, you heathen zipperheads!" Sally McClellan stood up and hollered.

"Sally, they're *not* Japanese!" Her husband Phil jerked her back down into her seat by the neck of her Brothers' Meeting Bobcats Booster jacket. "Now shut up. These assholes might have some stupid good-sportsmanship rule in effect. Do you want the boys to lose the game thanks to your big mouth?"

"No, dear," Sally replied meekly, then took advantage of the crowd's overwhelming roar to snarl, *sotto voce*, "Eat *me*, darling."

It was a game that would live forever in the annals of Little League and the casebooks of psychiatry. A play-by-play report would profit a man little who might strive to understand what happened that day on the grassy fields of Williamsport. Between Bennie and the Taiwanese pitcher it was a virtually scoreless game. The batting order prevented Vic Junior's visiting miracle from racking up more than one run every three innings, yet even so, it should have been sufficient.

It was not sufficient for some.

"Smite Thee, O Lord," Vic Junior said to Bennie in the dugout as they prepared to take their last turn at bat in the bottom of the seventh (this being Little League).

"Huh?" said Bennie.

"You know, *smite* them." Vic Junior gave his Savior a poke in the ribs. "Pour out Thy wrath. Drive them before Thee. Score us some more runs."

"We've got two runs and they don't have any. I'm up third. We'll have three runs and win the championship. What more do you want?"

"Winning it with *three* lousy runs? That's not a *man's* game." Vic Junior's sneer was much like his father's. "That's *pussy*!"

Bennie's face darkened. "Having enough to win isn't enough for you, huh? You want more runs. You don't *need* 'em, but you want 'em anyway. Is that all you *really* want?" It was asked in a tone of voice that should have set off whole carillons of alarm bells in Vic Junior's subconscious. It was the big bad brother of his Sunday school teacher's voice when she oh-so-sweetly inquired, *Do you* really *want to read that comic book instead of studying the Ten Commandments, Victor?*

It was a shame that Vic Junior's subconscious chose that moment to step out for a quick snack and a full-body massage, leaving his feckless conscious mind to eagerly reply, "You bet!"

"So be it." Bennie turned his eyes from Vic Junior's greed-glowing face to the scoreboard.

Numbers twinkled. Numbers crunched. Numbers skittered and fluttered like a yard full of chickens on speed. All the zeroes in the Brothers' Meeting Bobcats' Bennie-less innings mutated to tens and twenties and portions thereof. A murmur went up from the stands. The umpire, blind to anything save the play at hand, commanded that the Taiwanese pitcher stop gawking at the scoreboard and get on with it. The boy, badly unnerved by this Western mystery, actually lost control of his first pitch, leaving a startled Bobby Drummer to get a single.

"What are You doing?" Vic Junior seized Bennie by the sleeve.

"Just what you asked," Bennie replied. "I'm giving you more runs."

"Not *that* way!" Vic Junior moaned. "They're gonna think we dicked around with the scoreboard somehow and disqualify us!"

"'Dicked around'?" Bennie repeated, the picture of (no surprise) innocence.

"That's the first time I've ever heard anyone describe a miracle that way."

"Aw, Jeez, You know what I mean! I wanted us to get more runs on the board by *earning* them!"

"Oh." Bennie smiled and nodded.

The scoreboard winked one last time, then subsided. Its effect did not. Half of the Brothers' Meeting parents hooted, demanding that a higher score once posted ought to stay put. The other half shouted that it was all a ploy on the part of the visiting team to make it look like the Americans were cheating when everyone knew the computer system controlling the scoreboard was Made in Taiwan. Newsmen split and scattered throughout the stands, hoping to catch someone with unsportsmanlike foot in mouth, LIVE!

The coach of the Taiwanese team lost it. In the passion of the moment he forgot himself sufficiently to storm the Officials in their lair. The pitcher, stunned to see such behavior in a man he had previously thought less volatile than suet, let Jase McClellan connect with a double that placed a bewildered Bobby Drummer foursquare on third.

"I know what You're gonna do now," Vic Junior said, trembling. "You're gonna use this to teach me a moral lesson, like it's a parable or something. You let those guys get on base and now You're gonna miss Your first two swings on purpose and You're gonna let it get down to the one last swing and if You think I repented enough for being a greedy prick, you'll get that last hit and bring Jase and Bobby home, but if You think I'm not sorry enough You'll strike out and we'll just win the championship by two lousy runs."

An awful afterthought ran him through like an icicle to the heart. "Or—or maybe You're really mad at me, and You're gonna make the scoreboard wipe out all our runs and we'll—we'll *lose*! After everything we went through to get here, You're gonna make us lose the championship! You're gonna smite *us*! You're gonna pour out your wrath all over the Bobcats. That's what You're gonna do, right?"

"Who, Me?" Bennie touched the brim of his batting helmet in salute. "I'm just gonna play baseball." And he stepped up to the bat, leaving a white-lipped Vic Junior in the dugout behind him.

Maybe it's not a good notion to drop suggestions into certain Ears. When Nature comes up with new and improved ways to destroy big chunks of mankind, perhaps She's been cribbing over Humanity's shoulder. Heaven knows, we've done *our* part toward getting those pesky human stains off the face of the earth.

Heaven knows.

In any case, Bennie swung at the first pitch and missed. You'd think it was a bigger miracle than all the times he'd swung and connected for a homer, judging by the gasps that arose from the stands.

Bennie grinned. The Force that (Pick one: created/allowed Evolution to create) the emu, the mandrill, and disco music *has* to have an ironic sense of humor. He whiffed the second one too.

Watching from the dugout, Coach Vic felt a sharp pain in his chest. He looked down and realized he'd ripped out a fistful of hair through his shirt. Had he begged and beseeched and groveled before the Officials, wildly plea-bargaining for them to overlook the missing paperwork until post-game for *this*? ("Do it for *America*!" he'd implored. "Or I'll write up this whole incident and name names and send it in to *Reader's Digest*. You wanna be known as *The Men Who Stole the Children's Dream* for the rest of your lives?") The carpet burns on his knees still smarted.

What was it with Bennie? Sure, the Bobcats were set to win, but the kid's sudden attack of incompetence was no mere fluke. It felt more like a meaning-heavy omen, one that Vic wanted to see averted, and fast. The only hoodoo strong enough to do that would be seeing Jase and Bobby come home. Vic was too staunch a realist to believe that if his star struck out, anyone left in the batting order had the juice to do it, and he was sore afraid. He thought he heard the sound of much weeping and gnashing of teeth. He saw it was only Vic Junior having a conniption fit, babbling about Hell and wrath and smiting and Cooperstown. Coach Vic shook his head: That boy never did do well under pressure.

And then he heard a ghostly voice say unto him *Fear not*. He looked and lo, there was Bennie giving him the thumbs-up sign. The boy hunkered down at the plate. He'd only been toying with the Taiwanese, yeah, that was it. Vic didn't know much, but he knew baseball, and he knew Bennie loved the game too much to let it down.

"Hold it right there!"

The man vaulted out of the stands, bullhorn in one hand, a piece of paper in the other. He surged across the field to home plate. The Taiwanese pitcher threw down ball and glove, folding up into the Lotus position until these crazy round-eyes could get it in gear and play the game. A security guard jumped the fence after the man. He caught him within arm's length of the umpire. The man calmly swacked the guard straight in the face with his bullhorn. The guard folded up into a less classical position than the Taiwanese pitcher.

"Who the hell are—?" the umpire began. The man drew back his bullhorn in a gesture of invitation to a coma. The umpire bolted. The Taiwanese catcher dropped over backward onto his hands and scuttled away crabwise. The other players remained where they were, frozen on the field.

Alone at the plate with Bennie, the man raised the bullhorn to his lips and bellowed, *"There's been a mistake! This whole series doesn't count! The Bobcats should have been disqualified long ago!"*

"Who the fuck asked you?" Sally McClellan didn't need a bullhorn to make herself heard. Phil tried to make her shut up. He got a surprise out of her pack of Crackerjacks that the manufacturer never put inside. *"Who the fuck* are *you?"* she added while Phil fumbled for a handkerchief to press to his bleeding nose.

"I'm Ward Gibbon, goddammit, and I refuse to see this game destroyed by cheaters! Why don't you ask this kid who the fuck he is!" Ward pointed dramatically at Bennie.

From the dugout, Vic Junior stopped his hysterics, heart somewhere up around the soft palate. The black look Bennie had given him for his greed was nothing compared to the glare Ward Gibbon was now getting from the kid at the plate.

"My name is Yeshua ben Jose. Are you calling me a cheater, Mr. Gibbon?" Bennie sounded modest and respectful and toxic. No one seemed to think it odd that his voice carried as far and farther than Ward's and Sally's combined, though he wasn't shouting at all.

"I call 'em like I see 'em and this paper calls for plenty!" Ward rattled the sheet in Bennie's face, then waved it from side to

71

side overhead in Perry Mason style, as if the whole stadium could see what it said. *"I've smelled something fishy about this team for a long time, so I did some research. This is a permission slip! Every Little Leaguer's got to have one of these on file!"*

Sally McClellan told Ward Gibbon where he could file it. Two of the major networks turned cameras on her.

Ward was implacable. *"This slip was filled out for Yeshua ben Jose by his coach, Victor Harris, but this slip is* not *signed!"*

"Excuse me, sir." Bennie tugged at Ward's arm. "You mean that because that paper's not signed, I can't play?"

Ward lowered the bullhorn. "That's right, son." He didn't mean his smile for a minute.

"Can't Coach Vic sign it for me?"

"'Fraid not. It's a *parental* permission slip. Only your father or mother can sign it."

"Yes, sir." Bennie nodded his head obediently. "Coach Vic told me about that, but he said it was all okay because he'd talked to the Commissioners and if I get it signed later on—"

Ward clapped the bullhorn to his mouth and bawled for the benefit of the stands, *"And how much did your Coach Vic* pay *the Commissioners to overlook a FLAGRANT VIOLATION OF THE RULES? That's* bribery *we're talking about!"*

"You bastard!" Coach Vic was on his feet, shaking his fists at Gibbon. *"You're* the one who raised that stink over Bennie's papers!" He lunged from the dugout, howling for Gibbon's blood. A quartet of loyal Bobcats flung themselves around his legs to save him from certain doom. Gibbon was big enough to

snap their beloved Coach Vic into handy, bite-sized pieces one-handed, and he still had that bullhorn. Victor Harris got a good taste of diamond dirt when he went down. A helpful reporter was right there with a mike when he pushed himself up on his hands, spat dust, and shouted, *"I didn't bribe anyone!"*

"Well until you can prove that, that's all she wrote for playing this boy!" Gibbon countered. From the corner of his eye, he could see police streaming onto the field. They'd lock him up, but it would be worth it just to boot this miserable Jewboy's ass the hell out of the championship. "Sorry, son, you're history," he told Bennie.

"But I *love* baseball, sir. I really want to play." It was heartrending, that look in Bennie's eyes. It carried the distilled essence of nearly two thousand years of great Christian artworks portraying Jesus' suffering for Mankind's sins, plus a hefty slug of the ever-popular crown-of-thorns on black velvet portraits. Who could resist such an appeal? One guess. Two words. First word sounds like "Lord." Second word likes bananas.

Ward Gibbon's lip curled into a wolfish leer of triumph. "Tough, kid. You can't always get what you want."

History grants Mick Jagger the credit for originating that phrase, but the smart money knows it was first uttered by an unfeeling *hotelier* a couple of millennia ago when a weary Nazarene carpenter knocked at Ye Olde Inne door in Bethlehem and said unto him, "My extremely great-with-child wife and I want a room for the night." There's a lot that's been written about what kids remember overhearing from their time *in utero*. Believe it all, especially about *this* kid. He remembered it, He didn't like it then,

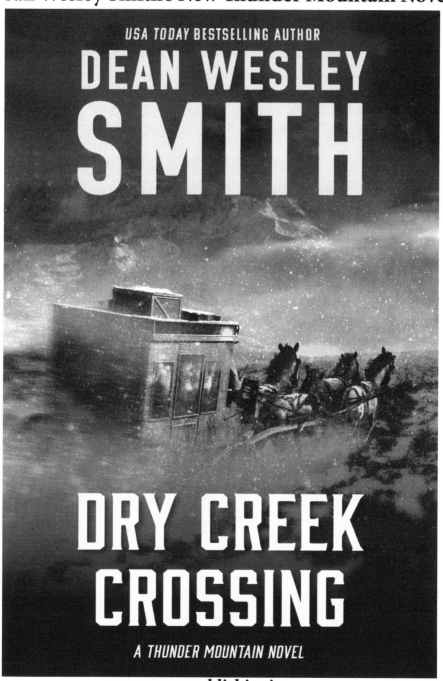

He liked it less now, and this time He was on the outside and able to make His anger felt.

"Sez you," He said. And lo, it came to pass.

The lightning bolt hit Ward Gibbon right up the bullhorn. You never did see a man achieve such instant mastery of hip-hop. Like that other famous Bush (the one that didn't need readable lips to make itself heard), he burned and was not consumed. Of course he yipped a lot.

But that was not all. This was no minor theological tantrum. No, this was a manifestation of the Divine displeasure, and that required more stage dressing.

The heavens opened. Rays of limpid light unfurled from the celestial heights, sending hosts of angels and gaggles of cherubs skidding down the heavenly speed slides. They hit the ground running and did beautiful springboard leaps to get airborne, then soared for the scoreboard. The numbers did that flicker thing again, this time mutating into letters that spelled out REPENT YE NOW, although because there were just nine spaces on the board it looked like REPNTYNOW. Sally McClellan said she was sure it was a city in Yugoslavia. The angels in their robes of glory sang hosannas. The cherubs, bum-nekkid, set up a counterpoint of "Take Me Out to the Ball Game." That's cherubs for you.

As the heavenly choirs perched upon the top of the scoreboard, legions of demons burst from the bosom of the earth. Waving pitchforks and wearing regulation umpires' uniforms, they cavorted along the baselines with hellish glee. On second, Jase McClellan covered his eyes and wet his pants. Bobby Drummer tried to crawl under third base. The Taiwanese infield all started shouting at the top of

their lungs. Either it was an ancient Oriental stratagem for driving off demons or they were just scared spitless, no one ever found out which. The demons abandoned the field and swarmed into the stands, throwing complimentary bags of piping hot Gluttony brand popcorn ™ to the crowd before they reached the top of the bleachers and vanished. It wasn't very good popcorn, but there was plenty of it.

As soon as the demons disappeared, Ward Gibbon stopped sizzling at home plate. He shook himself like a wet dog, astonished to discover he was still alive, though the bullhorn was past hope. He dropped the lump of slag and would have done so with the permission slip as well, only he could not stir hand nor foot. His sphincter was business as usual, though.

Aghast, astonished, embarrassed, he stared at Bennie and in an awestruck whisper asked, "Who are you?"

"Who do you say I am?" Bennie replied.

"Ungh," was Ward's best comeback.

The angels on the scoreboard held up placards reading 5.6, 5.8, 5.0, and so on. A cherub even jeered, "Throw the bum outa there!" Oh, those wacky cherubs!

Then, "Behold," said Bennie in a tone of awful majesty, and He did take His bat and lo, He did gesture therewith, and lo again, the object of his gesturing was the permission slip whereon were suddenly writ in characters of fire the four letters that are the Name of God.

That is, they might have been. There are no guarantees, and Lord knows, no hard evidence because, being characters of fire, they instantly reduced the permission slip to a smattering of ashes in Ward Gibbon's trembling hand.

"The slip's signed. The Bobcats' wins are legal. I'm going home before I smite someone," Bennie said. And without further ado, He did.

Well, would *you* have tried to stop Him?

After the paramedics took Ward Gibbon away and the Officials conferred and the angels wandered off and both teams took a much-needed potty break, a judgment call was made:

"There is nothing in the rule books against having God on your side. Play ball!"

Vic Junior went up to bat, hit a single off the frazzled Taiwanese pitcher, and brought his teammates home. Jase McClellan's cleats squished when he ran and he never teased Vic Junior again.

When it was over, both teams skipped victory/consolation outings to Disneyworld or Japan or even the nearest ice cream parlor in favor of a quick scamper into the nearest house of worship. The Taiwanese pitcher got separated from his group and couldn't find a church but he did find *something*. Later he got credit for bringing *Santeria* to Taipei, but that was about it as far as any repercussions worthy of the name.

***

VIC SENIOR WROTE UP the whole incident, couldn't sell it, and got that job at Four Corners Used Cars. When a story is an outright gift from God but the handwriting on the wall still reads *Mene, mene, tekel, does not suit our present needs*, the wise man finally admits it's time for a career change.

Barb wrote it up too, only she put in a lusty, long-legged, red-haired spitfire of a woman as the team coach. Later in the book she goes on to become the owner of a sprawling multibillion-dollar sports equipment and cosmetics empire. Everyone knows that the infamous midnight "sushi sex" scene between Barb's heroine and the Taiwanese coach on the pitcher's mound was what sold the book and a heck of a lot of raw fish, besides.

***

AFTER THE DIVORCE, Victor Harris went in for coaching Pop Warner football and tried to forget. And it worked, too, until the day at practice when he saw Vic Junior talking to a boy he'd never seen before. The stranger was about Junior's height, three times as broad, four times as muscular, and sporting an uninhibited non-reg beard the color of a thunderhead. He brought his own helmet. He was clearly a Vikings' fan.

The boy noticed Vic Senior staring at him and came over.

"Is this where the football tryouts are, sir?" he asked politely. "A mutual acquaintance said you might like to have me on your team." He stuck out his hand. "I'm Thor."

"Wait'll you're married," Victor Harris sighed.

M.L. Buchman might be known most as a bestselling and highly acclaimed military romance writer, but he writes in many other genres as well, including science fiction and thrillers. This story is solidly on the science fiction side and it has the heart his stories are known for.

Matt actually lives here in Lincoln City, making a living writing fiction full time. He and I try to do regular walking to keep in shape and talk business, since there is so much new business to talk about all the time.

As he said to me one day, he is amazed what he can do with a degree in geophysics.

I am just pleased his great story is helping this magazine get off the ground.

Inside the Sphere
M.L. Buchman

"THERE MUST BE SOMEWAY THROUGH HERE." Trevor Hollman fought the controls, but the plane didn't act as if it cared much. It was his fourth and final attempt to get the big plane and its fifty passengers down. If he missed again, low fuel would force him to land upstate and there'd be some seriously unhappy folks.

The array of instruments was useless for flying into the Sphere. No sensor had been found that could detect it. Automated drones stood no chance, it was only human flight, human instinct that could penetrate that closed space. Trevor had learned by trial and error where the protective layers lurked and how to slip past them.

The early morning updrafts jarred them to the left and a thousand feet up, and the runway didn't have the decency to shift with them. No, instead it shifted the other direction as if trying to avoid him and he had to apply heavy wheel-and-rudder control, first right then left in a gut-wrenching S-curve, to get them back to the center of the glidepath lights. They glistened a dangerous red until he corrected upward to reveal the green again.

There were portions of flying this route that he now truly despised. The sweat on his palms in their death grip on the wheel, more salty sweat stinging his eyes, and the bitter taste of fear deep in his throat, not so different from bile. He could gladly do without those but, with death always so close, he couldn't stop them.

On the plus side, there were also the parts that he still loved. The adrenal surge stoking his heart faster than even the very first time he flew, conquering the skies where no human belonged, and the final ease and exhilaration each time he made it back to *terra firma*.

Except the *terra* here was no longer so *firma*.

This time when the winds shifted, he anticipated both them and the runway, stayed in the green, slid through the last layers, and hammered his main wheels down on the numbers with the bright screech of rubber on tarmac before any other surprises came his way. The nose wheel plunked down with a satisfying thud easy as could be.

Damn he was good. He let himself think it now as he entered that last stage of a successful landing. Mike, his first flight instructor, had always said, "Any landing that doesn't end in a crash is a good one." And that was back before the Sphere which enveloped the city tried to kill you just for sport.

He let Zenna, his copilot, do the announcement back to the cabin as he taxied through the dawn light and onto the empty taxiways.

"Hi folks. We're pleased to welcome you to John F. Kennedy Airport, New York City. Please remember you're inside the Sphere now and your waivers are on file. We will be departing in forty-eight hours whether or not you're aboard."

"Whether or not you survive," Trev mouthed the thought silently.

"We wish you the best of luck in the Big Apple," Zen finished with a sincerity in her voice born of long practice.

Trev eased them up to the gate. This time the city decided to cooperate and the automated jetway mated with the plane rather than trying to block it or playing coy a half-dozen paces from the plane's door.

He cycled down the twin turbines and Zen shut down the radios and the useless nav system.

"You're a wicked wizard of the skies, Trevor. Just wicked." Her voice was warm, as if heated within by a deep-rooted excitement until it brimmed over. Unusual for her, typically so calm, cool, and a little distant. Friendly, but removed a half step.

"One thing I know how to do is fly."

"Let's see how you do in the big, bad city." She said it that way every time they returned.

He looked over at Zen. She hadn't looked like much to him at first, just a tall string bean with jet-black hair down her back. Her black leather armor shielding her from his appraising gaze as much as it averted some of the city's more hazardous denizens. But all he'd really needed to see was how she flew. He'd made dozens of scouting flights around the Sphere solo, but he'd needed a copilot as crazy as he was to enter the Sphere with a load of passengers. A woman who flew like that... After her first test flight, he'd announced the position filled.

When the city was awakened, if that's what had happened, it had killed almost a hundred pilots and ten thousand passengers on the first day before anyone knew what was happening. Of the few daredevils who had attempted the Sphere since, even fewer had returned.

Trev and Zen didn't have the corner on the market, but at ten landings a year, they were far ahead of all the other adventure airlines combined.

With time, he'd been able to see more and more of Zen, as if she were revealing herself as slowly as the city. The black hair set off the brilliant-blue eyes. The shining black leather followed a form that, while slender, had nothing to do with "string bean" and everything to do with sleek power.

There was an obvious pick-up line about what they could do with the forty-eight hours they'd be grounded in the Sphere, but the one time he'd given it voice, she hadn't even had the decency to laugh. She'd simply given him an arched, "You couldn't handle me" look which had pissed him off. Even more so because it just might be true.

Still, he was the only Sphere pilot with more than five successful flights and he had seventy-three. Some hit five and retired wealthy, but most never made it that far taking their plane and their passengers into the next world, if there was one, with a flash of fire and a pile of twisted metal.

"City, right." He spoke to cover the thoughts that crackled along his nerves. A burning need for sex went hand-in-hand with these flights to the city. His body, pumped high on adrenalin, didn't want to let go of that light-headed, all-powerful feeling just yet. But that wouldn't be happening until he managed to get them back in the air, out of the Sphere, and into the real world. Back home, for the world's most successful Sphere pilot, well, the pickings were not hard to find.

Zenna finished the shut down and clambered out of her seat.

"Where to this time, oh Great Zen Master?"

Her answering smile was brief and wicked, no, mischievous. That was another thing he hadn't noticed at first. Zen had a great smile. You could read it like a novel. It expressed joy, humor, derision, amusement, excitement, and a dozen other emotions with a dazzling brilliance. Again his body wondered how that smile would look in passion and again he added the question to his personal list to solve someday.

THE NARA REACTION

The Crash and Smash destroyed the most feared race in history.

All but one. Ri, the child warrior. Born of the shattered streets of Nara, Japan. Where books burn to heat the night.

Ri stands alone against death for all.

For this book and other
M.L. Buchman stories and novels
go to:
www.mlbuchman.com

He followed her out of the cabin and up the jetway. The passengers were already gone. The chances of seeing any of them in the city was pretty small. They'd already have flocked to the "A" train, cramming together rather than waiting for the next subway car that would automatically follow ten minutes behind, not wanting to waste a minute.

Trev liked following Zen. He used to lead the way, until he noticed how differently she moved inside the Sphere. It wasn't that she had a great ass as she walked ahead of him. Okay, it wasn't only that. She moved as if she came alive here. It reminded him of how he felt while flying.

Flying the Sphere wasn't merely a skill or there'd be a hundred pilots a week flying into JFK. It was also an art. The art of the possible, how to feel your way around the Sphere and slip a plane into her belly.

That's how Zen walked, like it was an art.

***

THEY HAD THEIR OWN car on the train as they start-stopped all the way through Brooklyn. The subway was immaculate and nearly silent. With few passengers and no surviving graffiti artists, the automated systems ran and flawlessly maintained the subway floating millimeters above the mag-lev rail in its underground tunnel.

A few lost souls wandered aboard before they crossed under the East River, but they looked directionless.

He and Zen played their normal game making up pasts for them.

The lady in the feather boa, one that might have been new when Trev was a teenager, he named as a famous Broadway actress still haunting the stages though they'd been empty for over a decade. She left a taste of lavender soap on the air when she passed them by with not even the slightest nod.

For the old guy with the pink Mohawk, so retro it might almost be current, Zen decided he was a business executive who'd dropped a megabuck for a flight into the Sphere, and never caught the flight back out. He smelled like he hadn't bathed since he landed.

The Sphere did strange things to people.

Trev had been to most of the Earth's big cities and they were just that, big. McD's in Delhi was just like the one in Seattle, except Seattle had ten million geeks rather than a hundred million Indians on its streets.

The Big Apple was different. Since the Sphere had wrapped around it ten years ago, it warped and woofed through time and space. People traveled here on the chance that the city would like, rather than despise, them. The outer world's stratosphere of the "super successful" was peopled with Sphere survivors. The best actresses, novelists, scientists… all had visited the Sphere.

But the risks were high. Some found incredible talent and wealth, others would never again form a cogent thought. Sphere survivors also peopled the darkest asylums.

Trev didn't come for the Sphere, he came for the flying. Like Neil Armstrong, the first and the best. Except Neil's flight, other than an insane level of risk on barely tested equipment, had been achieved mostly by science, planning, and huge infusions of cash. Trev's flights were about instinct. And each flight was as risky as the first. Neil had done his stunt once, survived, and been done. Trevor was shooting for a hundred. Just twenty-seven to go.

The Sphere never touched him. Oh, she fought his arrival, he'd always thought of the Sphere as a cranky old bitch, but he'd slipped in each time.

He glanced at Zen as the "A" train roared beneath the East River. She sat calmly, at perfect rest, her body weaving slightly with the sway of the rocking car as if born to it. He never knew why she came here. He'd asked, but she hadn't answered.

They always stuck together inside the Sphere. Even the first time, when they'd done little more than scout the airport, they'd, by some unspoken pact, moved together. Is that why the city didn't touch them, because they stayed together? He didn't know, but he wasn't going to experiment with the idea. If that was what kept them safe, he'd stick tight by her side.

For the month between flights, she'd evaporate, as if she didn't exist outside the flights and the Sphere. He'd considered following her more than once, but he wasn't so sure he'd like the answers.

***

THEIR SCOPE of exploration had expanded with each trip until now they traveled far and wide through the city.

Trev had learned to let Zenna choose their next destination. He'd been in the city twice before the Sphere had formed, and remembered little more than noise, dirt, and the world's most amazing pizza. She'd lived here for twenty-five years, then been on a flight to Chicago when the world changed.

She'd led him on walks along FDR overlooking the Hudson River, now a serene river flowing gently by with no boat traffic, not even a Circle Line ferry. They typically slept at the Plaza Hotel in the Edwardian Suite with its rich-wood period furniture, stunning view of Central Park, and two bedrooms, each with its own bath. They'd explored museums and even found a few restaurants that had been sufficiently automated so they could still get a decent meal despite the chefs being long gone. Zen was a sucker for the stacks in the New York Public Library, which typically left Trevor flipping through decade-old magazines until he discovered the "Best of Mystery Writing" anthologies section.

In all their trips here, neither of them had gone mad, nor brilliant. And no one had tried to kill them except once on the Brooklyn Bridge.

Trevor scratched at his arm, the itch running long up his left forearm, as they passed under the East River and the bridge. They'd walked across it once, and he'd nearly lost his arm to one of the "ghosts." That's what they called the people trapped inside the Sphere. The city had shrunk overnight from forty million to five or ten thousand. Those who remained had never left, nor apparently wanted to leave. The last permanent residents of the city.

Trevor had tried to engage one on the bridge to ask directions and earned a knife slice up the length of his arm. After that, he'd taken to wearing the same Kevron black leather that Zen wore. Violent ghosts were rare now, but during the first years, before the ghosts had accepted their fates, as many passengers had died bloody deaths in their two days on the ground as had lost their minds.

Trevor had tried to talk to other ghosts, even been commissioned to kidnap one and return it to the outside for study. Though the teenaged girl had been there when he'd taken off, she'd disappeared by mid-flight. He'd turned down every contract since to capture a ghost. The Sphere had left them alive for a reason, and he wasn't going to mess with them again.

The girl's eyes, as dark as Zen's were bright, still haunted his sleep from time to time.

He let himself settle into the subway car's rock and sway as Zen let stop after stop go by. Ghosts boarded and left. Once a glassy-eyed passenger from this morning's flight wandered aboard and sat near them with no sign of recognition. It wasn't the thousand-mile stare of someone in revelation, there was simply no one home any more.

Trev shifted, but the eyes didn't follow him. He knew this one represented an empty seat on the return flight or another brain-blown zombie for the asylums if the chrono on his wrist led him back to JFK. No, the chrono wasn't on his wrist anymore, though every passenger had been sent in wearing one with a strap that had to be sawn off to remove. This one definitely wouldn't make the flight.

"Let's get off." The guy was unnerving him.

Zen just shook her head, "Not yet."

They went uptown. Past Greenwich Village, where they'd poked through the shops for a couple of trips, and Soho, where they'd wandered through a hundred galleries. Trevor had been partial to some of the photo exhibits, Zen liked the odd 3D stuff, like statues from a world with no recognizable form. Times Square and its theaters, each stuck forever with a single movie playing five times a day. Columbus Circle and the Met, where neither opera nor symphony nor ballet had been performed in a decade.

They lost the zombie-guy somewhere in the mid-50s, Trev hadn't really noticed where.

He glanced at Zen, but she was quieter than usual, and more nervy. Usually the steady one, she was now in constant small motion. And grim. Her expression was fixed now, glaring at an old poster pasted on the inside of the glistening subway car. She'd apparently become transfixed by an ad for an off-Broadway play that he'd never heard of.

He had entered some sort of calm place he usually only found while flying, just letting the world rock around him, his body swung forward as the subway braked and opened its door with a sharp hiss-and-clank, then, after the sound in reverse, swaying back as the cars accelerated sharply away from the empty stations.

"Eighty-first," Zen slid to her feet in a single elegant flow. "This is us."

***

THEY'D NEVER GONE this far north on the West Side. Central Park and its empty and perfectly groomed lawns, yes, but not over to the Upper West Side.

Trevor always found it surprising when they emerged from underground. It was now bright morning and the sky shone a crystalline blue. An hour on the subway had disconnected him from the outside world and his reentry into day or night, rain, shine, or snow was always a bit of a shock. The air impossibly fresh. Everywhere else on the planet, the masses of humanity scented the air. Sometimes it was okay, sometimes harsh and nasty. But New York had been scrubbed clean of traffic, garbage, businesses, and most of humanity. It had the cleanest, freshest air he'd ever smelled.

The silence always bugged him, though. A dozen billion people didn't leave a lot of silence out in the world, but inside the Sphere, there was nothing. Not a peep. No birds flew, no cars whirred by on mag-lev or air cushion. Little wind, no rain or snow. If not for the ghosts, it would be frozen in time.

Zen checked her chrono. They'd been in the Sphere for under an hour. Usually he was the one constantly checking the time, this time it was her.

They walked around the corner from the subway, past a stand with no hotdogs, no seller, and no nice bite of mustard and sauerkraut saturating the air with...

Trevor rocked to a stop.

There it stood.

He'd read about it. You didn't make your living being one of the only pilots who could fly into the Sphere and not study what lay inside.

The Rose Center for Earth and Space filled much of the city block before them. A thirty-meter across silver sphere that housed the Hayden Planetarium floated in the center of the glass-walled museum. Inside the sphere, he knew though he'd never been, were two large theaters, Big Bang below and star projector above. A fifty-meter across glass cube wrapped it away safe from the elements. The giant silver sphere appeared to float in the cube's center, a hydrogen atom's nucleus on steroids. One had to really look to see the four slender supports that held the massive sphere aloft.

The space between glass and sphere had been left mostly open. A descending walkway for the Size Scales of the Universe exhibit curved from mid-Sphere back to a perimeter mezzanine walkway. The spheres representing the size and coloring of the various planets ranged randomly about the space. But for the most part, it was silvery sphere, open air, glass walls, and slender steel supports.

But it wasn't just the planetarium that he saw.

Sure it was an amazing piece of architecture, but so were the Two-Mile Towers in Jo-burg and the Cubic Mile city that stood where London had once thrived, its lower five stories submerged in the risen waters of the Atlantic.

What stopped him cold, so cold that an actual shiver slid up his spine, was that he was looking at the Sphere. In seventy-three flights and roughly another hundred failed approaches, he knew the shape of the Sphere that had encapsulated New York City better than anyone else living.

And there it stood, the perfect 3D model. The sphere of the planetarium was the same shape as the Sphere encapsulating New York City. And the glass cube it floated in was what admitted you to the Sphere.

But it wasn't that simple. The towering steel pillars that held up the glass had also somehow been projected into reality around the invisible Sphere encapsulating the city. Snag a pillar, catch a cross-brace, or hit a floating planet model and you and your load of passengers were dead. And the whole building had been attached to the north side of the massive edifice of the American Museum of Natural History.

He could see now why you couldn't approach up the Hudson, you'd hit the front of the Museum's monolithic structure. The massive northeast corner supports must have landed squarely on

La Guardia airport, completely block-
ing landings there.

The sphere of the planetarium was
suspended inside the glass cube, not
touching the ground. That explained
why no approaches by sea or land could
reach New York. And why the risen
ocean simply stopped around New York
rather than inundating it. The only way
into the Sphere was by air through the
maze that were the supports and exhibits for the Hayden Planetarium's outer
glass-box architecture.

"Come on, Trev." Zen tugged at his
arm, actually causing him to stumble forward.

His knees were no more certain
than a child's as she led him inside the
glass building then up a great curving
ramp that reflected the invisible arm
that swung from Roosevelt Island up
and over Washington Heights. Many
action-adventure planes had been lost
there by pilots who had thought to fly
around the city after they'd made it inside the Sphere. Trevor could see that at
JFK he'd slipped through a hole in the
outer architecture, ducked beneath the
spinning globes of the massive exhibit of models of the planets, and landed
in one of the few safe spots left in New
York City.

Dizziness spun through his head as he
twisted and turned to see the world that
had until now been instinct and, he could
see, a fair share of luck.

"Don't you see it, Zen?"

"Sure." Her single calm word stabi-
lized rather than upset him. She sounded
so certain of the rightness of it that his
head cleared and he was able to follow
under his own steam. There was more
there. Her voice wasn't just calm, it was
rough. And her smile was nonexistent.

She didn't give him a moment to
think more about it.

Through the double doors at the head
of the ramp, hundreds of deep, reclining
chairs encircled a central projector. He
sniffed for a hint of ancient popcorn, but
there wasn't any, just that odorless air left
by the cleaning machines.

"Sit. The show starts soon according
to the program by the door."

Trev collapsed into a seat. Zen settled
beside him. She rested her hand, warm
and slender, on his wide and rough one,
where their chairs shared a common arm.

It was as if she belonged here.

She did.

"You are…"

"Shh. Don't spoil it."

"But, why?" Before he had even completed the cogent thought, the question
had spilled forth.

She nodded toward the dome above
him as the chair tipped them slowly back
until they faced mostly upward into the
planetarium dome.

The lights began to dim revealing
a cloud-scattered sky glowing in the
last light of the day spread wide across
the half dome of the planetarium arcing
above them.

A piece of soothing classical music
eased the setting of the sun. The stars began to shine forth, first one twinkler, then
another. A dusting, a wash, and finally a
brilliant bounty shone across the heavens,
for the planetarium projector had somehow blurred the line between being a
ceiling and revealing the heavens.

Zen sighed.

"I always loved the sunset sequenc-
es. I grew up across the street," she whispered as if not to disturb all of the people
who might have once sat in the now empty planetarium.

"My grandmother brought me here probably a hundred times. I love this city and I love the stars, though this is the only place the two ever met. Between pollution and lights, this is all that I knew of the night sky."

Her voice lulled and washed over him.

A deeper voice, perfectly modulated, rolled from hidden speakers and began describing the constellations that the Greeks had placed across the sky to honor their gods. Projected lines of white light drew the pictures across the starfield.

"New York was dying." Zen spoke just a little louder than the recorded narrator. "At its heart, it was failing. And around the world, the ice was melting. I knew that soon it would inundate New York just as it did Shanghai, Mumbai, Los Angeles and so many others. They'd started the dykes, but the Netherlands disaster proved the ultimate pointlessness of that."

She slid her fingers between his and he held them tightly.

"I figured out how to save the city. But I didn't understand some of what I did. The effects that turns some visitors into geniuses and others into madmen, that wasn't planned. I just wanted to save and preserve."

Trev studied the face that the narrator informed him was the Greek goddess Athena, Virgo the Maiden. Zen had saved the city? The shock should have hammered into him, but somehow it didn't. It was as if he'd known all along that Zen and the city had some special connection.

"How?" Trevor finally found the question.

"Magic."

"No," he struggled up from the embrace of the chair sufficiently to look at her directly. Her face shimmered beneath the stars. "No, really."

"Woman's magic. Honestly, it's the best explanation I've ever found. Between flights all I do is research, trying to understand what happened here. I mean I know that it was me who did it, but I still can't figure out how. I've talked to scientists and religious leaders. I studied ancient texts and loony 'Net theorist blogs. All crap as far as I can tell. I finally found an old aboriginal woman in the Australian Outback. She told me a story from the Dreamtime, their name for the ancient past when creation occurred. She insisted that every thousand years a woman of power is born 'to preserve.' It's the best explanation I've found even if it makes no damn sense."

"And this is preserving?" Trev felt an anger rising. "What about the forty million who lived here? What about the ones we take back to scream in the asylums? What about the girl?" The one with the dark, haunting eyes who had simply faded away even as he watched. Was his anger a righteous declaration on behalf of all those others or on behalf of the ache in his heart at the loss of that one?

"I, I don't know." He heard the break in her voice.

Zen's voice never broke.

He still held her hand, now chilled, tightly. The stars turned above them to reveal a myth of a horse who could fly and save a fair maiden in distress.

"The aboriginal woman also said that she who preserved would be born of the one who destroys. I don't think my mom destroyed much. What if I'm the one who destroys?" Zen's query barely reached his ear.

That took the wind out of him and he fell back in the chair.

He didn't know why, but some instinct, probably a response to the pain in her voice, made him push the chair arm, which separated them, back between the seats and pull her into his lap. He held her, though she didn't weep as he half expected. She simply leaned in and let herself be held.

"It all started here," she told his neck as she rested her head on his shoulder.

Her hair smelled of paradise and citrus shampoo.

"I had an idea. Then I believed in it. That this beautiful city could be encased safely inside a sphere just like the Hayden Planetarium, all suspended in a great glass box that could keep out the sea and protect this city I love so much. I felt the change, I just didn't understand it at the time."

"I went to Chicago on business and New York disappeared behind me. You were my ticket back in. The way you fly, I knew you'd be the one who could find your way back in. I studied like mad so that I could fly with you. I had to see what I'd done."

Trev held her, her Kevron armor cool and smooth beneath his hand, her breath a warmth on his cheek. Her breath was fresh, like the air of her beloved city. Staring upward he watched beyond the stars, saw the city encased in a Sphere exactly the same shape as the planetarium.

Magic? Woman's magic? How should he know? It made as much sense as any of the thousand conflicting theories he'd heard about it.

"If you are the one who preserves," Trev tested the thought carefully. "Then this whole mess is just crazy enough to make sense. Maybe."

She nodded against his shoulder and he allowed himself to take advantage of the moment to rest his cheek on her impossibly sleek and soft hair. Just for a moment.

"But if you're the one who destroys…"

Zen froze in his arms, gone impossibly still.

She'd said something else. Some other magic.

"But if you are the one who destroys, which kind of fits better, when do you give birth to the one who preserves? And what does she do?"

"Well…" Zen sat up enough that he could see her bright eyes catching the starlight.

His hands slid easily to her waist. It struck him that he'd never touched her in all of their years of flying together. And that even through the Kevron, she felt smooth and perfect.

"I," she brushed her lips across his. "I had some ideas about how we could find that out."

Over the years, Dan C. Duval has kept amazingly busy either in the high-tech computer world or running a horse ranch or now running a bookstore.

I have always been a fan of Dan's stories and bought a number of them for Fiction River *volumes. His work has also appeared in anthologies out of DAW Books and one of his stories was selected for the* Year's Best Crime and Mystery Stories 2016.

This wonderful and nasty little story will give you an idea of why I want many more of Dan's stories in these pages coming up.

The Bee Man
Dan C. Duval

A LONG TIME AGO, there was a little boy, whose father supplied all the milk for an entire village. The little boy had the chore of milking the cows every morning and evening. He hated to do that because he wanted to run in the fields and play instead of milking the cows. He complained about his chores each day and muttered about them when his brothers and sisters slapped him for complaining aloud so much.

One morning, when the little boy was alone with the cows, slowly filling the bucket with milk, a fairy suddenly appeared beside him.

The fairy was a little person, even smaller than the little boy; not pretty but not ugly, it was not clear if it a boy or girl. In fact, the fairly looked more like a grown-up shrunk to be tiny, than like a young child.

The fairy said, "Little boy, why are not playing the fields? Why are you working so hard? Give me something sweet and I will do your chores for you so that you can go play."

The little boy knew that his father had found a nest of bees several days before, so he ran to the house and, sneaking by his mother and his sisters working in the kitchen, scooped a handful of honey from the bucket his father had strained it into. He ran back to the barn.

By the time he got there, the cans of milk were all lined up, waiting for his father to move them onto the wagon he used to take them into the village, each filled to the brim. Even the boy's milking bucket was full of milk, so that he could haul that into the house for the day's cooking.

The fairy sniffed at the little boy's sticky hand and tasted the sweet honey, licking at the globs squeezing through the little boy's fingers.

"If you will leave a handful of sweet honey out for me each night," the fairy said, "I will milk your cows for you, so that you do not have to work so hard and can go play in the fields." The fairy lapped up more of the honey.

The little boy asked, "Will you milk the cows for me after dinner?"

"Yes, I will," said the fairy and sipped more of the honey.

The little boy asked, "Will you milk the cows for me tomorrow morning?"

"Yes, I will," said the fairy. "Your cows will be milked for you every morning." The fairy took another mouthful of honey. "And every evening" The fairy sipped again. "Forever. But you must put some honey on the doorstep for me every night."

The little boy said, "I will do it!"

The fairy said, "Every night, remember."

The fairy grabbed the little boy's hand and sank its teeth into his thumb. The little boy cried out and tried to pull his hand away, but the fairy held on and began to suck at the blood streaming from the wound. The fairy took no more than a mouthful of the blood before it let go of the little boy's hand. The little boy stuck his thumb into his mouth, the honey making the blood sweet and sticky.

The fairy frowned and said, "A handful of honey every night or I will take sweet blood, instead of sweet honey."

With that, the fairy vanished.

After dinner, the little boy went to the barn to see if the fairy had milked the cows. As he slipped inside the door, he found all of the cans already filled and lined up waiting to be moved onto the milk wagon.

So the little boy spent the evening playing in the fields and poking about the woods and thought nothing of the chores he did not have to do. The next day, the milk was waiting for him when he went to the barn and the little boy played instead of working.

But the little boy was a lazy little boy.

He left the honey on the doorstep for the fairy for several nights, but one night it was too cold and he was too tired from playing and running all day and he didn't get out of his warm bed to put the honey on the doorstep.

In the morning, one of his older sisters was found dead in her bed, her throat torn out as if by a wolf. Though his father and older brothers searched, they never found any wolf, nor could they figure out how a wolf would have gotten into the house.

The little boy was very frightened. It was all his fault, but he couldn't face his father and admit it: he would tell the fairy to stop milking the cows and it would all be back to what it was before.

But he never saw the fairy, not when he called to it, not when he stayed on the doorstep all night himself, not when he

In the morning, one of his older sisters was found dead in her bed, her throat torn out as if by a wolf.

stayed in the barn with the cows all night. He was very careful, though, to make sure there was honey on the doorstep before he went to sleep.

It was only a few days more, though, before the honey his father had found was all used up, so instead of playing he had to search the woods to find more honey. Instead of running free, he climbed trees to search the notches between branches and the abandoned holes where bees might make their nest. When he finally found one, he was stung many times trying to steal some of the honey.

The honey he found did not last long and he did not want to be stung the next time he got more honey, so he stole some cheesecloth his mother had set aside and wrapped it around the edge of one of her old church hats that she no longer wore, to guard his face from the angry bees. His winter mittens would protect his hands.

So he was able to supply the fairy with its honey every evening.

At least, for a time.

He took so much honey from the bees, though, that they moved their swarm elsewhere. He had to go farther from the farm to find more nests.

By the end of spring, all of the hives near the farm had been raided to the point where the bees had left. One day, the little boy had to go so far to find a nest that he wasn't able to get home that night and was lost in the dark woods. In the morning, when he got back to the farm, he found that one of brothers had been killed in his sleep, his throat torn out.

The little boy could not let that happen again, so he went to the last nest he had found and captured all the bees in a sack. He took large pieces of their honeycomb and put that in the bag, too. He brought the sack home and put the bees in a box.

But the bees left the next day and he spent days losing, searching for, and finding the swarm before he discovered that he needed to put a small hole in the box, too small for the largest bee in the nest to leave, but small enough that the other bees could go out and collect the honey. The bees would not leave the large one behind so they stayed in the box, even when he took some of their honey. But while learning this lesson, another of his sisters was killed when one day he could not find the swarm and had none of the honey that he needed to leave for the fairy.

His private bee's nest gave him all the honey he needed during the summer but he saw that his bees were barely able to give him enough honey to feed the fairy and themselves and he was afraid they would not be able to make enough to last through the winter, when there were no flowers.

That meant he needed to catch more bees, make more nests, so that honey he took would leave the bees enough to last the winter. He searched for more nests, careful to make sure that he was home each night to leave the honey out, which meant he had no time to play or to run in the fields. When he ran, it was to and from the woods, to find more bees and return home with them.

As it turned out, he found enough nests to fill plenty of boxes with bees and had enough honey to last the whole winter, with even some extra for his family in the coldest, darkest parts of winter.

Over the years, the little boy became an older boy, and the number of his tamed bee's nests grew. Within a few years, he was able to feed the fairy and have enough left over to sell honey to the whole village. By the time he was married and had his own children, he was known far and wide as "The Bee Man" and people came from faraway places to learn what he knew about keeping bees.

And still each morning and each evening, the cans of milk would be waiting for him in the barn, even after he'd sold the cows, thinking that maybe the fairy would go away if there were no more cows to milk. He moved to a different farm—careful to take his bees with him—and still the milk appeared, even though he had no cows, so he bought more cows rather than have people wonder how a man who had no cows ended up having so much milk.

Each morning, too, the offering of honey was gone.

All would have been fine but there were years where there was little sun, so fewer flowers, which meant less honey. And then there was the bear that tore

open several of the hives and scattered the bees, before it could be driven away. And once all of the bees just died, for no reason he could fathom. When he did not have honey to set out for the fairy, one of his brothers or sisters died in their sleep, their throats torn open, until he had no brothers or sisters left.

The evening after his last sister was found dead, he did not leave any honey out, because he had no more brothers or sisters for the fairy to kill. Being an old man by then, he did not care if the fairy came for him.

But in the morning, his oldest daughter was found dead, her infant still suckling at a bloody breast. After that, the Bee Man tried everything to rid himself of the fairy, even having the Bishop himself perform an exorcism. Still, every day, the milk appeared and the honey disappeared.

The Bee Man had told only his confessor about the fairy during his whole life, an old priest who had seemed relieved

Coming Issues from Pulphouse Fiction Magazine
www.pulphousemagazine.com

when he died himself and no longer had to keep such a secret. One night, though, when he felt Death creeping up on his shadow, he called his youngest son to him, the one who had taken over the old man's bees and was himself becoming known as the Bee Man. He told the boy about the fairy and about the milk and about the honey and all that he tried to do to be rid of the fairy, and about the agreement that had to be kept. The old man made his son promise to leave the honey out for the fairy every night.

When the old man died, the bees did not buzz but stayed sullenly inside their boxes, the cows lowed mournfully, and even the fresh morning milk did not seem as sweet. The young Bee Man had not believed his father's story and, himself saddened by the passing of his father, did not leave any honey on the doorstep that night. In the morning, he found that his oldest brother, who had married the miller's daughter and taken over the village mill, was found dead in the mill, surrounded by the stone of which it was made, his throat torn out as if by the teeth of a wild beast.

He never failed to leave the honey out after that.

Unlike his father, the young Bee Man told the story to each of his children, so that they would understand how important the bees were to them (and especially to their brothers and sisters) and how important it was to leave the sweet offering every night.

That is why our family has tended the bees for so many generations. You will someday be the Bee Man yourself. Well, as long as your father doesn't forget to leave the honey on the doorstep one night and the fairy comes for YOU!

~

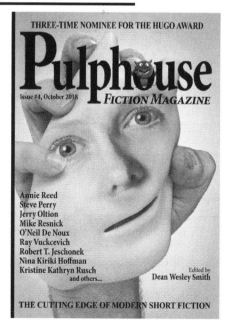

Coming Issues from Pulphouse Fiction Magazine
www.pulphousemagazine.com

Not only did Mike Resnick sell me stories to the original Pulphouse: A Fiction Magazine, *he and Barry Malzberg did a regular and wonderful column as well. To say it is an honor to have him back in this new start is an understatement.*

Mike is the all-time leading award winner in short science fiction, living or dead. He has been nominated for a record thirty-seven Hugo Awards for his work.

On top of the all the novels and short stories, Mike is also an editor, including over forty anthologies in which he bought a number of stories from me over the years. Right now he is editing Galaxy's Edge Magazine *as well as* Stellar Guild Books.

For those of you who know the history of science fiction, this wonderful story will have an extra level. But even if you don't know the history, the story is a great romp in the western tradition of great classic science fiction.

Catastrophe Baker
and a Canticle for Leibowitz
Mike Resnick

I WAS STANDING AT THE BAR in the Outpost, which is the only good watering hole in the Plantagenet system, lifting a few with my old friend Hurricane Smith, another practitioner of the hero trade. Somehow or other the conversation got around to women, like it always does sooner or later (usually sooner), and he asked me what was the most memorable name I'd ever found attached to a woman.

Now, man and boy I've met thirteen authentic Pirate Queens, and eleven of them were called Zenobia, so that figures to be a mighty memorable name, and the Siren of Silverstrike was pretty original (at least in my experience), but when it came down to choosing just the single most memorable name, I allowed that there was one that won hands down, and that was Voluptua von Climax.

"You're kidding!" said Smith.

"I wish I was," I told him. "Because a deeply tragic story goes with that name."

"You want to tell me about it?" he said.

I shook my head. "It brings back too many painful memories of what might have been between her and me."

"Aw, come on, Catastrophe," he said.

"Some other time."

"I'm buying for as long as you're telling it to me," Smith offered.

And this is the story I told him that night, out at the most distant edge of the Inner Frontier.

***

IT ALL BEGAN when I touched down on the pleasure planet of Calliope, which abounded in circuses and thrill shows and opera and ballet and theatre and no end of fascinating rides like the null-gravity Ferris wheel, and of course there were hundreds of casinos and nightclubs. I moseyed around for a few hours, taking in all the sights, and then I saw *her*, and I knew I'd fallen hopelessly and eternally in love again.

Trust me when I tell you that there ain't never been a woman like her. Her face was exotic and beautiful, she had long black hair down almost to her waist, beautifully rounded hips, a tiny waist, and I'll swear she had an extra pair or two of lungs.

She was accompanied by a little guy who seemed to be annoying her, because she kept walking away, which kind of reminded me of jelly on springs, and he kept following her, talking a blue streak.

I knew I had to meet her, so I walked over to her and introduced myself.

"Howdy, ma'am," I said. "My name is Catastrophe Baker, and you are the most beautiful thing I've seen during my long travels throughout the galaxy. Is this little twerp bothering you?"

"Go away and leave us alone!" snapped the little twerp.

Well, that ain't no way to speak to a well-meaning stranger, so I knocked out eight of his teeth and busted three of his ribs and dislocated his left shoulder and kicked him in the groin as a mild reproof, and then turned my attention back to the beautiful if beleaguered lady.

"He won't bother us no more, ma'am," I assured her, and it seemed likely since he was just laying there on the ground, all curled up in kind of a ball and moaning softly. "How else can I be of service to you?"

"Catastrophe Baker," she repeated in the most beautiful voice. "I've heard about you." She kind of looked up and down all six feet nine inches of me. "You're even bigger than they say."

"Handsomer, too," I said, in case she needed a hint.

"You know," she said thoughtfully, "you might be just what the doctor ordered."

"If I was the doctor, I'd be more concerned with helping your friend here," I said, giving him a friendly nudge with my toe to show there wasn't no hard feelings. I really and truly didn't mean to break his nose with it.

"You misunderstand me," she said. "I heard you were kind of a law officer."

"No, ma'am," I told her. "You've been the victim of false doctrine. I ain't never worn a badge in my life."

"But didn't you bring in the notorious McNulty Brothers?" she asked.

"No-Neck and No-Nose," I confirmed. "Yeah, I brought 'em in, ma'am, but only after they tried to cheat me at whist."

"Whist?" she repeated. "I find it difficult to picture *you* playing whist."

"We play a mighty fast and aggressive game of it out on the Frontier, ma'am," I answered. Which was true. At one point in the second hand No-Nose played a dagger, and I topped him with a laser pistol, and then No-Neck tried to trump me with a blaster, but I finessed him by bringing the barrel of my pistol down on his hand and snapping all his fingers.

"Well, if you're not a lawman, what *are* you?"

"A fulltime freelance hero at your service, ma'am," I said. "You got any heroing needs doing, I'm your man." She stared at me through half-lowered eyelids. "I think you might be the very man I've been looking for, Catastrophe Baker."

"Well, I *know* you're what I been looking for all my life," I told her. "Or at least since my back molars came in. You got a name, ma'am?"

"Voluptua," she replied. "Voluptua von Climax."

"Well, Miss Voluptua, ma'am," I said, "how's about you and me stepping out for some high-class grub? Or would you rather just rent a bridal suite first?"

"All that can wait," she said. "I think I have a job for you."

"Is anyone else bothering you?" I asked. "Laying out men who prey on women—especially women with figures like yours—is one of the very best things I do."

"No, it's much more serious than that. Come with me, Catastrophe Baker, and I'll introduce you to the man I work for, and whom I hope you will soon be working for as well."

So I fell into step alongside her, and soon we were in the Theater District, which is this three-block area with a whole bunch of theaters, and then we saw a sign directing us to *Saul Leibowitz's Messiah*, which was the first indication I had that there was more than one of them.

Anyway, we entered the theater, and she led me backstage to a plush office, and she opened the door without knocking, and we walked in and found ourselves facing a very upset man with thinning gray hair and the biggest smokeless cigar you ever saw. She walked right up to him and gave him a peck on the cheek, but he was too upset to notice.

Finally she spoke up and said, "Solly, this is Catastrophe Baker, the famous hero, here to help us in our time of need."

That woke him up, and he stared at me for a minute. "You're really Catastrophe Baker?" he said.

"Yeah," I said.

"The same one who got kicked off Nimbus IV for—"

"They told me they were in their twenties," I said in my own defense.

"All eleven of them?" he said. "I suppose they must have added their ages together. What did the judge say?"

"The judge complained," I said. "The press complained. The constabulary complained. But no one ever heard the girls complain." I turned to Voluptua. "I hope you'll file that fact away for future reference, ma'am."

"That's neither here nor there," said the guy. "My name is Saul Leibowitz, and I am in desperate need of a hero."

"Then this is your lucky day," I said, "because you just found one. Just set me the challenge, name the price, and let's get this show on the road."

"Price?" he repeated. "But I thought you were a hero."

"Heroes got to eat too, you know," I told him. "And when you're as big as me, that comes to serious money."

"All right," he said. "You name any reasonable price and I'll pay it."

"Let me hear the job and I'll decide what's reasonable," I answered.

"I'm producing a new musical," he began.

"I know," I said. "I saw the sign for something called *The Messiah* on my way in."

"Actually," he sniffed, "the proper title is *Saul Leibowitz's Messiah*."

"And what's the problem?"

"I'll be honest with you," said Leibowitz. "The play was in serious danger of folding. Then I hired the famous show doctor, Boris Gijinsky, to fix it. Yesterday he added the most beautiful canticle in the second scene, the cast and director were sure everyone

would love it, and we were set for our official opening next week—and then, last night, our only copy of the canticle was stolen. I need it back, Mr. Baker. Without it I'm probably destitute by next week."

"I don't want to cause you no consternation," I said, "but I ain't never seen a canticle before."

"It doesn't matter," said Voluptua. "*I* know what it looks like, and I'm coming along."

"Are you sure?" asked Leibowitz. "It could be dangerous."

"That's no problem," I said. "I'll be there to protect her from danger."

"Who'll be there to protect her from *you*?" he said.

"I'll be fine," Voluptua assured him.

He turned to face me. "She's twenty-six. Just remember that you like 'em young."

What I mostly like 'em is female, but I didn't see no sense arguing the point, so I did some quick mental math, and told him I'd do the job for ten percent of the first month's gross.

"Five percent," he countered.

"Split the difference," I said. "Nine percent, and I'm off to find the bad guys."

He seemed about to argue, then just kind of collapsed back on his chair and sighed deeply. "Deal," he said.

"Okay," I said to Voluptua. "Let's get going." I accompanied her to my ship, then came to a stop.

"I don't want to put a damper on your enthusiasm," I said, "but I ain't got the slightest idea where to go next."

"That's all right," she said. "I have a pretty good idea who took it."

"Why didn't you tell Mr. Leibowitz?" I asked.

"All he'd do is go out and hire a hero," she explained. "And he already has."

"So where are we heading?" I said, as I ordered the hatch to open and the ramp to descend.

"Stratford-on-Avon II," she said, as we entered the ship. I relayed our destination to the navigational computer, and a minute later we'd shot up through the stratosphere. Then she turned to me. "Change course," she said.

"I beg your pardon, ma'am? Ain't we going to Stratford-on-Avon?"

"That's what we want them to think," she said with a triumphant smile. "And that's why I said it: in case we were being overheard. But I'm more than just a pretty face."

She took a deep breath, and I was happy to agree that she was more than just a pretty face.

"Take us to Back Alley IV."

I passed the order on to the computer.

"We will traverse the MacDonald Wormhole and will reach our destination in seven hours and three minutes," announced the computer in its gentle feminine voice.

"Well, Catastrophe Baker, it looks like we've got some time to kill," she said, starting to slip out of her clothes. "Have you got any ideas on how to make it pass more quickly?"

I allowed that she was giving me more ideas than I could handle, and then she was in my arms, and I got to say that she felt even better than she looked. A minute later I carried her to my bunk, and we spent a vigorous few hours killing time, and I can testify that she was mighty well-named, and I feel sorry for those who think a climax just has something to do with the end of a video. For the longest time I thought the ship had developed a new vibration, and then I finally figured out that what was vibrating was *her*. She was a mighty good

kisser too, and every now and then she'd get carried away and give me a bunch of little love bites, and a couple of them even drew blood, which probably wasn't that surprising considering how white her teeth looked when she smiled.

"Approaching Back Alley IV," announced the computer in what seemed like no time at all.

A minute later it said, "I'm not kidding. We're entering the atmosphere."

Another minute and then it said, "Will you get your hand out of there and put your pants on before we land? I've never been so humiliated in my life!"

"All right, all right!" I muttered, swinging my feet over to the deck. "Keep your shirt on."

"Tell that hussy to keep *hers* on!" said the computer.

We finished getting dressed just as the ship touched down, then opened the hatch and walked out onto the planet's surface. As far as I could tell, Back Alley wasn't much of a world: no trees, no flowers, no animals, nothing much but a Tradertown that had sprung up maybe half a century ago judging from the shape of the buildings. It was night out, and four little bitty moons were racing across the sky, casting their light down onto the bleak surface of the planet.

"I don't mean to be overly critical, ma'am," I said, "but what makes you think the canticle is here? It's a mighty big galaxy, and there can't be five hundred people, tops, in this little town—and as far as I can tell, there ain't no other towns on the planet."

"You're right," she said. "There's just this one town."

"So what makes you think it's here?"

"Because I know who stole it," she answered.

"Then why didn't you say so back in Leibowitz's office?" I asked her.

She shrugged, which is a mighty eye-catching thing to do when you're built like Voluptua von Climax. "He'd want to know how I knew, and it would just lead to an awkward scene."

"Now that we're here and he's a few light years away," I said, "how *did* you know?"

"Because he stole it for *me*," she said. "He's madly in love with me, and he thought if he stole it Solly would go broke and then he'd have a clear path to my affections."

Now personally I hadn't noticed her putting up any blockades to her affections, but even so it made sense that he'd want to get rid of the competition, at least the part he knew about, and it had the added advantage that sometime in the future he and Voluptua could resurrect the show with the missing canticle, whatever that was, and make a fortune.

"What can you tell me about him?" I asked.

"He's mean through and through," she told me. "I think you should sneak up behind him and subdue him before he knows you're there."

"That's again the heroing codes of ethics and sportsmanship, ma'am," I said.

"But they say he's the dirtiest fighter on the whole Inner Frontier!"

"Good," I said. "I hate it when a fight ends too soon."

She stared at me. "How long do your fights usually last?"

"Oh, maybe six or seven seconds," I answered.

She blinked very rapidly. "Really?"

"Heroes don't never lie, ma'am."

"I find that very exciting," she said, throwing her arms around me and nib-

bling a little on my lower lip.

I kissed her back, then disengaged myself. "We got time for this later," I said, "but right now I think I should be confronting this villain and getting back what was stolen. Where's he likely to be?"

"Probably in one of the bars," she said, "carousing with drunken friends and cheap women."

"He got a name, ma'am?"

She wrinkled her nose and frowned. "Cutthroat Hawke," she replied.

"He any relation to Cutthroat McGraw?" I asked. She just stared at me. "I guess not," I said. "Well, let's go find him and retrieve Mr. Leibowitz's goods."

She led the way past two well-lit taverns to a little hole in the wall with bad lighting and a worse smell. I stood in the doorway and looked around. There were a bunch of aliens, most of 'em kind of animal, at least one vegetable, and a couple I'll swear wasn't even mineral, and none of 'em looked all that happy to see me.

Then I spotted the one human, sitting alone in the farthest corner, and I knew he had to be Cutthroat Hawke. He was wearing a leather tunic, and metallic pants, and well-worn boots, and it was clear that shaving wasn't his favorite sport. He was nursing a glass of something blue with a bunch of smoke coming out of it, and he didn't pay me any attention at all when I took a step or two into the room.

"Cutthroat Hawke!" I bellowed. "Your destiny has found you out! Are you going to turn over what you stole and come along peaceably, or am I going to enjoy the hell out of the next half minute?"

"Who the hell are you?" he demanded.

"I'm Catastrophe Baker, freelance hero by trade, and I'm here to right the terrible wrong you done to Saul Leibowitz and Voluptua von Climax."

"Voluptua?" he repeated, looking around. "Is she here?"

"Never you mind," I said. "You got your hands full with *me*."

"*She* put you up to this, didn't she?" he snarled.

"I won't have you defaming the woman I momentarily love," I told him harshly. "Now, are you coming peaceably or are you coming otherwise? There ain't no third choice."

And no sooner had the words left my lips (which were still a little sore from all those love bites) than half a dozen aliens got up and blocked my way.

"Leave him alone," said one of them ominously.

"I can't do that," I said. "He's a thief and a villain."

"He robbed a human," replied the alien. "We approve."

"I don't want no trouble," I said, "but you're standing between me and the object of my noble quest."

He reached for a weapon, and suddenly he wasn't standing between us no more. And I'm sure he'll walk again someday, once he gets out of whatever hospital they took him to after I got a little hot under the collar and flang him into a wall forty feet away. Then a snake-like alien started coiling himself around me and squeezing for all he was worth, so I grabbed him by his neck (which was about twenty feet long, but I latched onto the part right behind his head) and did a little squeezing of my own, and I don't doubt for a second that they can fix all them vertebrae I shook loose if he ever stops twitching long enough for them to go to work on him.

The other aliens suddenly decided they had urgent business elsewhere, and suddenly I found myself face to face with Cutthroat Hawke. Well, let me be more precise: suddenly I found myself looking down the barrel of Cutthroat Hawke's blaster.

I was too far away to grab it out of his hand, so I decided to try a heroic ruse.

"Not only that, she said my cigar was bigger than yours."

"Hey, Cutthroat," I said, "your shoelace is untied."

"I wear boots," he replied.

"And your fly is unzipped."

"I use magnetic closures."

"And there's something with about fifteen legs crawling up your sleeve."

"Boy," he said, "if you're the best and the brightest, the hero business has fallen on hard times."

He'd have said something more, but just then the fifteen-legged spider bit him on the shoulder, right through his sleeve, and he turned to slap it away, and whilst he was doing so I kicked the blaster out of his hand and picked him up by the neck and held him a few feet above the ground.

"Now ain't you sorry you put me to all this trouble?" I said.

He tried to answer, but he was turning blue from lack of air, and finally he just nodded his head.

"And if I put you down, you ain't going to try to escape or go for a weapon, right?" I said.

And I'm sure he'd have said "Right" if he'd still been awake, but he'd passed out from lack of air while I was asking the question, so I just released my grip and he fell to the floor in a heap.

I examined his pockets, but there wasn't anything there except a few credits, just enough to pay for his drinks, so I walked to the middle of the bar, stuck a couple of fingers in my mouth, and whistled to get all the aliens' attention.

"I need to know where Cutthroat Hawke stored his worldly possessions," I announced.

They all just stared at me, sullen and silent.

"I'd really appreciate your help," I said.

No answer.

"Okay," I said, busting a chair apart and holding a leg up. "I guess one of you is going to have to volunteer to help me look for it."

Suddenly every alien in the joint was telling me that he kept his goods in a box under his bed in room 17 of the boarding house next door. I walked out, met Voluptua, told her to keep an eye on Cutthroat Hawke (not that he was going anywhere), and then I went up to Hawke's room.

Sure enough there was a small box under the bed. In it was a diamond ring and a matching bracelet, wrapped up in some old wrinkled paper. I looked around for something that might be a canticle and couldn't find it, and finally figured, well, at least Mr. Leibowitz could pawn the diamonds to keep the play running an extra week or two, so I stuffed the whole package in my pocket.

I gathered Voluptua and Hawke up, carried him over a shoulder to my ship, bound his hands and feet with negatronic manacles for safekeeping, stuck him in a corner where we couldn't trip over him, and a minute later we'd reached light speeds and were headed back to Calliope.

Once again Voluptua decided it was too warm for clothes, and she doffed hers and came over and started helping me out of mine. Finally I felt a certain familiar sense of urgency and carried her over to the bed.

"But you're still wearing your pants," she protested.

"But unlike Hawke's," I said, "mine got a zipper."

And I demonstrated it to her, and then she demonstrated some things to me, and then it felt like the ship was vibrating again, and then she was covering me with

painful (but loving) little bites, and finally she plumb wore me out and I fell asleep.

I woke up when I felt a hand in my pocket that almost certainly wasn't mine, and sure enough it belonged to Voluptua.

"What's going on?" I said.

"I was just smoothing out your pants pocket, my love," she said.

"From the inside?" I asked.

Before she could answer I got the distinct impression that something was missing. I sat up and looked around, and it turns out that what was missing was Cutthroat Hawke.

Well, let me amend that. *Most* of him was missing. What was left were his clothes and a few bones.

I walked over to make sure, though in my experience mighty few people walk off and leave their bones behind.

"What the hell happened here?" I demanded.

She gave me an innocent smile. "I have no idea what you're talking about."

"I'm talking about losing an entire prisoner while we're cruising along at light speeds," I said.

She gave me an unconcerned shrug. "These things happen."

"Not on my ship, they don't!" I said.

She gave me a very unladylike burp.

I looked from the bones to her to the bones and back to her again.

"You *ate* an entire prisoner?" I said.

"I'd have saved some for you, my love," she said, "but they don't keep well."

"You ate him!" I repeated.

"What are you getting so upset about?" she said. "I didn't use your galley, and I cleaned up after myself."

"If you were hungry, why didn't you just say so?" I said. "I'd have been happy to stop off at a restaurant."

"I was going to have to kill him anyway," she said. "He betrayed me."

"How?"

"He was my partner. We stole the canticle together, but then he decided not to share the proceeds with me." She made a face. "He was a terrible man! I'm glad I ate him!"

"Do you do this a lot?" I asked.

"Steal canticles?" she replied. "This was my first."

"I meant, eat your partners," I said.

"My partners? Not very often."

"Well, I ain't no policeman," I said, "so I ain't turning you in. We'll let Mr. Leibowitz decide what to do with you."

"You don't have to tell him," she said, putting her arms around me. "I love you, Catastrophe Baker."

"I know," I said. "And I got the love bites to prove it."

"You know you loved them."

"It was an interesting experience," I admitted. "I ain't ever been an appetizer before."

She laughed, and while she did I took a quick look to see if her teeth were filed.

We talked about this and that and just about everything except our favorite foods, and finally the ship touched down, and a couple of minutes later the two of us walked into Leibowitz's office.

"That was fast!" said Leibowitz, obviously impressed. "I didn't expect you back for two or three more days."

"Us heroes don't waste no time," I said. "I'm pleased to announce that the culprit that robbed you is no longer among the living."

"You killed him?" asked Leibowitz.

"No, your ladyfriend put him out of his misery."

He looked surprise. "Really?"

"Ask her yourself," I said.

He turned to Voluptua. "How did you do it? With a blaster? A knife? Poison?"

"You got seventeen more guesses," I said, "and my bet is that you're going to need 'em all."

He got up, walked around his desk until he was standing right in front of her, and hugged her. "As long as you're safe, that's all that matters," he said.

He kissed her, she kissed him, he flinched, and I could see he was missing a little bit of lip when they parted.

"Always enthusiastic, that's my Voluptua," he said, turning to me. "And did you bring me back my canticle?"

"I'm afraid not," I said, pulling the package out of my pocket. "All he had were these diamonds."

I started unwrapping them when he grabbed the wrapping paper out of my hand, unfolded it, and held it up to the light.

"My canticle!" he cried happily after he'd read it over.

"I always thought a canticle was some kind of a fruit, like a honeydew melon," I said.

He laughed as if I had made a joke, then summoned his staff to tell them that he'd got his canticle back, and since everyone was busy admiring the canticle and praising Voluptua for her bravery, I decided no one would notice or mind if I kept the diamonds for myself, since they didn't rightly belong to anyone, or at least anyone that wasn't thoroughly digested by now.

And that's the way I left them: Leibowitz, Voluptua, and the canticle.

***

HURRICANE SMITH downed his drink.

"So how much was your nine percent of the play worth?" he asked.

"Nothing," I said. "The damned thing closed on opening night. The critics said it was the worst hymn anyone ever heard."

Hurricane chuckled. "That's critics for you. They're never happy unless they're convincing you that what you like just isn't any good." He poured himself another one. "Still, it was an interesting story. They still together, the producer and the lady?"

"Far as I know," I answered. "I guess it *was* pretty interesting at that. Maybe I'll write it up for one of them true adventure holodisks."

"Why not?" he agreed. "You got a title?"

"I thought I'd call it *A Canticle for Leibowitz*."

He shook his head. "You may get top marks as a space hero, but you ain't ever going to make it as a writer if you think something called *A Canticle for Leibowitz* is going to sell more than ten copies."

"It does lack a little punch," I admitted. "What would *you* call it?"

"That's easy enough," said Hurricane. "I'd call it *A Cannibal for Leibowitz*."

It made perfect sense to me, and if I ever write this heroic epic up, that's exactly what I'm going to call it, unless some effete namby-pamby editor changes it to something else.

Jerry Oltion has become the most prolific author in the history of Analog Magazine *with all his wonderful short stories. And he sold a number of stories to me in his spare time back in the first incarnation of this magazine.*

He even found the time to sell me this story back in the mid-1990s when I was editing the fiction section of VB Tech Journal. *(Yeah, I did that for two years after the first run of* Pulphouse.)

Besides continuing his regular science fiction writing, Jerry is also a major amateur astronomer and does a regular column these days for Sky *and* Telescope.

Jerry said this story was born from once living next to Yellowstone Park.

Back to Nature
Jerry Oltion

DENNIS BLEW THE LANDING SIREN FOR THE THIRD TIME. Through the house's open front door, he could see Anne walking through the living room toward the kitchen, searching for anything she might have forgotten. It was her third such transit.

He unsealed his window and shouted, "Will you come on! We're only going to be gone a week! If you've forgotten something we can do without it. This is a camping trip, remember?"

A moment later Anne stepped through the doorway with another armload of stuff. The door slid closed behind her as she walked down the steps to the car. Dennis helped toss the things she had brought—all the snack food he had intentionally left behind, by the looks of it—behind the seats. "We'll never eat all this stuff," he grumbled.

"If we don't, then we can bring it back home with us," she said, sliding into the passenger seat. "We've got room."

"I just hate the idea of dragging something halfway across the galaxy if we're not going to use it." Dennis slammed his door tight and started the engine. He waited for the idiot lights to go out one by one, then lifted away from the house into the traffic streaming by overhead.

The autopilot edged the car in a little below and behind a homie, a yellowish-white conglomeration of living bubbles stuck haphazardly around a central drive frame that couldn't have been much larger than Dennis and Anne's. Air resistance kept it moving far below sonic speed, and it bobbed up and down with every patch of turbulence, cutting them off every time the autopilot tried to pass.

"Stupid idiot." Dennis thumbed on the manual override, dived beneath the homie, and shoved the throttle to full. With a gratifying whoosh of splitting air the tiny car shot under the other vehicle. Dennis pulled back on the steering yoke the moment they were past, ignoring the proximity alarm, and stood the tail on the planet. "Eat gravitons, homie," he muttered as the orbital drive kicked in and the car streaked out of the atmosphere.

Anne released her hold on the armrest. "'Stupid idiot' is redundant," she said with a weak grin.

"So's a homie," Dennis retorted. "It's been centuries since cars needed to be self-contained. What do they think they're going to do, colonize a parking lot somewhere?"

Anne shook her head. "You're supposed to be taking this trip to relax."

"I am relaxing. I just don't want to spend my whole vacation staring at the ass end of some slow-brain throwback to the exploration age."

"Throwback?" Anne asked.

Dennis nodded. "It's the pioneer mentality. They've got to take everything with them wherever they go. They pack their whole lifestyle into those things, then go on vacation to 'get away.' It's like they don't even trust the air wherever they're going. They're trying to be pioneers in a populated universe."

"There are still unexplored planets."

"Sure, but you won't find these guys going there. Oh no. You'll find them parked side-by-side in mini housing developments on some of the best camping country in the galaxy. Earth is teeming with them."

"Then why are we going camping on Earth?"

Dennis smiled. "Because I'm not going to let the homies have the most beautiful planet in the galaxy."

"Oh," Anne said dubiously.

"Don't worry about it," Dennis said. "It's a big planet."

While the autopilot threaded the way through the jumble of orbiting colonies and factories and communication satellites, he switched on the long-range navigation computer and gave it their destination. When they were clear he turned on the hyperdrive, then settled back to watch the light show as the stars slid by.

***

EARTH WAS A MOTTLED BALL of blue and white below them when they shifted out of hyperspace two hours later. Dennis spun the car around until they could see it out the front window.

"Where do you want to go?" he asked.

Anne yawned and blinked. "I don't know. I've never been here before."

"I've only been once. I stayed in Australia then, but it's winter there now. We want someplace around forty degrees north latitude, and maybe one or two o'clock local time if we want to keep our biorhythms in sync."

"That puts us about there," Anne said, pointing at the planet's image on the navigation screen in the dash between them.

Dennis expanded the view until they could see land features. "Looks like prairie," he said. He moved westward until a mountain range slid into view.

"There," Anne said. "Kind of off by itself. See?"

"Yeah. It's not part of the main range. Maybe there won't be anybody there." Dennis switched on the orbital drive and took them down in a steep descent.

"Where is everybody?" Anne asked, eyeing the approach radar's blank screen. There were no space stations or factories, and hardly even any traffic.

Dennis grinned. "Nowhere. Earth's classified uninhabited. There's no industry in space around it at all."

"Uninhabited? I didn't know that."

"Sure. It's protected. Nobody lives here anymore; it's just for sightseeing."

"Who decided that?"

"I don't know. The last people off it, I guess."

As they dropped closer, the mountain range began to take on detail. The center of the range stuck up above tree line in a jumble of rocky peaks, but the lower ridges were heavily forested and nearly every valley was dotted with lakes. Dennis and Anne flew slowly over them, looking for the perfect spot. They eventually found four lakes in a chain, the highest just above tree line and the rest surrounded by thick forest. Dennis eyed each lake for potential campsites as they passed. Over the third one he slowed to a hover.

"What do you think?"

"It's beautiful!"

"How about that ledge up there, with the waterfall coming over the rocks beside that little grove of trees? We can pitch the tent in the grass there in front and have a view of the whole valley."

"I think I could live with that."

"Okay, I guess that's home for tonight, then." Dennis let the car drift on downstream.

"Where are you going?" Anne asked.

"To the parking lot. This is a backpacking trip, not a picnic." At the lower end of the last lake he set it down at the edge of a clearing and turned off the engine. "Last one out's a homie," he said.

THE SENSE OF DISCOVERY

At long last, Jerry Oltion is making his short stories available online.

He's working through them chronologically and having a blast, revisiting many of his old favorites. You can do so, too!

For this book and other
Jerry Oltion stories and novels
go to:
www.jerryoltion.com

***

THE VALLEY was even more beautiful from the ground. The trail from the parking area wound through the trees, following the stream part of the way, then switchbacking up the side of a ridge for a view all the way up and down the valley before dropping back toward the lakes. It took Dennis and Anne almost five hours to walk the distance they had flown in as many minutes.

"This is what it's all about," Dennis said as they sweated their way up one of the switchbacks. "Get out in the woods, get the blood pumping, and put some *real* air in it to pump. The very molecules that helped us evolve. Just think, Vincent Van Gogh breathed this same air!"

"That's why...I'm not getting any... energy out of it," Anne puffed from behind. "Hold up a minute."

Dennis stopped to wait for her. "I think we're almost there," he said. "I can smell the lake."

"I thought it was me."

"All right, witty. Just take a deep breath. You can smell the water in the air."

Anne panted a few times. "I guess so. Whew." She swallowed, said, "I'm not looking forward to explaining to Mom why we travelled thirty-six light years just to walk the last five miles. Right now I'm not sure I have a good reason."

"Sure you do. Because there's nothing so beautiful in all the universe as walking the last five miles on humanity's home planet. Unless of course it's you in the middle of it all."

She blushed. "Don't give me that. I'm sweaty and smelly and my hair's a mess."

"And you're still beautiful."

"And you're hopeless. But I'm glad I married you anyway."

"Me too."

Anne found a flat-topped rock and sat down, letting the rock take the weight of her pack. "Now I know why you wanted me to leave most of this stuff behind," she said. "I didn't think about having to carry it every step of the way."

"Ah, but you're carrying it. That's what counts. That's the whole idea behind backpacking. It's kind of, what—pride? Knowing that you can get by with just the things you can carry on your back. And not only get by, but enjoy yourself."

"I'm looking forward to it."

"What, enjoying yourself?"

"Joke. I'm having fun walking. But I think I'll like it even more when I can get out of these sweaty clothes and stand under that waterfall."

Dennis raised an eyebrow. "Need someone to wash your back?"

***

THEY STOPPED at the edge of the lake just long enough to catch four fish— quick, dark brookies with bright red spots on their sides—then climbed up the ridge to their campsite. Hunger overpowered both fatigue and the urge to bathe; Anne unpacked the food they'd carried while Dennis set up the portable microwave oven and cooked the fish, then they sat down on the grass to eat.

The tails of the fish were singed, and their eyes had bugged out and turned milky white. Anne frowned dubiously as she stripped the meat from the bones, but when she took her first bite she smiled and said, "Wow. Who'd have guessed?"

"You like it?" Dennis asked.

"Yeah. It tastes...I don't know, kind of primeval. I don't think I'd like it much at home, but there's evidently something about being on Earth that brings out the primitive instincts."

Dennis laughed. "Well now, that sounds encouraging." A glint of light in the sky caught his attention, and he lost his smile. "Damn," he said.

"What?" Anne looked up, squinting.

Dennis pointed at the cluster of living bubbles reflecting the afternoon light. He wished he'd thought to bring along a weapon. Not to shoot them down with, but a warning shot across their bow might make them think twice about landing.

He hadn't brought one, though. The homie dropped down out of sight behind a ridge and for a moment Dennis thought he and Anne might be spared, but then it rose up again and moved out over their lake.

"Maybe they're just looking around," Anne said, but even as she said it the homie began to descend, stopping beside a grove of trees just a little below them, and not a hundred yards away.

It settled to the ground with a crunch of rock and breaking branches. It lifted again, moved over a few feet and settled again, then lifted once more and moved back to its original resting place. The pilot cut the antigravs and it settled another few inches.

It sat there, a silent, ugly intruder.

A door opened at its base and a small, furry gray dog scuttled out. The dog stopped, sniffed the air, and began barking. Behind it came a boy, about ten years old. He looked around at the trees and the lake, then picked up a rock and threw it in the water. The splash startled the dog, which stopped barking for a second before starting in again at an even more frenzied pitch.

"I don't believe it," Dennis growled. He got up and stalked to the brink of their ledge. Cupping his hands, he shouted, "Go away!"

"Dennis!"

"They don't have to camp right there. Damn it, we were here first. Get out of here, homie!"

The boy ran back inside, and a moment later an older, white-haired man stood in the doorway. He shielded his eyes and looked up at Dennis.

"We were here first!" Dennis shouted. "There's three more lakes in this valley; why don't you go find one for yourself?"

The man looked up at Dennis for a few more seconds, then went back inside without a word. The dog stayed outside and barked. A moment later the side of a living bubble folded out to make an awning, and an arm that had been concealed beneath it lowered a skycycle to the ground.

"Ohh, that does it, that son of a—" Dennis started down the slope.

Anne said, "Dennis. Come back here. If you go down there, you're just going to get in a fight."

He looked back at her. "That's kind of what I had in mind."

"That won't solve anything. It'll just make them more determined to stay than ever."

"So what are we supposed to do? Just let them screw up our campsite?"

"I don't know. Let's at least finish dinner, okay?"

Dennis scowled, but he turned away from the lake.

"Maybe they're nice people," Anne said.

"Nice people don't park a houseship in front of somebody else's camp. Nice people don't take that kind of ugliness into this kind of wilderness in the first place."

"Just this morning you were condemning them for parking all together in campgrounds."

"They *belong* in campgrounds. No, that's not true. They belong in scrap dumps. They belong in toxic waste sites, where their surroundings match their sense of aesthetics. But they most assuredly do not belong in places like this."

Anne sighed. "All right, agreed. I don't like it either, but shouting won't help."

"What do you suggest? Avalanche, maybe? I think I could get a few rocks to move from up above there..."

"No! Ignore them. Go fishing, or hiking or whatever we want to do. Let's don't let them ruin our vacation."

"They've already done that as far as I'm concerned." Dennis turned back to look at the homie. "Look at that. They even brought a skycycle. I'll bet you anything that damn kid will be flying all over the place, screaming his head off and scaring every animal for miles. And what he doesn't scare, that stupid dog will."

"Your fish are getting cold."

Dennis looked at her, his teeth clenched. "Fish," he said. He walked over to the rock he'd been sitting on, grabbed a fish from his plate in either hand, then turned and hurled them down at the homie. "There! Have my fish, too! You spoiled my day and ruined my campsite, you might as well have my dinner, too!"

One fish hit the top of the awning and slid to the ground. The other banged off the side of one of the bubbles. The dog screeched as if it had been hit, then started barking again.

Anne stood up. "Dennis, stop that right now!"

"No. You said do what I want to do; well I want to throw fish at them."

Down below, a woman emerged. She wore a shapeless pink gown of some shiny material that made her look about a hundred pounds overweight. She looked up at Dennis on the ledge above her, and put her hands on her hips.

"Woo, now I'm scared," Dennis said. "Go back to Aldebaran, where you belong!"

Dennis felt a tug on his arm and turned to scowl at Anne. "Let go of—what are you crying for?"

"Because I want to, damn it! Come sit down." She led him back to their camp and pulled on his arm until he sat. She handed him his plate and put her second fish on it. "Now shut up and eat."

Her hair had fallen in her eyes, but she made no effort to brush it aside. She stabbed her fish angrily and swallowed, sniffing, not looking up.

"Hey, I'm sorry."

"You should be."

"They've screwed up the whole thing."

"You haven't done too hot either, hero."

"What do you want me to do? You want me to ignore them? Fine. I'll ignore them from home. Let's get out of here."

Anne was silent for a long time. When she did speak, it was almost a whisper. "You leave and you'll be doing it without me."

"What?"

She looked up. "I said I'm not leaving. You're not the only one on this camping trip. I like it here. Nobody's going to spoil my fun, not them and not you. You got that?"

Dennis nodded, his eyes wide. He'd never heard Anne talk that way before.

She'd always just gone along with him, let him rant and rave until he was done, but she'd never talked back before. He didn't know what to say.

"Uh, you, uh..."

"Just be quiet and eat your dinner. And when you're done, go catch some more. I'm still hungry."

"Right." Dennis picked up his fork off the grass and began to eat.

***

HE CLIMBED AROUND the ridge rather than have to go down in front of the homie. He didn't want to get any closer to it than he had to. Damn homies. Not only had they spoiled his vacation, but they had somehow managed to screw up his marriage too.

Not true, he told himself. It's not screwed up, not yet, not if you can just calm down about this whole thing. It's you shouting and acting irrational that's got Anne all mad.

All right. His marriage was more important than the homie. If Anne wanted him to ignore it, then ignore it he would. He'd go fishing and hike around the hills and swim in the lake and hate every minute of it, but he wouldn't ruin Anne's vacation too.

He stomped down to the edge of the lake, extended his pole out to its full ten-foot length, and cast the fly out into the water with a savage splash. The homie was still visible off to his right, a multi-colored abomination almost as tall as the trees beside it. Dennis turned to put it at his back and cast again.

After his fiftieth cast or so, he just let the fly sink to the bottom and lie there. He was too mad to catch fish. Besides, the kid had taken the skycycle out over the lake, and the fish could evidently sense the agrav unit, because they had all disappeared under the rocks.

He sat on the bank and contemplated murder. If Anne weren't around...

No, he wouldn't. Knock them around a little, yes, but not murder. Not that knocking them around would do any good either, but it would *feel* good.

He realized that the kid had stopped and was hovering only a few yards from the shore next to the homie ship, staring up toward Dennis and Anne's camp. Dennis looked up to see what the kid was staring at, but rocks and trees obscured the view.

Something had to be going on, though, because the fat woman was standing out from under her awning and shouting something up there too. Shouting and shaking her fist.

Shouting at Anne. Dennis threw down his pole and started running for the homie. Nobody shouted at his wife, not if he had anything to say about it. Oh, this *was* going to feel good.

Suddenly the fat woman turned and spoke to the boy. He somewhat reluctantly moved the skycycle toward shore, never taking his eyes off the sight above. Dennis looked up again, and now that he had run a few hundred feet he could see what was causing the commotion.

Anne was bathing in the waterfall.

He slowed to a walk, then stopped completely.

With the evening sun striking her and the water splashing off her shoulders in sparkling spray, she looked like something supernatural, a goddess caught in a moment of solitude.

A pagan goddess, he thought as she cupped her breasts in her hands and let the water splash over them and spray out in front of her. A luscious goddess of lust. She saw him staring at her and beckoned with outstretched arms.

A few minutes later he heard the homie lifting off behind him, but he was too busy climbing to really care.

***

LATER STILL, in a quiet moment on the grass, he propped his head up on one hand and asked, "You knew they'd leave if you did that, didn't you?"

"Mmm hmm."

"How?"

"Because of something you said."

"What?"

She tugged at a stem of grass. "I never would have dreamed of doing something like that back home, but here it's different. It's like I've left all my irrational hangups behind at the car. But you said that homies always packed everything with them. I figured if that was really true, then there's no way they'd have left their taboos behind. And it looks like I was right."

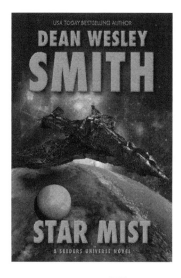
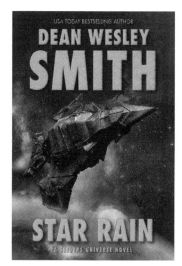
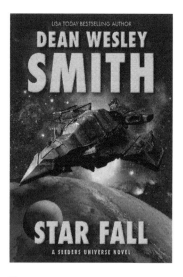

Steve Perry has been around this business for as long as I have, which is not saying he is old. He started very young. And along the way he has been nominated for an Emmy and spent more weeks on The New York Times *bestseller list for more projects than can be counted.*

He and Esther Friesner (also in this issue) are the only two besides me to have written Men in Black *novels as well. Is it any wonder we are all here in this magazine?*

Steve wrote for Batman: The Animated Series, *did the novelization for* Star Wars: Shadows of the Empire, *and wrote numbers of books with Tom Clancy on the Net Force Series.*

Plus when he has a moment, he writes what he calls Wild Hair stories and sends them to me or Kris, depending on what we are editing at the time. I have loved every one of them. Fantastic to have one of the Wild Hair stories in this first issue.

Chrome Bimbos
Steve Perry

I WAS EATING SUPPER at the 76 in Brookshire just west of Houston when somebody slapped me on the back so hard I thought I was going to lose my teeth. I had a steak knife in my hand and I felt the urge to turn around and gut whoever it was.

"Hello, Perfessor," my attacker said.

Well, shit. It was Sweet.

Sweetbrier Mott slid uninvited into the booth across from me, next to the phone. Behind him, somebody was feeding quarters into the juke box, the new one shaped like the front of a truck and done all in green. Johnny Cash cranked up and started singing about fire.

Sweetbrier Mott didn't look like what most people think truck drivers should look. Oh, he was big, an easy six-four barefoot, built like a bodybuilder, wide shoulders, narrow hips, tight and hard, but he didn't dress the part. Instead of boots, he wore Italian leather loafers; instead of jeans, khaki slacks; where most of us would wear a T-shirt, Sweet had on a colorful blue cotton print from Hong Kong. He had thick, wavy blond hair in a sixty-dollar cut, a smile you could use to sell toothpaste, and a face that a movie star would kill for. He was also as mean as a stepped-on rattlesnake and just as dangerous, but he could pass for a yuppie in any college town in America—until he opened his mouth.

"How's it goin' motherfucker?" Miss-issippi dripped from his voice.

I chewed on my suddenly tasteless steak and shook my head. Maybe he'd go away if I pretended he wasn't there.

In the background The Man in Black was twanging on about how that ring of fire burned and I knew just what he meant.

The waitress was new, and she hadn't been working in the truck stop long enough to learn she should stop wearing a skirt. She was young and pretty, maybe nineteen, and she came to stand next to the booth, smiling at the handsome and attractive façade that was Sweet. "Hi! Can I get you something?"

Sweet grinned like a big tomcat, reached over and slid his hand under the waitress's short skirt and up her inner thigh as far as it would go. "You sure can, pretty woman. What time you get off work?"

The girl was stunned for an instant, but she was quicker and braver than I figured. Her smile went away and she stabbed down with her Bic pen, catching Sweet on the forearm halfway to the elbow. Punched a hole in him, she did, and blood welled in the little crater when she jerked the pen back. Most men would have yelped and snatched their hands away in a hurry, but Sweet never even blinked. He clamped his fingers hard into her soft thigh, the muscles in his arm dancing, and the girl went white with the sudden pain. "Shouldn't have done that, puss," he said, the edge sharp in his voice. "Now I'm sure as hell gonna find out your address. And when I drop by, I'm gonna poke you with something a lot bigger and harder than that pen. All night long and in every hole I can put it. You ain't gonna be able to walk, talk or sit for a month."

For a moment the girl stood there in terror. I gripped the knife tighter and thought about leaning over the table and burying it in Sweet's belly, but it was a fantasy. I gave

away seventy pounds and six inches of reach and if I didn't kill him with the first stab, he would beat me to death. He had put three guys I knew in the hospital for crossing him, one of whom wasn't going to drive again unless he got used to doing it one-eyed.

Sweet let go of the girl's thigh. When he pulled his hand out, he casually lifted her skirt. I could see all the way to her panties, and she was going to have a big ugly bruise where he'd grabbed her.

"Peekaboo," he said. "Mm. Nice twat," he said, smiling up at her.

He dropped her skirt. "Run get me a Coke, will you darlin'?"

Ashen, the waitress hurried away.

"Not a bad-looking cunt," Sweet said, flashing his beautiful smile at me. "Bet she gives me a hell of a ride." If the stab wound oozing ink and blood on his arm bothered him, he didn't let on.

Sweet had no use for women, save one, and he indulged himself in that at every opportunity. Old, young, single, married, willing or not, it didn't matter to him. I kept hoping somebody's armed boyfriend or husband would catch him and blow him away, but so far it hadn't happened. He was one of the guys who gave the male sex its bad name.

"So, Perfessor Dunsmuir, where you headed?"

Before I started driving, I did a year and a half in junior college in Santa Monica. Thus, "Perfessor."

"L.A.," I said, hating myself for being afraid not to answer. "I'm taking Jeff Louis's Transcon run. Jeff broke his foot changing a tire."

"I thought Transcon was out of business."

"No."

Sweet leaned back, bored. He picked up the booth phone and punched in a number. "Hey, hon, guess who? Yeah. I'll be there in about ten minutes. What? Hey, I don't give a shit, get rid of him. Send him out for cigarettes or something. I got big plans for you, you understand. *Big* plans."

My steak had grown cold. My appetite had grown cold, too. Sweet left before the waitress came back with his Coke.

When she returned, she stood there clutching the big glass, trembling. She'd bitten her lip.

"Listen," I said, "You don't need this job that bad. Leave, now, don't tell anybody where you live if you haven't already. Find your application and take it. If you stay here, sooner or later Sweet will remember to get around to doing what he said. If you leave now, he might forget."

The girl was shaking so bad the Coke began to slosh out over the rim of the glass. She nodded. I felt a little better, not much. I didn't expect I would ever see her again. I hoped I wouldn't.

***

IT WAS ABOUT TEN P.M. before I got a call for my shower, close to eleven when I headed out for my rig. Late July in that part of Texas was hot, even as far along as the night was. Insects buzzed the yellow lights, too stupid to know they couldn't see them; the smell of diesel from idling tractors and the stink of still-warm oily macadam filled the air. There were probably thirty rigs in the big lot, lined up like dragons stoking to take off or asleep for the evening. The moon was still waxing, but almost full, and its silvery glow blended with the truck and building lights.

People don't understand trucking, why it calls to us drivers the way it does. Rolling along at two a.m. in the middle of New Mexico at seventy-five miles an hour under a trillion stars and feeling unstoppable is part of it. Being the last man on Earth, just you and the jackrabbits and the armadillos in the night is part of it. Moving, leaving places behind, reaching new places, that's in there, too. Kind of hard to bundle it all up, but there's an aspect of it that's like being a lone gunslinger riding into town.

Last of the samurai, ronin, walking the roads to your own timing and own tune. It's a lot more fulfilling than non-drivers think, controlling a big truck. You can get a real feeling of accomplishment manhandling the eighteen wheelers with more forward gears than you can shake a stick at, chewing up the road and spitting it out behind you again. Kind of got its own mythology, the famous speed runs, the drivers from the early days before the interstates, the stories of famous pile-ups, the haunted highways, like that. Yeah, sure, there are bad people in the business, but there are some people you want to avoid everywhere.

Speak of the Devil. As I was climbing into my cab, Sweet's rig pulled around the line and started out. He'd gone to see some woman, finished with her, and gotten back already. Probably half the drivers in the lot were sleeping but damned if Sweet didn't hit his horns twice as he crossed the lot, two long blasts. Look out you limp dick fuckers, the horns said, here rides Sweetbrier Mott!

Sweet owned his own truck, he was an indy, and it was some rig to behold. He drove a Freightliner Aerodynamic, double sleeper, painted midnight black with silver pinstripes, pulling a Fruehauf trailer, neither one more than three years old. Expensive setup, top of the line, but that wasn't the half of it. Sweet's rig made a mall-sized Christmas tree look plain. Both tractor and trailer were outlined with orange and yellow lights, twice as many as I'd ever seen anybody else carry.

Then there were the chrome bimbos.

Some guys will put the bimbo on their mud flaps, behind the rear tires of the trailer. She's a shiny silhouette of a sitting naked woman, one leg stretched out straight, the other leg drawn in so that

her knee is up, leaning back on one arm, breasts outthrust. That's the basic configuration, thought there are variations. You can buy her in any big truck stop in the country, ranging from a hat pin to damned near life-size. She comes with mounting bolts and nuts so you can put her on the flaps, but if you've a mind to, you can punch holes in metal and stick her on the truck or trailer itself. Some guys will do that, put up one or two shiny naked women on their tractors. Hey, I may not know art but I know what I like, they say. Naked fucking broads.

I never met a woman who had anything but contempt for the chrome nudes and I made it a point not to drive rigs that wore them. Not that I have anything against naked ladies myself, but being educated has its pitfalls. Along the way I found out that women have feelings, too. Hell of a thing for a truck driver to discover.

Sweetbrier Mott had *dozens* of the chrome bimbos on his rig, all sizes, so that his vehicle looked like nothing so much as an advertisement for a heavy metal brothel. It was way over the line, even for spit-on-the-ground-macho truckers, and to call it tacky would be kind. Sweet's rig was a caricature, a slap at the world's face, an especially ugly sneer at women. It pretty much summed up Sweet's attitude, no way to mistake that: Hey, you're all whores, good for nothing but fucking and *I'm* the guy to do it, so bend over babe.

God must have a soft spot for sexist bastards, to have made so many of them. Not that I'm immune to my own lusts, but hey, I'm educated. At least I know I ought to know better.

The garish truck moved past mine and into the Texas night and I shook my head. Whenever I get depressed, I can always console myself by thinking, *Well, things could be worse, pal. At least you ain't Sweetbrier Mott.*

***

PRETTY MUCH the biggest truck stop along I-10 once you get into Arizona is Rip Griffin's Texaco, at Tonopah, about an hour west of Phoenix. I'd stopped in El Paso for a few hours' sleep, and I was six or seven hours behind the eighteen or nineteen it would usually take from Brookshire to Tonopah. The day had been a killer for hot, hundred and sixteen degrees in the shade through much of New Mexico and Arizona, and only a little thunderstorm outside of Wilcox had broken the heat for a while. It's mostly desert country, cactus and sagebrush from Tucson on into California, dust devils twirling in the day, bugs spattering your windshield with their yellow and green insides at night. Yeah, it's dry heat, but inside a non-refrigerated trailer between Phoenix and Palm Springs, the desert sun will cook the resin out of hundred-year-old wooden furniture. And my Transcon tractor wasn't air-conditioned, so I was sweaty and worn out as I pulled into Rip Griffin's.

I found a table in the restaurant and was waiting for my order when I saw Sweet swagger in. He didn't see me, or if he did, he didn't let on, which was just as well. I was tired enough that I might have said or done something stupid and gotten myself killed.

Sweet sat at a table near the window by himself, and I put him out of my mind as my Mexican dinner arrived. Fuck hum, life is too short to spend on guys like Sweet.

I was considering pie for dessert when the woman walked into the restaurant. It was like one of those old cowboy movies when the bad guy enters the saloon and everything stops cold, even the piano player. In the loose-jawed silence, the click of the woman's six-inch heels on the floor echoed like gunshots.

She was drop-dead gorgeous, absolutely. Tall, maybe five nine, platinum blond hair to her shoulders, wearing a tight black sheath of a sleeveless mini-dress that might as well have been Saran wrap for all it hid. She had full lips, high cheekbones, icy blue eyes and when she smiled, teeth so straight and white as to make Sweet's look crooked and dirty yellow. Oh, and yes, she had the body to go with the face. Just short of lush, wide hips, perfect legs under black stockings, large breasts, but, of course, no sag. She looked twenty-two or twenty-three and there probably wasn't a man in the place who didn't picture that long hair spread out on a pillow. A wet-dream come to life.

It was more than that, though. Looks don't mean much, I know. Take Sweet, for instance, he would con you if you didn't know him. This woman turned heads, sure enough, but there was something else about her, something in her attitude that marked her as more than just a beautiful woman. She had a kind of confidence, an aura that shined through her, born of something deeper than her physical attraction. Yeah, maybe I was fooling myself, thinking that somebody who looked that good had to *be* good, too, but I didn't think so. It was like that feeling you get sometimes when you meet somebody and you somehow know they are bright and clever and deep and it turns out they are. Some subtle signal in a gesture, some soul-to-soul call that defies logic or reason so that you just *know*. There was no question in my mind in that moment that this woman was more than the sum of her visible parts. My mouth went dry and my breathing speeded up. What would I say to her? Surely she would recognize me as her soulmate? Hi. Do you need a ride somewhere? Which way are you going? Why, yes, I'm going that way—whatever damned direction it might be. To hell with the load. A man might not get another chance like this in his life, a perfect match only came along every so often. Just give me a sign, lady, and I will go with you anywhere, forever…

But no. Gunshot heels firing, the woman of my dreams flowed across the silent room…straight toward Sweetbrier Mott.

Oh, God. I should have stabbed the son-of-a-bitch back in Texas.

Truly, I decided, truly there ain't no justice. Maybe I was wrong about her. She could be Sweet's counterpart, beautiful on the outside and scrap iron and broken glass on the inside, but I knew to my core that wasn't the case. There was more to her than she showed. How could she not see him for what he was? How could she waste herself on him?

The woman sat across from Sweet without a word, and I saw him trade smiles with her. If these two made babies together, people would pay just to watch the children walk by. They looked the ideal couple.

Too much. I had to get out of there before I lost my supper. When I passed him, Sweet was too busy to notice me. They were already holding hands across the table, and I figured they'd be halfway to bed somewhere before I got my rig started. Damn! How could there be a God, to let this happen? Sweet was scum! As was I, for letting him live.

***

I WAS MORE TIRED than I thought. I knew I should make the run across the

desert at night, but I also knew I'd wind up pulled over in the sleeper before more than a couple more hours passed, so I figured, what the hell, I'll get a room. Rip's was full, but there was a little hole-in-the-wall trucker's motel a couple of miles west, at the new off-ramp, so I headed that way and checked in.

I couldn't sleep. The temperature had dropped so that it was maybe eighty-five at two-thirty in the morning, and the air-conditioner in the room was gamely trying to outfight it, but I was too tired to do more than roll around. I was parched. I felt cheated. I felt desolate. I got up and slipped on a pair of shorts and went to find the Coke machine. Maybe a cold drink would help.

I was on the second floor, my room facing the desert and parking lot. There were a couple of other trucks there, including—goddamit—Sweet's. Shit, I couldn't seem to get away from him. It was made worse by knowing that he was probably screwing his few brains out with that vision of beauty, right down the way a few doors.

I found the pop dispenser, only it was a Pepsi machine and there wasn't anything in it I wanted. Shit. I grabbed a handful of little square cubes from the icemaker next to the bright humming drink machine and sucked on the cold instead. A dry and dusty moth bounced off my head on its way to the Pepsi light.

I started back to my room, circling around the tiny swimming pool, taking a different route.

Halfway there, I heard Sweet laugh.

I don't make a habit of sneaking around cheap motels at three in the morning peeping into windows. But I was tired and restless and the sound of Sweet having a good time was too much. And there was *her*, the woman who had to be more, but who had turned out to be less. I found myself drifting toward the sound of Sweet's laughter, drawn like the moth to the pop dispenser. It wouldn't hurt to walk past, I thought, but that was a lie: it already hurt.

The door to Sweet's room was not closed, there was a gap almost two feet wide and anybody who happened to be passing and accidentally glancing that way couldn't miss them. There weren't any lights on in the room, but the moon had to be full and it had gotten to an angle where it shined straight through the open door.

"Like this?" she said. Her voice was honey-on-glass smooth, smoky and hot and dark and full of mysterious delights. Of course. Oh, man.

She was sitting on the bed, naked, and had assumed the pose of the chrome bimbo of whom Sweet was so fond. She was leaning back slightly, chest pushed out, one leg cocked up, the other stretching to the end of the bed. She wet her lips with her tongue, smiled, and it made my heart ache to see her. Well, yes, it made another part of me ache, too, worse than my heart. My shorts turned into a tent. No justice. Certainly no *fucking* justice. In the cool moonlight, her skin had a silvery tone to it, and she could have been the model for what Sweet had bolted all over his rig. I would have given anything to touch her.

I couldn't see him, the door blocked him, but he must be standing next to the bathroom. "Yeah," Sweet said, "just like that. Oh, baby, I'm going to pump you bowlegged!"

I stood there, a bug in amber. I shouldn't be doing this, I told myself. I'm not a pervert. Turn around and get on back to your room, Dunsmuir. Move it.

"Wait a second, hon," the woman said.

For a wild second, I thought she had read my mind and was talking to me. Then I realized she wanted something from Sweet.

"I want you to do it for me," she said in that female Darth Vader voice.

"Do what?" Sweet said.

"Come sit on the bed and pose for me. You're so beautiful."

"Men ain't beautiful," Sweet said, but I could tell he was pleased by her remark.

"Come on. Please? I'll make it real special if you do. Like nothing you've ever had before."

She slid off the bed and turned so that her back was to me. She was as perfect from behind as the front, and I throbbed at the view. Not a blemish, just like one of those air-brushed stroke book centerfolds. I live to be a hundred, I will never forget the sight of her there in the moonlight. Impossibly perfect, as though carved from chrome herself.

Sweet came into view and moved to sit on the bed. Men don't do anything for me that way, but I had to admit he was as good looking as they got. His muscles were all ridges and hard planes as he slid into the pose.

"Like that?" he said.

"Just like that," the woman said. "Hold it for a second."

Then she turned and looked straight at me. I realized immediately she'd known I was there all along. She walked to the door as if she had all night. I stared at her, paralyzed, my mouth as arid as the desert behind me. Full front naked, she was almost shimmering in the light of the gravid moon. She reached the doorway and stopped, no more than five feet away from me, and smiled. She reached out and caught the edge of the door. "You don't really want to see this," she said softly, almost a whisper. She closed the door.

"What'd you say, puss?" Sweet said, his voice muffled by the closed door. He hadn't seen me.

"Nothing," she relied. "Don't move.'"

I might have stood there another ten seconds before I shook myself from my hypnosis and hurried away. I heard Sweet moan and I didn't want to hear any more of that, my erection was so hard my dick ought to be humming in the breeze, shorts notwithstanding, and the thought of them together was more than I could possibly stand.

Back in my room I masturbated to a quick release, then I tried sleeping again, but gave it up after only an hour. Might as well drive. I couldn't stay here with her in there with Sweet. I hurriedly packed my gear and went toward my truck. The moon had settled some but dawn was still half an hour or more away as I reached my rig. I cranked the engine up and sat there for a moment, diesel idling.

Sweet's truck came to life fifty feet away.

Oh, man, how could he do it? Get up and leave a woman like that? I would have stayed there in that bed with her until I starved if it had been me. But find 'em, fuck 'em, forget 'em, that was Sweet's motto. Bleed the lizard and hit the road. Damn.

I flicked on my lights just as Sweet's truck passed in front of me.

But it wasn't Sweet driving.

I blinked, and it took a second for it to register. By then the tractor was past, and I was looking at the side of the trailer. Looking at the jumble of chrome bimbos plastered all over the side of the big Fruehauf unit, shining in the remnant of the moonlight, my headlights, and the orange and yellow outliners. And the bimbos were all there like before, but they had changed.

***

IN SOME OF the bigger truck stops you can find the new variation on the chrome bimbo now. They just suddenly seemed to appear there shortly after that late July night in Arizona. It's the same pose as the old model, one leg out, one knee bent up, leaning back, chest pushed out, as shiny as ever. But there's a big difference—the new bimbo is male. I suppose some of the women drivers buy them, maybe gay drivers, though there aren't many of those I know of.

A male bimbo.

Exactly like the ones on the side of Sweetbrier Mott's rig when it left the motel parking lot in Tonopah, Arizona, on that hot July night, with the smiling, naked, *shining* woman of my dreams driving it, waving goodbye to me.

And where was Sweet? Nobody seems to know. Nobody claims to have seen him again, at least not in person. Most of the drivers figure some husband caught up with him, but it wasn't a man who did Sweet in. Or even a woman, in the strictest sense. There are stories about the rig, though, half-seen in the distance, or whipping past somebody in the middle of the night in the middle of nowhere, the whole thing spangled with male bimbos, but nobody talks about that too much. And female chrome bimbo sales are down lately too, so I hear. Somehow word about this kind of thing always gets around.

There *is* some justice in the world, after all.

~

From WMG Publishing
COMPLETELY SMITTEN
A Fun Kristine Grayson Fates Novel.

New York Times *bestselling writer Kevin J. Anderson might be the busiest writer working in modern fiction. And one of the most prolific as well. He has published more than 140 books and he and his wife, bestselling writer Rebecca Moesta, founded Wordfire Press eight years ago as well.*

Kevin is known for Star Wars, X-Files, *and* Dune *novels, as well as his many original science fiction novels. But back in 2012 he started something a little different for him, a series of humouous horror mysteries featuring Dan Shamble, Zombie P.I. Okay, if that doesn't sound like a* Pulphouse *story, I don't know what does.*

Thankfully, Kevin let me put a Dan Shamble story right here in this issue. And there will be more coming in later issues as well.

The Writing on the Wall
A Dan Shamble, Zombie P.I. Adventure
Kevin J. Anderson

1

"**THAT ZOMBIE WROTE** *FU* right there on the side of my store!" said Howard Snark, the human proprietor of Stakes 'n Spades, the only full-service hardware store in the Unnatural Quarter. He put his hands on his hips and fumed as he stared at the dripping spray paint.

Howard was normally a pleasant, soft-spoken man with salt-and-pepper hair, a full salt-and-pepper beard, and a salt-and-pepper personality. Standing there, I adjusted my fedora and inspected the graffiti. I could understand why he was upset, since his store had been defaced, but I thought he was misinterpreting.

"Actually, I think it says *FA,* Howard," I said. As a zombie detective, I have to pay close attention to details.

Beside me, my partner, Robin Deyer, leaned closer and nodded. "Dan's right. It's *FA.* Zombies don't have the best penmanship." She sounded apologetic.

We all stood together outside Stakes 'n Spades responding to the complaint, along with Officer Toby McGoohan, or McGoo. While walking his beat, he had apprehended the zombie tagger right as he was scrawling the letters with a can of lime green spray paint.

"It's still a violation," said McGoo, "regardless of the spelling."

The zombie graffiti artist looked dazed and confused, staring perplexed at the spray paint can in his grayish hands, as if he couldn't remember what he'd been doing.

Howard snatched the can away. "What were you thinking, Eddie? You're one of my regular customers. What did I ever do to you? I'm just trying to make a living here."

Howard had opened Stakes 'n Spades in the Unnatural Quarter because he saw an unfulfilled need. After all, monsters needed plumbing equipment, tools, lumber, nails, duct tape, and other building supplies as much as anyone else did. He had once lived in Silicon Valley, where many of his friends and colleagues became successful millionaires by working in software. Howard, on the other hand, had a vision that his own fortune lay in *hardware.*

When a rich, old aunt died and left him a modest inheritance, Howard built his store in the Quarter. Then, after he'd spent the entire inheritance, the rich, old aunt came back as a ghost and demanded some of the funds back. It could have been an inter-family argument with many consequences—legally speaking, the undead could sometimes reclaim their material wealth, depending on the amount of vagueness in the deceased's last will and testament—but, Howard and his aunt reached an amicable settlement. He gave her enough money to go on a retirement cruise with other ghosts, and he downsized his store slightly, but made it more profitable. Howard Snark had faithfully served the Unnatural Quarter for years, even becoming chairman of the Chamber of Commerce for a two year stretch.

Now, McGoo stood with his report pad out, frowning at the zombie graffiti artist, ready to write a citation or make an arrest, whichever was necessary. "Well, Eddie, what have you got to say for yourself? You were caught red-handed."

Eddie looked down at his hands where some of the messy spray paint had covered his fingers in a neon-lime color. "I don't know."

He wasn't as well-preserved a zombie as I am, but he wasn't a horribly decaying shambler, either. His pants were slung low so that his waistband encircled the bottoms of his hips, while the waistband of his plaid boxer shorts was pulled high up on his back. Apparently, his demographic considers that sort of dress "stylish."

"What were you trying to write?" asked Robin. "FA...what else?"

"I don't know."

McGoo took off his policeman's cap and wiped a hand across his freckled forehead. His reddish hair was rumpled. "I don't know why these deadbeats can't just take an art class." He looked up at me. "Maybe you can solve this one for me, Shamble. There's been a rash of incomprehensible graffiti in the last day or two. None of it makes any sense. You're the detective—can you figure out what goes through a teenager's mind when he does stupid things?"

"That's beyond the skills of the most talented zombie detective," I replied. "And I *am* the most talented zombie detective—or so I've been told."

"That's what you tell yourself, at least," McGoo muttered.

"Did the other graffiti writing make sense?" asked Robin. When she decides to work on something, Robin is intense and dedicated. When she'd gotten her law degree, she decided to help the unnaturals who needed legal representation. She and I have been partners for a long time, both when I was a human detective, and now that I'm a zombie detective. When you have a good working relationship, you keep it.

McGoo flipped back through his pad. "First time, two days ago, some zombie just wrote *HE*—and then never went further." He looked at me with teasing scorn. "You zombies don't have a lot of follow-through."

"Some of us have ADDD. Attention deficit disorder of the dead."

McGoo looked down at his pad, turned the page. "Another zombie scrawled *I'VE* on a brick alley wall. Another one just wrote *LP,* whatever that means."

"I don't know," said Eddie again, even though we hadn't asked him the question.

"Maybe he was inspired." On the street corner in front of the Stakes 'n Spades hardware store sat a long-limbed zombie artist with a set of multicolored spray-paint cans and a stack of shiny hubcaps. Goch was a marginally popular street artist who specialized in painting designs on hubcaps, then selling them to curious human tourists who came into the Quarter to see everyday monsters in their natural habitat. Goch claimed that he "found" the hubcaps, although more likely, they had been stolen from parked cars. He had very long arms and legs that he folded up like a spider's, and long hair that made him look like an aging post-mortem heavy metal rock star.

Now, Goch held a spray can in his hand as he swirled a jet of color around on the hubcap. "When the muse takes you, you gotta paint."

"Well, he doesn't gotta paint *my store!*" said Howard.

Eddie slouched his head and his shoulders as much as his pants slouched. "I'm sorry, Mr. Snark…I don't know what came over me."

Dan Shamble, Zombie P.I.

New York Times Bestselling Author
Kevin J. Anderson

TASTES LIKE CHICKEN

Dan Shamble, Zombie P.I. faces his most fowl case yet, when a flock of murderous chickens terrorizes the Unnatural Quarter.

And a cute little vampire girl who may or may not be his daughter.

For this book and other
Kevin J. Anderson stories and novels
go to:
wordfirepress.com

Howard let out an exasperated sigh. "Eddie, you're a good kid. All right, if you sweep up in the back, break down some boxes, and help run the store for a day or two, we'll call it even. I won't press charges—this time. I've got work to do. An entire new shipment of mallets and stakes came in, so we're having a special sale in honor of Bram Stoker's birthday."

Howard was always good at marketing.

McGoo put away his pad. "Doesn't bother me not to make an arrest. Less paperwork that way." He looked at me with gratitude. "I guess you didn't need to come out here after all, Shamble."

"We didn't come here for you," I said as Robin and I turned to go. "We're working on a case. We've been hired to see Angina, Mistress of Fright."

2

DESPITE HER WORLDWIDE fame before the Big Uneasy—the mystical event that unleashed all of the monsters, ghosts, and legendary creatures back into the world—few people had seen Angina, Mistress of Fright, since she'd retired from show business and become a recluse in the Unnatural Quarter.

She was a much beloved screamfest hostess, who had become quite a star on *Nightmares in the Daytime,* a monster movie double feature that had played first on a cable channel out of Chicago on Saturday afternoons, before it caught on and spread around numerous syndicated channels.

With her scanty outfit, large breasts, and campy, as well as vampy, personality, Angina had become a cultural icon. Few people actually watched the bad black-and-white horror flicks she hosted; the audience was much more interested in her goofball comments, and her cleavage, during the breaks.

But when the breasts started sagging and crows' feet appeared around her eyes, Angina—whose vanity was legendary—retired from public life, preferring to be remembered as she was in her femme-fatale heyday.

That was all before the Big Uneasy a decade ago. With real monsters setting up shop and interacting with normal society, the demand for old horror flicks dwindled, so Angina had picked the perfect time to retire. And she found the right neighborhood for her retirement home.

Even though she chose the Quarter as her "unnatural habitat," Angina built high fences, barricaded herself in her house, and became a total recluse. She interacted with no one, had groceries and supplies delivered by golems who were sworn to secrecy. And she never left.

But recently an admirer, a dedicated fan, had engaged Chambeaux & Deyer Investigations to make contact with Angina. It was our job to make our client happy.

The Angina house was a rickety, bent-over affair (designed that way on purpose) with peeling wood siding, slatted shutters that hung askew on the windows, black shingles on the roof, a belfry complete with bats, seven gables close together. The house was surrounded by a brick wall topped by fierce-looking wrought-iron spikes and a dash of barbed wire (probably electrified). The rusty gate was padlocked shut. At the cornerstone of the brick wall, I saw the engraved notation, "Chas. Addams, Architect."

Everything about the Angina house looked rundown and dangerous—which was perfectly acceptable décor in the Unnatural Quarter, in accordance with the neighborhood homeowners' association covenants.

Just outside the padlocked gate I found a speaker and an intercom button. "Would you like to do the honors, Robin?"

I could see she was barely suppressing a giggle. "I confess, I'm a little nervous, Dan."

Robin had faced horrific monsters, fierce demons, and powerful black magic, but now she had butterflies in her stomach because she was actually a big fan of Angina, Mistress of Fright. She pushed the intercom button. "Hello?"

A loud, harsh, female voice burst out of the speaker. "Go away!"

"We're here to see Angina. We have a request—I hope you can help us out."

No answer—only dead silence.

My turn to push the button. "Is anyone there?"

"I want to be left alone!"

Robin's turn. She pushed the button. "We were hoping for an autograph, if it's not too much trouble."

"No trespassing!"

Robin and I looked at each other, and she seemed very disappointed. "A person has a right to privacy. We can't intrude if Angina doesn't want us."

Robin was always a stickler for the rules, which had worked much to our disadvantage many times. I've often found it more effective to apologize afterward than to ask her permission before I did any questionable activity.

I didn't give up so easily, though. "The cases don't solve themselves, and we have an obligation to our client to try everything possible. We've got to figure out a way."

Back at the offices of Chambeaux & Deyer, clients normally just walk through the door, whether it be a golem seeking justice for his comrades caught in an illegal sweatshop, or an opera-singing ogre who had lost his voice, or even human clients whose interactions with unnaturals hadn't gone well. (That happens more often than you might think.)

This time, though, we received our engagement letter via the mail. Jackson B. Hayes introduced himself to us as an avid collector, insisting that he was Angina's "number one fan!" Then he went on to reassure us that there was nothing obsessive about it, like Annie Wilkes of *Misery* fame, but that he really, really, really loved Angina. He had grown up captivated by her, watched every episode of *Nightmares in the Daytime* cinema, collected a Standee figure of her, posters on the walls. He had DVDs of her movies, VHS copies of her older ones, even Betamax copies of older ones still.

Jackson had sent us a black-and-white glossy photo, one of the beautiful head shots that showed Angina in her prime: alabaster skin and eyes with enough mascara and shadow to make an Egyptian sarcophagus jealous. The canyon of cleavage between her breasts was large enough and prominent enough that it could have been a national park, or at least a national monument.

"I desperately want to get this photo autographed," wrote Jackson. "It would mean so much to me."

So, he engaged Chambeaux & Deyer Investigations to break Angina's legendary reclusive barrier just long enough to get a signature. "And make certain it's an *authentic signature.* I've been duped before."

He described how he had purchased a signed photo from a collector on the internet, but because Jackson B. Hayes was an Angina expert, he recognized the forgery immediately.

"Angina always signed her autographed photos to her fans with a special exclamation point drawing the dot in the shape of a heart. She said it symbolized a stake going right into the fan's heart. So endearing! Since the photo I purchased had a normal exclamation point, I knew it was fake."

Sheyenne, my ghost girlfriend who also runs our offices, brought the package to Robin and me. "Here's a new case."

"Sounds like an easy job," I said. "Everyone knows where the Angina house is."

Robin's eyes were sparkling as she began to gather our information, gazing at the beautiful black and white photo. "I'd really love to meet her myself."

I'd never seen my partner turn into a fangirl before. It was charming.

Sheyenne had used her poltergeist powers to dial the phone and let Jackson B. Hayes know that we would start work right away. All we had to do was get a minute of Angina's time.

Now, as we stood outside the imposing brick wall and padlocked gate, Robin clutched the black-and-white photo in its protective envelope. She wasn't sure what to do.

I pushed the intercom button again. "We won't go away until we see you, Angina."

The response came back loud and gritty. "Keep out! No trespassing!"

Robin pushed the button. "Please, we don't mean to be a bother, but—"

"I want to be left alone! Go away!"

This was starting to sound redundant. I pushed the button again. "Is this just a recording? Is there anybody in there?"

"No trespassing! Keep out!"

Robin looked at me, worried. "Maybe we could try again later. Perhaps a phone call? Send a package in the mail?"

"Zombies can be persistent," I told her.

"Not as persistent as lawyers," Robin said.

3

THE UNNATURAL QUARTER really got hopping after dark, when all the nightbreeds, vampires, and shadowy creatures felt their metabolisms rise. But it was after official business hours for Chambeaux and Deyer. I decided to relax with Sheyenne and watch a movie. Considering our Angina case, though, it was a work-related date.

Since my girlfriend is a ghost, she can't touch any living, or formerly living, thing, which makes it difficult to hold hands. She passes right through my flesh. But when she really gets into that spectrally romantic mood, she can don a polyester glove and make her grip feel almost lifelike. Since at times I can be almost likelike, too, we make a good couple.

Sheyenne has been with me longer after death than we were a couple when we were both alive. Of course, our relationship and some unsavory acquaintances was what led to our respective murders in the first place, but neither of us let that dampen the post-mortem romance.

We sat in the conference room with a portable TV set and the lights turned down so we could watch a DVD of Angina, Mistress of Fright's *Nightmares in the Daytime.* The movie itself was an old stinker, *Revenge of the Grinning Skull,* whose effects were so bad the director must have gone home every night hanging his head in shame; the acting was so bad, the cast must have done the same; and the writing was even worse, so the screenwriter probably didn't bother to go home at all, for fear of facing his family once they'd seen the film.

But when Angina came on screen during the breaks, she was really something. The Mistress of Fright had a sparkle in her dark eyes, and she laughed so boisterously that sometimes her artificial fangs fell out—which she played for laughs, as well.

She groaned at a particularly awful point in *Revenge of the Grinning Skull.* "Angina must have gone out of her way to pick movies so bad that they would make her look good."

Her polyester glove levitated and I reached up to hold her hand. A fresh-popped bowl of popcorn sat on the conference room table in front of us, mainly for ambience, because a ghost can't eat and I usually don't have much appetite.

Normally, I would have gone to the Goblin Tavern to share an after-hours beer with McGoo, but that night I told him I had a date. "Must be nice, Shamble," McGoo had said. "You're dead, and you still get more girls than I do."

"Yes, that's me, McGoo. Always been a babe magnet."

"Me too. But I think my polarity is the opposite of yours. I just repel them."

McGoo was probably still walking the beat even this late at night; he didn't have much to go home for.

A few hours after Robin and I came back from our unwelcome reception at the Angina house, McGoo called to tell me that he had found more incomplete zombie graffiti scrawled on a wall in the Quarter. Another young zombie with the same intellectual capacity as Eddie had spray painted *"LLEN AND I"* before running out of steam.

McGoo had caught the deadbeat as he stood there looking at the can of spray paint in his hands. When McGoo demanded to know "Who's LLEN?" the zombie didn't seem to know. No surprise there.

Now, while Sheyenne and I watched the movie, Robin was burning the midnight oil in her office, poring over cases, studying legal precedents, writing up briefs. She's still alive but she doesn't have much of a life—except with us. I didn't want this talented young woman to work herself to death, but I knew that working on cases and hammering out briefs was how Robin chose to relax. She was more stressed when not working.

Robin came to stand at the door of the conference room, peeping in so she could watch the movie too. "You're welcome to join us," I said.

She looked at Sheyenne and me holding hands. "I don't want to interrupt your date."

"You're not," Sheyenne said. "This is about as far as Beaux and I were going to get tonight."

"Always stuck on second base," I said.

Robin snagged the bowl of popcorn. "I will take this if you're not going to eat it. It smells delicious, fills the whole office."

She stood munching on a handful of popcorn, captivated by *The Revenge of the Grinning Skull.* "I remember this one!" When Angina came on, we all laughed aloud as a man in a rubber Creature from the Black Lagoon mask did pratfalls and fell into a half-full bathtub.

"Angina certainly has stage presence," Robin said. "With those looks, that body, she used to be quite a dish."

"And now she's just leftovers," I said. "No wonder she's a recluse."

Sheyenne said, "Maybe she just wants people to remember the way she was on screen. You never age there."

"Right," I said. "Like the Blu-Ray of Dorian Gray."

The phone rang. Even though it was after office hours, everyone knew that zombies and ghosts—and dedicated lawyers—worked all hours anyway.

Sheyenne flitted out of the conference room while I paused the movie. She didn't bother to use the door, simply passed right through the walls to get to her desk. Robin munched popcorn while we both listened to the phone conversation in the reception area.

"All right, McGoo, I'll send her right over. I'm sure Dan will want to come, too." After hanging up, Sheyenne flitted back to the conference room. "More trouble at Stakes 'n Spades. Goch, the hubcap artist, has been arrested, and he's demanding to see Robin as his lawyer."

I groaned. "What did he do?"

"Defacing private property, but he denies it. Said he's got to have Robin right away."

Robin set down the popcorn. "Sorry about your date and movie."

But Sheyenne understood. She always did.

4

IT WAS THE DEAD OF NIGHT, but that's when the dead really got lively. At the hardware store, the street lights were bright, and McGoo stood there flustered, disappointed, and at his wits' end.

Goch was in handcuffs, his long legs shaking so badly that his knobby knees knocked together. His colorfully painted hubcaps were strewn around, like a going-out-of-business sale for bad artwork. Several spray-paint cans lay tipped over on the sidewalk.

Outside the hardware store, Howard Snark wrung his hands and shook his head. "I barely got the other graffiti cleaned off!" He shook his fist at Goch, who cringed. "Why can't you get a life?"

"Because..." said the zombie artist.

But Howard wasn't listening. "I am pressing charges this time, Officer McGoohan."

"I thought you might," McGoo said.

Scrawled in gigantic letters across the front of the hardware store, were the words *"CAN'T GET."*

It didn't make any sense to me. *"CAN'T GET* what?"

Robin stepped up to the artist, using her most understanding voice. "You've got us all confused, here, Goch. What does it mean?"

The zombie heaved a long sigh. "You don't ask what art *means."* He looked pleadingly at Robin. "It was the Muse—it must have been. I couldn't control myself. You have to defend me, Ms. Deyer. It's about artistic expression."

"I'd like to express myself all over your face!" Howard slapped his forehead. "I sold you that paint. I even bought four of your hubcap creations for my store—and this is how you thank me?"

When Goch trembled, his handcuffs rattled like the chains on a restless spirit.

Other unnatural spectators had gathered around—two vampires who had just come back from a nightcap at a Talbot & Knowles blood bar, a partially unwrapped mummy who was still in stitches from a show at a comedy club, and several slack-faced and curious-looking young zombies.

As Howard Snark and Goch continued to argue and McGoo wrote up the citation, one of the young zombie spectators shuffled forward, picked up a discarded can of pink paint, and walked over to the door of the hardware store. As we stared in disbelief, he started painting—right in front of us.

I lurched forward. "Hey! Stop that."

McGoo and I seized the arms of the disoriented young zombie who was moving listlessly like a...zombie. I grabbed the spray paint out of his hands.

He'd had time to paint the word *"UP!"* Oddly enough, the dot of the exclamation point was a cute little heart.

Howard groaned, exasperated. "What is wrong with you undead people?"

"UP with what?" Robin said to the dazed zombie. "You knew you'd be caught!"

"UP yours," Howard said. "You're going to pay to clean my building."

I paused and stared, though, looking at the words.

CAN'T GET and *UP!*

Then, I remembered the afternoon's new graffiti—*LLEN AND I*—and the incident that had called us here early in the day, *FA.*

The first graffiti McGoo had reported to me was just the word *HE,* but I recalled what else we'd seen. *I'VE* and *LP.* I was sure I was putting them in the correct order of how the graffiti had actually been written.

HE

LP.

"McGoo, it's a message. It all goes together. The graffiti is telling us something—and we'd better listen."

I felt a chill rush through my embalming fluid as I realized that the spray-painted letters spelled out that terrifying mantra so dreaded by senior citizens everywhere:

HELP I'VE FALLEN AND I CAN'T GET UP!

"Who?" McGoo said, "Where? How do we respond to this? Shamble, you're onto something."

I pointed to the stylized exclamation point with the little heart. "It's Angina. And she's in trouble."

5

AS WE RACED to the Angina house, I placed a phone call to Sheyenne. "Spooky, we might need you." She's always happy to help, and I seem to solve cases better when she's around. At least, that's what she says.

An emergency with a person potentially in peril took precedence over arresting a zombie vandal with a side career in hubcap painting. Besides, we knew we could always find Goch again, since he was a well-known street artist, not a particular flight risk.

Howard said, "I'll hold Goch for you in the meantime. Stakes 'n Spades has a full line of chains, padlocks, and rope."

Robin, McGoo, and I arrived at the Angina house, which looked even more corny and stereotypical under the full moonlight. Sheyenne joined us just as we arrived; she's a powerful poltergeist who is not bound by the restrictions of physical travel as are human cops, determined lawyers, or shambling zombies.

Remembering the imposing padlock that held the main gate shut, I had planned ahead and asked Howard for a sturdy set of bolt cutters. He showed me the options from his store, gave me a sales pitch about the craftsmanship and the warranties of each. I just took the biggest one.

McGoo punched the gate's intercom button. "Ms. Angina, we're here to help. Are you in trouble?"

"Keep out! Go away! No trespassing!"

"Sounds like she's fine." McGoo lifted his eyebrows. "Though not very friendly."

"It's a recording," I said. "Same words every time."

"She's definitely in trouble," Robin said. "We've got to do something."

I grasped the bars to rattle the gate, and I was shocked, literally, when sparks crackled through my body. I yanked my hands away. Fortunately, zombies don't have to worry about being electrocuted.

"She means business," I said.

Robin sounded desperate. "Given the evidence, there's a reasonable expectation that this person is in danger. If it's to do a wellness check on a person who hasn't been seen in a long time, we have sufficient cause to break in. We're on sound legal ground here."

I lifted the tool. "And I've got a big bolt cutter."

"There's an easier way." Sheyenne took a shortcut by flitting right through the gates. "At least let me switch off the current."

Once through the wall, she deactivated the electrified fence, and I used the bolt cutters to snap the chain. We pushed open the gate and raced up the flagstone walk that was artfully surrounded with scraggly weeds.

Sheyenne vanished directly through the front door of the vintage haunted house. And, since my ghost girlfriend had just gone inside, it was now, quite literally, a haunted house—but in the best possible way.

McGoo, Robin, and I ran up the rickety wooden porch steps, and we heard a loud series of thunks as multiple deadbolts were turned. Sheyenne pulled the door open with a loud nerve-jarring groan and hovered in front of us, pale and glowing, but her expression was distraught.

"We're too late," she said.

I went inside first, with my hand on my .38 in its holster. McGoo had already drawn his service revolver, though there was nothing threatening inside the haunted house.

Just a dead body.

The foyer of the Angina house was a large receiving hall, with two towering grandfather clocks, ostentatious furniture, marble tiles, a dramatic curving staircase. And Angina, Mistress of Fright, sprawled at the bottom of the stairs on the marble tiles. Obviously dead. And for several days from the looks of her.

Even though we had just watched *The Revenge of the Grinning Skull* on Angina's *Nightmares in the Daytime,* I barely recognized the famous horror film hostess. Angina had retired from the public eye and gone into hiding years ago. I suppose the kindest way to describe it was that she "had not aged as well as a fine wine." Angina had gained another film hostess's worth of weight, and her lush, black hair had gone gray and fallen out in clumps. Her skin showed numerous age spots (other than the normal discoloration of having been dead for several days).

"I guess we didn't have to run so fast."

Then the air above Angina's body shimmered, and a figure appeared—an indistinct and barely visible image of Angina, like the ghost of a ghost, a watermark in the air. She was just a flickering afterimage, compared to Sheyenne's bright and intense ectoplasmic form.

"It took you long enough!" She was indignant, but her voice sounded as if it came from a great distance. "Didn't you get my message?"

McGoo and I looked at each other. Robin said, "Not right away. It wasn't clear."

The ghost of Angina let out a disgusted snort. "Zombies are lousy messengers."

In sharp contrast to the decrepit old, overweight, and age-spotted corpse of the Mistress of Fright, Angina's ghost looked as if she had stepped right off of one of her pristine DVD images: beautiful face, voluptuous body, fine skin tone, and bodily curves that went gently in and out rather than just out.

"You're a ghost, just like me," Sheyenne said. "Don't you have poltergeist powers? Couldn't you just walk through the wall and get out?"

Angina's ghost let out a metaphorical sigh. "I tried, but I couldn't walk through walls, and I don't have any poltergeist powers. Looks like I washed out as a ghost, just like I washed out as a serious actress. I'm weak, and I'm trapped inside this house, but I feel that I'm supposed to move on. I needed help."

I made the connection. "So you possessed those zombies to put out your message."

"Zombies are very poor conduits, but they were the only thing I could use. Undead slackers—they're hard to control for more than a few minutes at a time."

I tried not to sound testy. "Some of us are well-preserved zombies."

"And a lot of them aren't well-preserved at all," Angina snapped. "It was an ungodly challenge to get them to write

"I knew I should have stayed in clown college."

down one or two letters before their attention would wander off somewhere. The whole thing took days!"

Robin nodded solemnly. "Yes, ADDD."

"I couldn't leave the house, and I was stuck here, fading away, like my career. But at least you finally came."

"We were too late to save you, though." Robin frowned.

"Oh, don't worry about that. It was quick—I tumbled down the stairs, and... then I was a ghost. Besides"—she drew herself up, touched her breasts, ran her spectral hands along her spectral waist—"look at me! Quite an improvement, I'd say. That old body was quite a burden, and I'm glad to be rid of it. I like this much better.

"But after I died, I was trapped in this house, and I just couldn't figure out how to let anyone know." She glanced at Sheyenne, gave one of her signature Mistress of Fright winks. "Now, I may not be a poltergeist, but after all the movies I hosted, I remember damn well that ghosts can possess people—particularly weak-willed people. And who's more weak willed than a zombie?"

I chose not to take offense at that.

"I just didn't realize it would be so tedious just to get one line right. Ugh, it reminds me of some of the actors I worked with."

"Well, we're happy to have found you now," Robin said. "We'll let you out of the house. Even as a ghost, you'll be welcome in the Unnatural Quarter. You'll fit right in. A lot of monsters watched your show, too. And..." She seemed embarrassed. "I'm a big fan, too."

Angina shook her faint, spectral head. "Oh, I'm not going out there! I need to move on. I know I do."

After the Big Uneasy, the undead were a common sight—vampires, zombies or ghosts—but not everyone came back for an encore. Some people died and stayed dead...and they liked it that way. I was glad that Sheyenne had come back to haunt me, but Angina just felt trapped.

"Then I'm not sure I understand," I said. "What do you need our help for?"

"I died here alone, under violent circumstances. My body needs a proper burial before I can head toward the light."

"You sure that'll work?" McGoo asked.

Angina huffed. "Mister, do you know how many hundreds of horror movies I hosted? I've seen enough to know that's what you have to do."

6

THE QUARTER offered several services that could take care of Angina's needs, such as ghost-removal services and licensed "proper burial" teams with all the bells and whistles. There were budget plans and extravagant ones.

Angina, of course, needed to have the best.

Once released from her house, Angina had followed us out the front door, and now she hovered around the Chambeaux & Deyer offices, waiting as we wrapped up the details. Sheyenne described the ins and outs of being a ghost, but Angina wasn't really interested, since it wouldn't matter for long.

But I had other cases as well, and I always keep my clients' needs foremost in my mind. While we arranged for the proper disposition of Angina's corporeal remains, the real client who had started this whole mess—or adventure—was the autograph collector, Jackson B. Hayes. I wanted to wrap up that case while I had the chance.

I pulled out the black-and-white head shot that the fan had lovingly sent to us. "We were trying to get your autograph, Ms. Angina. That's why we visited you in the first place."

I showed her Jackson's letter, and faint fuzzy tears appeared in her translucent eyes. "I was always good to my fans."

"Is there any chance…?" I held up a pen. "An autograph would mean so much. Then we could close out the case."

Sheyenne drifted closer. "But if she doesn't have any poltergeist powers, Beaux, she can't scrawl her name."

"My penmanship was very neat," Angina said. "I would never scrawl."

"Maybe we could just get a photo of me holding up the glossy with you in the frame," I said. It was all I could think of.

Robin joined us. "She's very faint. I doubt the ghost image would even show up in the picture."

Angina, though, had a bright idea. "You're a zombie, Mr. Shamble. I could do what I did before. Hold onto that pen and empty your head of thoughts."

"That's easy enough for him," Sheyenne teased.

I couldn't let her get away with that. "Not when you're around, Spooky. I have lots of thoughts."

Robin was uncertain. "You want to possess Dan, so that he can write, just like the other zombies did with graffiti?"

"I can try," said Angina.

Whatever it takes to wrap up a case. I dutifully cleared my head, held the pen, and felt a strange presence enter through the bullet hole in my forehead, which was a very strange experience.

My hand moved of its own accord, flexing my wrist, limbering up, and then with a flourish I signed, "To my Number One Fan—Best Wishes, Angina, Mistress of Fright." For veracity, Angina possessed my hand and forced me to make the final exclamation point, complete with a cute little heart for a dot.

"There," Angina said. "See? A stake headed straight for the heart."

Robin witnessed the signature and signed a certificate of authenticity to verify for Jackson B. Hayes that Angina herself had autographed the photo. She also made a secondary notation that this was guaranteed to be the last signature Angina ever gave to a fan. Jackson would love that.

Within an hour, the proper disposal service had been completed, Angina waved farewell and then winked out of existence heading off to a better place where she hoped to find a new audience for her work.

After Angina vanished, I stood next to Sheyenne, who looked somewhat wistful. "I could've gone on at one time, but I stayed behind to seek justice, to find my killer…and to hang out with you, Beaux."

I didn't know what I'd do without Sheyenne. Unlife was so much better with her around. "You're not going to leave me, are you, Spooky?"

She smiled and snuggled close. I felt a tingle, but little else. It didn't matter, I knew she was right there, and her presence warmed my cold blood.

"No, Beaux. I'm here on purpose, and I intend to stay. We've got a lot more cases to solve."

~

I flat loved this story from Sabrina Chase. It struck me as a perfect Pulphouse *story from the moment I read it.*

Besides writing novels and wild short stories, Sabrina Chase works as a software test developer, writer, and recovering physicist. Not sure if there is a 12-step program for that last part. Sounds tough, actually.

She resides right here in the Pacific Northwest, but a distance from the home of this magazine.

Coyote and the Amazing Herbal Formula
Sabrina Chase

OLD WHITE WOMAN sat on her porch enjoying a morning smoke one fine spring day. "Somethin' gonna happen," said Old White Woman. She peered up at the sky with one eye, the one that was just a little brighter than the other. "Good. Figger I'm due."

Not long after a figure like a man came staggering down the dirt road from the mountain. He was so dusty a cloud surrounded him as he moved. But what was especially interesting, to Old White Woman's clearest eye, was the dust was grey—when the dirt of the road was rusty orange.

"Ooooh," said the stranger. "Water to keep me from crumbling right up in a pile of shavings. Think of the mess, and me so harmless and weak." He grinned and collapsed on the steps of the porch.

"Mighty fine teeth you have there. Don't look so weak to me, Sneaky One," said Old White Woman. "I got the way of seein' and your tricks don't work on me."

The stranger slumped even further. His head drooped, his ears drooped, and he pretty near drained through the cracks to the ground. "Was it the fur? I'm so weary I could die—which is a thing not so easy for me—and I haven't done what I set out to do." He gave a little howl.

"Don't carry on like that. It ain't fittin' for an old spirit like you. Set you there and I'll fetch some water, and you'll repay me by tellin' me a tale. Ain't heard a new Coyote story since my granny's time."

Old White Woman grabbed her cane, heaved to her feet, and stumped into the cabin. She came back with a tin pitcher of cold well water. Coyote took it and drained the whole thing in one gulp, changing just a bit to stick his snout down inside and lick it dry.

"Brought a little corn squeezin's too. Yer still droopin' like a chewed string."

Coyote took a hearty swig from the bottle, wheezed, then took a more respectful sip. "That's the best liquid fire I ever drank, but it's not enough for what ails me."

"And what precisely ails you?" asked Old White Woman. "Yer lookin' pretty hale on the outside."

Coyote reached into his pants and removed his detachable penis. It slumped on the palm of his hand, raw, weeping, and limp as a rotten cucumber.

"Salted green horny toads, that is the saddest peter I ever seen in all my born days," said Old White Woman. Coyote's penis turned its one eye on her and seemed to sigh. "What in tarnation have you been doing with it, diggin' post holes for a five-mile fence?"

Coyote gave her a measuring look. "You're closer than you know, you and your seeing eye. I'm grateful for the drink but all I have to offer is a story that is not finished. Perhaps your wisdom can help me through to the other side of it. You see, I've been busy for the last few centuries making love to the Grey Mountain Spirit. She's hard and unyielding and made a bet with me that I could not move her with pleasure. And this," he said, waggling his depressed member, "is the result. I fell asleep at some point. I must go back and win my bet, but how can I with *this*?"

"Oh, I reckon you won, if that's the mountain in question," Old White Woman said, pointing with the stem of her pipe back up the road Coyote had traveled. "We don't get earthquakes much in these parts, so people remember 'em. Was in my granny's time. You been sleepin' a while, Old Man."

"And I am refreshed!" said Coyote, jumping up. "I am *refreshed*," he said pointedly to his penis. The penis tried a little hop, and straightened just a bit, then fell and drooped over the sides of Coyote's hand. "How can you just lie there when I have a debt to pay?" yelled Coyote. "She's saved us both, you ungrateful lovestick!" The penis just twitched.

"Ain't interested, thanks all the same. I know where it's been," said Old White Woman.

"I was just thinking, you living alone and all," Coyote sulked.

"My man's been gone ten years now, but we had us a handful a children. Not sayin' I don't miss him and some parts in particular, but I'm set in my ways and I don't need some wild lover with a tail."

"Where are these children?" Coyote asked. "They leave you alone here, abandoned? I smell your scent, but no one else."

Old White Woman snorted. "Abandoned? I talk to 'em alla time. See, while you were sleepin' off yer rock-rubbing we got 'lectricity an' tellerphones and all manner of clever contraptions. My daughter sent me the latest device just last month. A box full of the Innernet! We can send letters and I don't even need to lick a stamp. You can find out most anythin' with that box. It's a marvel."

"You don't say!" said Coyote, greatly impressed. "Do you think it would know how to make this stand up and do its duty?" He waggled the penis again.

"I get messages all the time sayin' they got the stuff ta do it. Come take a look-see."

Coyote followed Old White Woman into the house. Inside was the magic box, which had a glowing window and strange things tied by their tails to the box that made it work. It was exactly as Old White Woman had said. Many, many medicine men claimed to have exactly what was needed to make his manhood harder, longer, wider, more enduring, and remove unsightly back hair. Coyote ignored that part.

"How do I get these medicines?" Coyote asked.

"Sez here you gotta give 'em the numbers offa them little plastic card things they use for money nowadays. Then they send a package with the medicine to you in the mail."

"But I don't have a plastic card, and mail would take too long. I need a cure now. There's centuries of lovemaking I have to catch up on!"

"You'll be wantin' a softer lover this time, don't forget," said Old White Woman. "Keep on like you've been and you'll break the little guy past fixin'."

Coyote sniffed at the magic box. It had very faint scents, strange and new.

"How do these Internets work, then? How do the messages get in the box?"

Old White Woman shrugged. "It's a mystery to me. All I know, you gotta have that thick wire there plugged in just right or it don't work for spit."

Coyote sniffed the wire. The strange scents were stronger there. "I am the best tracker and hunter in the world, am I not? I will track these messages back to where they came from, and ask there for the medicine." He looked at the messages again. One in particular had a scent that made his nose twitch. HerbaPotenz.

THE LONG WAY HOME

Moire Cameron ran to protect her secrets, ran to the heart of an interstellar alien war. But a false name and fake ID can't conceal her or help fulfill her last order, given by a dying man eighty years ago. To do that she must find a reason to live again.

For this book and other
Sabrina Chase stories and novels
go to:
http://chaseadventures.com/

"How you gonna fit in that little tiny wire?" Old White Woman asked.

"Shapechanger," Coyote said and smiled, the smile with all the teeth. "I will send you a lover that is not wild and does not have a tail, for you have helped me and I will help you in return." He crouched and sprang into the magic Internet box.

It was very much like swimming in a river of tiny lightning bolts inside the wire, and the river branched so fast Coyote had trouble keeping the scent he wanted.

One of the trails had an end. He poked his head out. A bleary-eyed young man with black hair and a beard sat at a desk with another magic box, staring at him dully. There was a sour smell.

"Is this the place I can find HerbaPotenz?" asked Coyote.

"*Ne,*" said the young man. "This Bulgaria. Get off my screen, dog-faced man. Are you a virus?"

Coyote sniffed, and learned. The young man was something like a trickster, but he did not enjoy his tricks and did them only for power and the numbers on the little plastic cards. Coyote ducked back inside the Internet box, leaving his own trick for the Bulgarian. Now every time he used his magic box, a picture of a coyote would appear just for a blink and laugh at him.

Coyote found a better track and followed it to another end. This time when he looked out, there was a woman with big yellow hair and big breasts in a small dress and when she saw him, her eyes became very big too.

"HerbaPotenz is here! I can smell it!" Coyote said. "Look, I need some desperately!" He waved his chapped penis at her.

Big Hair Woman had big strong lungs too. She screamed and flailed her hands at Coyote, who didn't mind at all because it made her big breasts move like wrestling bear cubs. He jumped out of the magic box to get a better view, but that made Big Hair Woman scream even louder and run away.

"Wait!" called Coyote. "I need the medicine! Where is it?" He ran after her. Now there were lots of screaming and running people. They all ran into a big room with a tall roof and many large metal shelves with boxes in them. A big fat man was driving a machine that lifted boxes up and down, but when he saw Big Hair Woman being chased by Coyote he stopped and jumped out. All the people ran out a door that went to the outside. Big Fat Man stopped in the doorway and faced Coyote. Coyote could smell he was afraid, but he did not move.

"Leave EllaBeth alone! What the hell are you?"

"I just want some HerbaPotenz," Coyote said, "Where can I find some?"

Big Fat Man looked at him suspiciously. "That's all? You're not after EllaBeth?"

Not at the moment, Coyote thought, but he knew better than to say so. "That's all I came here for," he said, opening his eyes wide to look innocent.

"In those boxes, second shelf," Big Fat Man pointed. Coyote ran and jumped up. "No, not that one, it's teeth whitener. You sure don't need that. Other one."

Coyote pulled out a container and opened it. He sniffed. He frowned. "This does not have the power. I smelled it here, and this has much the same scent, but it is not the thing I need."

Big Fat Man scratched his head. "I dunno. I just run the forklift. That's the

stuff we send out, but I don't know how it's made. Mister Brett, he might know." He glanced up at some windows that looked down on the big room with the shelves. There was another small room up there, and Coyote could smell an even stronger fear coming from it. He ran up the metal stairs to the small room.

"Are you Mister Brett?" Coyote asked the man hiding under the desk. He had three hairs on top of his head that had been glued in place with strange-smelling fat, and he peeked at Coyote from behind his hands. Three-Hair Man nodded. "I need HerbaPotenz, the real medicine. This is not really HerbaPotenz," Coyote said, tossing the container through the window with a crash. Three-Hair Man cringed. "You have it, I smell it on you."

"I used it all!" Three-Hair Man cried. "We changed the formula. It was too expensive to make it like the old guy said. He sent a sample, though, and of course I had to try it, right? I don't have any left!"

"Why don't you ask this medicine man for more?" Coyote asked.

"Well, he'd want to know why we needed it when we told him it wasn't selling," Three-Hair Man said, wriggling uncomfortably. "He's supposed to get a percentage."

"You are making fake medicine and cheating the one who gave it to you?" Coyote growled. "Tell me where to find this man, or I will bite you!"

Three-Hair Man whimpered, and scrabbled at the top of his desk for a big pile of papers. He took one and held it out, shaking. "That's all I have! Now go away!"

"What, no email?" Coyote said, disappointed. He rather liked using the Internet now.

"He's old; why would he use email?" said Three-Hair Man.

Coyote snarled at him until he curled up in a tight, smelly ball. Then Coyote pinched off a little bit of his shadow and tossed it in the corner, so Three-Hair Man would see it and remember Coyote and always be afraid. Then he set out to find the medicine man.

He followed the address to a big house with many windows, and Coyote was pleased to see it. Only a wealthy medicine man could afford to live in such a big house. Then he smelled that many, many old people lived there. The man he was searching for lived in a small room in the big house, and had very little.

"Are you the one who made the HerbaPotenz?" asked Coyote.

"That is what they are calling it, I am thinking," said Old Medicine Man. "*Mannerwurtzenmittel* was my name for it, but they said nobody could pronounce it and it sounded like something for insects anyway."

Coyote told him his story, including the display of Exhibit P. "Please, can you help me?"

"I believe so," said Old Medicine Man. "I kept a little, for the memories. My dear wife, may she rest in peace, was very fond of it." He took his cane and went to the little cabinet that held his belongings, taking out a fat round glass bottle with a glass stopper.

Coyote caught the scent, and quivered with delight. "That's it!" He took the bottle, pulled the stopper out with his teeth, and poured the medicine over his penis. It bounced up and down, growing stronger and wider with each bounce. Soon it was back to its regular form and ready for action.

"Oooo, I can feel it working. I can't wait to try it out," sighed Coyote. "Now I can have fun again! But before I do—Old Medicine Man, how can I repay you?"

Old Medicine Man smiled sadly. "I always wanted to live in the country, but that would be too much to ask. Perhaps I could move to a room where I could see some trees outside?"

"How about a whole forest, with a mountain? Possibly even a nice older lady to love? I do *not* mean the mountain." Coyote put the medicine bottle back in his hand. "You may need this." He lifted the Old Medicine Man into the chair with wheels and ran to the big room where all the people met, for he had seen a magic Internet box there. "We'll just make a few stops on the way."

Coyote jumped into the magic box, holding Old Medicine Man close. He remembered one of the tricks the Bulgarian had, and he could use it to take money from Three-Hair Man that really belonged to Old Medicine Man. The magic box, as Old White Woman had said, was indeed powerful. He could even go to the machines where the money came out, because they were also connected to the lightning river like the magic boxes.

And so it was Old White Woman saw Old Medicine Man suddenly appear in her house, a glass bottle in his hand and his pockets full of money. He looked very confused.

"I am apologizing for the intrusion, but there was this...strange person, and he—"

"Don't tell me. Lots of teeth, kinda hairy around the edges?"

Old Medicine Man nodded.

"Why don't you just set a while and tell me all about it. I do love a good story," said Old White Woman.

~

"What do you mean, I look 'long in the tooth'?"

Not only does T. Thorn Coyle fiction fit perfectly in this magazine, but she fits as a person as well. She's the author of an alternate-history urban fantasy series called The Panther Chronicles *and in the Spring of 2018 her* Witches of Portland *series will launch.*

Her multiple non-fiction books include Sigil Magic for Writers *and* Evolutionary Witchcraft. *She has taught magical practice in nine countries, on four continents, and in twenty-five states.*

She also wanted me to know she has been arrested four times and it will take a cup of tea or really good whisky to get her to tell me about it.

Salt
T. Thorn Coyle

ONCE THE RANDOM ITCHING settled down, the water soothed him. Just around body temperature, it was dense with salts that hugged his body, offering him a cradle of buoyancy. The sensation wasn't exactly one of floating—not like the summers he spent floating on Lake Berryessa when he was a boy—it was a suspension. Suspension in a substance that was not quite liquid, but not solid, either. His body, which felt almost too big to fit inside this tank, was a large object in suspension. His broad shoulders, the biceps and massive thighs he worked on three days a week at the gym with its blasting techno and pretty men, allowed just enough space to surround his body with the salt solution. His belly rose above the thick water, the one thing the gym would never take away.

He was a towering mass of fat and muscle, but in here, he felt almost light.

"Still your mind." The memory of his teacher's voice rang in his ears. He had tried. He'd done all the practices she gave him: slowing down his breathing, concentrating on a candle flame, imagining he was a mountain with a still pool at its center. Nothing had served to block out the clamor of their voices.

They were always seeking him. Except here. The darkness, silence, the lack of smell, the warm air and water, these all put him in a state of being he hadn't felt in many years. He wasn't sure whether this temporary stasis allowed him to finally reach the state his teacher had asked him for, or if the voices simply didn't like the salt. Many things avoided salt: slugs, snails, and spirits.

That was one other thing she had taught him: to make a magic circle out of salt, to keep unwanted forces out. That worked half the time, but they could still find the inner crannies of his head.

Suspended in warm darkness, there was no sound except his breathing, and sometimes, when the dense salt water cradled his ears just right, the slow beat of his heart. Jasper took a deep breath in, willing himself to relax.

Once a week he visited the flotation tanks. If he could have afforded to, he would be here every day. It was the only time he really rested. Even sleep was just a weary tussle between exhaustion and the voices in his head.

The magic and meditation helped a little, but his teacher finally suggested he seek out a different type of help. "Just in case it's in your mind," she said. The psychiatrist he went to wanted to give him drugs. He tried that for six months before quitting because it didn't help, the drugs just dulled his senses and left a chalky taste in his mouth, so food tasted all wrong. And they made him unable to have sex. He hated that the most. Sex was something he really enjoyed, and the only thing that actually kept the voices from intruding in his consciousness—flesh slamming into wet flesh, mouths, tongues, cocks, and hands in motion, the smell of another man's arousal in his nostrils, and

those few moments of head blinding, body spasming orgasm—brought relief, and a still state of expansiveness just after.

Then —magic, drugs, or sex— the voices would return.

The drugs had muffled the voices, but took away what was good in life. And while the voices were less loud, they were still there, along with the accompanying emotions: fear, anguish, rage, and terror. They never fully went away because it turned out the voices did not *originate* inside his head. It was just that no one else could hear them. Not his teacher, not the psych, no one.

The voices had showed up during puberty. Jasper was now 52 and counting. It was too long to live with the grief and anger of the dead. Too much to learn about the terrible end of life in myriad forms. He did not want to know the different ways someone could die. But someone had to listen, they insisted. And that person, by some fluke of bent synapses or psychic opening…that person turned out to be him.

The voices whispered at him. It seemed like nonsense at first. Things he could not quite comprehend. Then he began to hear more clearly. The voices grew louder, asking him to help. Asking him for revenge. Asking Jasper to fix things. Sometimes—and this was the worst—the voices would scream. They would beg. They would wail and gnash their teeth, trapped in a temporary hell, unable to find the doorway out.

When it all began, Jasper couldn't fix anything. Jasper was thirteen and trying to fit in. Then he was fifteen and trying to figure out if it was safe to kiss Harley. Harley, with his short black hair. Harley who swam laps every morning in the high school pool, long muscles bunching and releasing down his back.

Jasper's cock rose gently from the salt solution. He hadn't thought of Harley in a long time, but the memory never failed to move him. He exhaled, and settled his attention back within the cradling womb of the flotation tank.

There was no way Jasper could have helped anyone back then. His mom worked two jobs, paying rent on their shitty apartment in the shitty part of town. It was his job to keep the place clean. He actually didn't mind that part. Jasper liked things to look good. Getting a job after school in a local charity shop, Jasper would sometimes bring home an old piece of furniture he'd worked on in the back room off hours.

He would sand out the scratches and cheap veneer, repaint the whole in black, or days when he wanted something different, bright blue, or red. Once that was done, he spent hours painting fanciful scenes that ran down the arms of chairs, or snaked up the sides of squat bookcases. Their apartment looked nicer after that, more interesting, and Jasper started selling his remade wares at the local flea market one Saturday a month. That was where he made his real money. The thrift store barely paid, but it helped him get his hands on goods. He and his mom started eating better.

On top of that, he had school to manage, plus his secret crush on Harley, and movies with his best friend Sandra on Sundays. He had no time to help the dead.

Didn't being dead make them beyond help? Beyond hope? He'd learned that wasn't the case. The dead had needs, and wishes, just like everyone else.

Jasper tried to slow his breathing even more, floating in the dense, warm water. The buoyancy felt good. Not only did the time in the tank ease his mind, it eased his back which ached from hours bent over the furniture. His furniture business

TO RAISE A CLENCHED FIST TO THE SKY

was pretty high end these days. Not rock star high end, but collectible enough to pay the rent on a two-bedroom bungalow tucked under a redwood tree in a pretty decent mixed neighborhood where they didn't mind that he was gay. All they cared about was that he kept his yard picked up and watched out for the kids.

He wasn't doing too well stilling his mind today. Something kept him from surrendering to the powers of the flotation tank. That shit from last weekend was still bugging him. The ghost. This one ghost. She had started screaming in his mind around three in the morning. Jasper had just gotten home from the bar, a night out for drinks and dancing with some other bears, the big, hirsute men like him. The men he'd learned to love and lust for, once he got over the slim-hipped boys like Harley, boys who never really paid him much mind, unless they decided to use him for practice. Jasper let them. He always let them. And they always broke his heart.

***

JASPER LOVED the bulk of the men at the bar, their muscled arms and rounded bellies covered in soft hair. He'd been talking with a man named Steve, whose arms bulged out from beneath a leather vest. Steve had a full brown beard, just edging toward gray, and beautiful eyes, a hazel green that changed according to light and mood. In the light pooling on the long oak bar, that set the rows of liquor bottles shimmering, Steve's eyes were dark with interest and the beginnings of lust.

Steve wanted to come home with him, but Jasper had too much work to do on Sunday to spend all night breaking

the bed. He'd extracted a promise for a date this coming Friday. Dinner first, then maybe some drinks. Then more kissing of that lovely face, with soft lips nestled inside the thicket of beard. It was better that way, anyhow. Sometimes he wanted to take things a little slow. He wouldn't mind falling in love.

Jasper had just dropped off to sleep that night when the screaming started. She was terrified. Something really bad had happened to her and he couldn't tell what it was. He sat straight up in bed, chest heaving from his startled breath and pounding heart. Sweat dotted his face, and the sheets were damp where it had pooled under his arms and between his thighs.

"YOU HAVE TO HELP ME! HE'S COMING. HE'S COMING BACK!"

He scrambled up from the sheets and twisting blankets. Knocked his big hand against the nightstand and heard his phone drop to the wooden floor.

"Shit!" The screaming kept on and on. Jasper practically fell out of the bed, trying to get away from it, and trying not to step onto his phone. He found it. Punched the button to check the time. Three fourteen. Which meant the screaming had started at three thirteen, on the dot.

The shouting would have been deafening, if it was coming from outside. As it was, his skull felt like it was fracturing, building a headache behind his eyes that would take hours to recede. He tried to home in on her: what she looked like, what the tenor of her voice was beneath the volume, how old she was. He tried to calm his own panic, center himself, like his teacher taught him, slowing all his bodily functions down, and opening his other senses. The pressure and pain in his head made this more difficult, but he kept trying.

Finally. Finally. He found the still pool at the center of the mountain, and dropped in. He opened up his inner eyes. And there she was.

Floating through the air, mouth an open rictus of pain. Brown eyes wide, panicking. He made a gesture in the air with his right hand and the sound slowed down, then stopped. But he could see she was still screaming. She was so thin. Skinny even. Fourteen years old? He threw her a lifeline. A cord of glistening light, silver and blue. She grabbed hold of it, feet kicking in panic, body writhing through the air.

Jasper pulled. And pop! The ghost was through. He fell back, butt cheeks slapping the wood floor through the thin boxer briefs he'd worn to bed. Wrapping the gossamer cord around his left hand, he got to his knees, and then pushed up to his feet.

He had to get to the altar. Call upon some spirits. Get some help.

***

HE COULDN'T STOP thinking about it.

The quiet in the tank was the best part. The tanks had become a refuge like no other. If it were not for that ghost, he would be thoughtless in here after ten minutes, which meant he would have a full fifty minutes of complete calm. No intrusion. No worries. No tension. No fear.

But he couldn't get rid of the thought of her. He went back over his actions. Had he done the right thing? He did his best. Lit some candles. Offered up some incense. Inscribed the sigils of protection in the air. He drew a circle of salt around them both, and held her as best as his fleshy body could hold one such as her. He soothed her with his mind, stroking her hair, and stilling her sharp hands as they wound around each other, kneading nothing.

"Ssh. You are safe for now. He can't pass through the salt." Whoever *he* was.

She rocked within his arms, which extended themselves out from his body to make a space. Even though he couldn't really feel her, she was there. Thank the Gods Steve with his bright green eyes hadn't come home from the bar. Nothing ruined the afterglow of sex like a ghost screaming in your head. He'd lost more than one lover that way, over the years. Another reason to slow things down a bit: it gave him time to prepare his companions for the possibility of disruption.

As if anyone could really be prepared. His teacher had barely been, saying his work was beyond her ken. She taught him what she could: how to work the energies, light the candles, tap the tides of moon and sun. How to protect his dreams. How to make a Sending if he had to, though he never, ever should. But she told him that even she did not know what his work would become. All she knew was that it would be something needful, and something very strange. That was how she talked. Needful. He got what she meant by that, now. When your work was so specialized and intermittently urgent, it filled a need that most people barely knew was there.

The ghosts were filled with need. *This* ghost was filled with need.

How had he, a furniture maker, ended up a counselor and savior for the disembodied? A low rent psychopomp? He was no priest who held rites for grieving families, presiding over funerals, or opening great pathways at the festivals when the veils between this land and that were thin. He was just…here. Living his life. Painting fancy furniture from castoffs and selling it to people who had money to burn. Hanging with the leather daddies at the bar. Lighting his candles in the evening, and rising every day with a prayer, just like his teacher taught him.

Somehow his life had become a beacon for the desperate dead.

Jasper didn't mind helping them out and showing them the door. He had learned how to help them shuffle off this plane and into wherever they needed to be next. But they kept wanting more than that. They wanted revenge. Or closure. Or for him to solve some crime. Or the thing that felt worst: they wanted a reason. A reason for their death. A reason for their torture. A reason they ended up floating down a river, or tied up in a box, or dead from a stray bullet shot by cops looking for someone else.

This one, this girl, she wanted to feel safe from whatever was still hunting her, even now that she was dead. She was still there, enclosed in a salt circle in his bedroom. At least, he assumed she was. He hoped that she was safe. Having no idea why someone would hunt a ghost down, he also hoped he could figure out what to do. He had tried to send her through the doorway to the Great Unknown, but she had balked at that and started screaming again that He was still out there. Jasper had gotten stray, shadowed thoughts from her, like a sped up spool of film. Flickering images too grainy and fast for him to figure out.

He groaned. The tank was useless today, and his hour was two-thirds in. Barely enough time to reach theta state. Jasper willed himself to relax again, tensing up his muscles and releasing them to the salt water's embrace.

"OK ghosts. You win this round. I give up. Give me twenty more minutes. Twenty more minutes *alone*, OK?" That wasn't really fair. Jasper knew the ghosts couldn't get through the tank's environment, but he felt like blaming them anyway. They were the cause of his worries. He exhaled a mighty breath, just like she taught him. "Clear away everything you carry that isn't your own," she used to say. He pushed the memories out from his body, imagining the salt absorbing it all, neutralizing the terror and the pain. Leaving him alone.

He let himself drift off then. His mind finally slowed toward stillness. The water cradled Jasper like strong and gentle arms. Like he imagined Steve's arms might feel, snuggling in the night. Jasper knew the salt water would hold him and protect him, better than a circle, better than anything else. He just wished he had more time. In this state of deep relaxation —finally— a stray thought surfaced from somewhere deep inside him. Just one thought. He hoped it was all he needed. Then it drifted away, just as the low lights inside the tank flickered back on, bringing him back to the world. Too soon. His time was up.

After showering off the thick salt and rubbing almond oil over as much of his skin as he could reach, Jasper pulled on his boxer briefs and jeans, donned a black "Plays Well With Others" T-shirt and headed home. He thought he knew what he needed to do. He hoped the ghost was still inside the salt circle. While he couldn't imagine how she could get free, all bets seemed off this time.

The bungalow was quiet when he got home. He dropped his small gym bag just inside the door, and plopped his wet towel on top. Shadows lengthened across the hardwood floors, and up the dark wood wainscoting that lined each room, up to the goldenrod walls. Jasper headed down the hallway toward his bedroom. The only sounds were the clicking over of the fridge, a few birds, and a couple of kids playing basketball outside. His head was quiet, which was strange. He had braced himself for her screaming as soon as he put his key in the door.

Nudging open the bedroom door, he looked around the large, white room. High bed with dark blue pillow cases and plum comforter. The altar in the corner, set up on an old dresser he'd remade ten years before. The circle of salt was still there, next to the altar. He could just see the outlines of the girl, huddled there.

Jasper froze. On the other side of the altar, a figure occupied the chair Jasper sat in to take off his shoes, or throw his jacket. It was the figure of a man, whose face kept changing from young to old, chubby cheeked to lean, pale to dark. The man was slightly blurred around the edges, more solid than a ghost, but slightly transparent. Jasper could just see the back of the chair with its painted animals through the man's collared shirt and blazer. It was as though the man was a filter laid over the chair. A hologram. A Sending.

"You have my ghost." The voice, at least, was clear. His lips moved, but the man spoke inside of Jasper's head, soft. Direct.

Jasper turned toward the altar, hairs on his arms at attention, all his senses aware of the Sending. Keeping the figure in his peripheral vision, he started opening dresser drawers. Took out saltpeter for just in case. Frankincense. The dried petals of night blooming jasmine. A charcoal disc. One of the un-dyed beeswax tapers he saved for times when the magic had to be unimpeded, pure.

His teacher had told him, "If a magician makes a Sending, make sure you remain calm. They can travel your emotions and get inside your dreams. They can haunt you until you are a shadow, a husk. At best, you'll die. At worst, you'll end up in a padded room, or doing the lithium shuffle down a green hallway."

He carefully set up the clean, silver candlestick. The incense dish. The knife.

"Preparing to do magic, are you?" The figure laughed inside his head, sending a sharp flare of anger inside Jasper's belly. Jasper could feel the figure try to grab the anger before he released it on a breath. Just like the mind, emotions could be stilled. He had learned that in his second year of practice, though it took years to master the trick. He lit the candle and held the charcoal disc up to the flame. It caught at one rim, hissing out sparks and sending up a plume of acrid smoke. He placed it in the censor, waiting for the smoking to stop and the rest of the disc to turn glowing red.

While he waited, he breathed. The Sending shifted in the chair, still talking inside his head. Jasper ignored the voice and spared a glance to the salt circle. The ghost of the girl was watching the man in the chair. She had backed as far toward the edge of the circle furthest from the Sending as she could.

Jasper tapped fragrant lumps of resin onto the glowing charcoal, and added a few petals of the jasmine. Sweet smoke rose up, twining around his head, mixing with the honey smell of melting wax. It was time to ask for help.

"Diana! Protector of the innocent! Huntress! Heed my call! Bring your arrows of protection to this girl!" He had called the Gods many times in the past, and made offerings to them twice monthly, and whenever the seasons changed. But he didn't know what would happen in a case like this. Would Diana appear, like the Sending or the ghost? Or would she refuse to heed his call?

It was funny, Jasper knew that magic worked. He knew the ancestors and ghosts were real. But the Gods? Sometimes he wondered. And then his spine snapped upright as though a piece of metal ran up his back. The muscles in his arms flexed. His gaze grew sharp like steel. His right hand picked up his blade, but it felt to him like he held an arrow's shaft. "Diana?" he whispered.

The Sending cackled. "You think you called her here? You think that she can help? That's your great magic?" The Sending began breathing in great draughts of air. The edge of the salt circle began to tremble and the ghost started shrieking inside of Jasper's head. "HELP ME! GET HIM AWAY FROM ME! HELP ME!"

Jasper moved to stand between the ghost and the Sending, arms out, blade poised in hand. The pain in his head was increasing and sweat popped out on his skin. He could taste the salt of it in his mouth. It stung his eyes. It was too much, these voices in his head. The screaming ghost, the laughing Sending, and the sense of the Goddess Diana, just inside his skin.

"Know. Your. Work." The voice of the Goddess was as steely as the gaze she trained on the Sending.

"What?" The words made no sense to him. He felt a flash of irritation. Not his. Hers.

"Know. Your. Work. Vanquish him. Act."

With a great bellow, Jasper shot forward toward the Sending, steel blade moving through the holograph until blade met wood, parting the grains of the painted chair, pinning the Sending to the wood.

The Sending battered at his mind, the girl was still screaming. Jasper didn't care. The blade grew hot in his hand. He could sense the rope that anchored the Sending to the magician and powered the personality of the thing. And he saw what he had failed to see before: the thread of silver and red that tied it to the ghost. Somehow, the cord passed through the salt, attaching itself to her heart. The red was her life's essence, bleeding slowly back along the cord to the magician. No wonder she was scared and screaming. No wonder she couldn't move on: she was still dying. The magician was bleeding out her soul.

"Diana, what now?" He was gritting his teeth, sweat pouring off his face, burning tiny holes into the Sending as the drops fell. The Sending was still writhing against the chair. "Help me." He could feel the foreign magic growing in his mind, adding to the pressure and the chaos.

But he didn't have a headache. He wasn't panicking. He felt okay. He just needed to know what to do.

"Cut the cord from ghost to Sending," came a voice. "Set her free."

Okay. He knew how to do that. But he only had one knife. How the hell was he going to pull this off?

Then he knew. Right hand still on the blade, Jasper grabbed his T-shirt with his left, pulling it up, exposing his massive, sweating belly. Then he leaned in. The Sending starting shrieking as the salty sweat ripped giant chunks of ether from its body. Jasper leaned until his belly was pressing against the hilt of the knife, then he rolled to one side of the blade and pulled.

The knife yanked free from wood and Sending and he sliced the cord that bled the ghost. A second, swift cut sliced the cord that held the Sending to the magician. Then he fell forward on the chair, head smacking the wall behind it before he could lever himself away from the wall with his left hand. Jasper's breath was heaving. He could hear the ghost weeping in his head. It sounded like relief.

Carefully, very carefully, he pushed himself back from the chair and took two limping steps toward the altar. He pried his fingers from the hilt of the blade. Grimacing, he dropped the knife onto the altar with a sigh. The palm of his hand was red and starting to blister. But he wasn't done.

There was a ghost to see to, and a wall to wash down with lavender water. A house to re-ward, setting fresh protections all around it. A hand to clean and bandage. He would need to study Sendings, and increase his magic work. If stuff like this was possible, there was a lot he didn't know. When he had his bright idea in the tub —to magic up Diana, patroness of girls— he had no idea it would end up this way.

Oh yes, there was a Goddess to thank for her help. He'd do that, too.

But first things first. Jasper turned to the salt circle. "Are you ready?"

The ghost nodded, whimpering. Still scared, but willing to move on. *Able* to move on. Jasper raised his blistering right hand and drew a sigil in the air. He traced a doorway shape behind it, and saw it limned with light. Carefully, one foot rubbed at the circle, scattering salt across the hardwood floor.

The ghost rose from the circle. Jasper opened up the door.

She floated through.

Dayle A. Dermatis works across many genres with her novels and hundreds of short stories. And no matter what genre she picks to write in, the stories and novels soar with fine writing, intelligence, and heart.

Sounds like I am a fan. And I am. You want to see why, go check out her website at DayleDermatis.com.

This little short-short originally appeared in Clowns: The Unlikely Coulrophobia Remix *and was shortlisted for the* Best Horror of the Year Volume Nine. *Knowing that there was no chance on the planet I had read the clowns book, Dayle sent it to me as a hunch I would like it. She was right and I have a hunch you will as well.*

Queen and Fool
Dayle A. Dermatis

ARLECCHINO. FUNNY, SAD HARLEQUIN. Trapped in the never-ending cycle of wooing Columbina but never having her. The audience laughs.

The truth runs deeper. So does the suffering.

***

YOU MAY NEVER have Columbina, but she has you. Imprisoned, weeping clear tears. You can never find release because the cage doesn't allow you to grow. Lust brings frustration, with a color as red as the crimson diamonds on your costume.

Your mask, with its ridiculously long nose—Columbina designed it. You've worn it so long, it's an extension of you. When she strokes it, the audience laughs at the bawdy entendre. They think you laugh, too, but soundless crying is too easily mistaken for laughter. Because when she strokes it you imagine that caress elsewhere—you *feel* it elsewhere, but that place can never grow long like your mask's nose.

You ache for her. You throb. You weep.

You're known for your exaggerated gait, your ridiculous wide steps. Only you and Columbina know you move that way because the cage chafes, a constant reminder

159

of your helplessness. Open your legs wide for the cartwheel, Arlecchino. Flip around the stage as if you are free.

You are never free.

***

THEY SAY the beginnings of your story are rooted in hell—that you were a demon serving at the devil's bidding.

The truth is simply this: You are in a hell of your own making. The hell of love, and lust, of hopeless adoration and a deprivation so frustrating you cannot think, only feel, only pray for surcease.

If there is a devil, it is Columbina—but Columbina is your possessor, your heart, your very air. Your angel of anguish.

***

AT NIGHT there is no rest for you, because Columbina comes. You give her pleasure with your mouth and hands, tasting her sweet nectar, her thick scent filling your senses. Behind your mask, your eyes plead for mercy, for release.

Unstrap this monstrous cage from me, you beg without words. *Touch me, just once. Once is all it will take…*

Oh, she does touch you, but while you are trapped, the caresses and whispers of hot breath bring no pleasure, only greater punishment. Tears leak from behind your mask even as they leak through the cage as you writhe.

You know if you speak, she will treat your words the same way the audience does, as jests and japes to bring amusement.

That is the one spark of hope left to you: that you bring your beloved Columbina amusement, and pleasure. She could never do the things she does to you if you did not love her so, worship her so. Your denial of pleasure is *her* pleasure, which somehow brings it back to being *your* pleasure.

It makes no sense, but then, isn't your role, your very being,

Columbina will always be the queen, and you will always be the fool.

Funny, sad, tormented Arlecchino.

～

Over thirty years ago, Kristine Kathryn Rusch and I started Pulphouse Publishing. Kris did the editing, I did the publishing stuff, and Pulphouse grew quickly into the fifth largest publisher of science fiction, fantasy, and horror.

Kris not only was the executive editor of all of the Pulphouse lines of books, but she edited the award-winning Pulphouse Hardback Magazine *for its twelve volume planned run. Then she stayed on as book editor, but her short fiction editing took her to* The Magazine of Fantasy and Science Fiction, *where she stayed as the only woman editor for six years. She is the only person in history to win a Hugo Award for both her editing and her writing.*

With her going to F&SF, we decided I would edit this magazine, keep the high quality fiction, just put it in a different format. She stayed at F&SF from 1990 until 1996 and I edited the first incarnation of this magazine from 1991 until 1996. To say our house was full of manuscripts and stories in those years would be an understatement, since we both got over a thousand per month, in large envelopes. (shudder)

Since then, she has written hundreds of novels and even more short stories and won just about every award that is offered in the different genres of fiction. I talked her into letting me publish this story here and I have a hunch you are going to love this story as much as I do.

Hand Fast
Kristine Kathryn Rusch

THE MOST ROMANTIC GIFT anyone ever gave me? A gun.

Valentine's Day, ten years ago. Ryder. God, what a sweet man. Six-three, all tattooed muscle, black hair shorn off that year to accent his dark, dark skin.

We were on the roof of his place, trying to keep candles lit in the cold breeze blowing across the Hudson, eating take-out sushi with custom-made chopsticks clutched in our frozen fingers, sitting on lawn chairs wedged into the ice-covered snow.

Ry gave up on the candles midway through, decided to go to his apartment to get a lantern—he said—and did come back with one. Battery operated, large, already on. And in his other hand, a Tiffany's blue box big enough for a cake, tied with the ubiquitous white ribbon.

Despite the box, he couldn't afford Tiffany's. Not even something small, and certainly not something that large. Even if we could have afforded Tiffany's, we wouldn't have bought anything there.

We were militantly anti-ostentation back then. It went well with our lack of funds. But we *believed* it, acted on it, maybe even looked the other way when someone in a silk suit and shiny leather shoes ventured into the wrong alley, stepping in only when that rich bastard looked to be in trouble for his life—never stepping in to save his wallet.

I opened the box with trembling fingers, stuck the ribbon in my pocket and stared at a small lockbox that looked old and well used.

Ry nodded. He wanted me to open it. So I did.

And saw the gun.

It wasn't any old gun.

It was custom-made, silver, and, I later learned, it glowed slightly when its owner touched it. It also designed its own bullets—silver for werewolves, holy-water-laced for vampires, and laser-lighty (filled with fire) for the unknown magical.

I long suspected—and never tested—that the miracle weapon could transform its bullets into whatever the owner imagined.

We handfasted me to the weapon. He claimed he had another one, but I never saw it.

Handfasting required the candlewax (he was planning ahead), a bit of mercury, a touch of burnt almond. And some other magical oil-based concoctions I'm not going to describe, just in case.

And yeah, handfasting—pagan term for wedding. But it also meant a bargain struck by joining hands. I thought then that applying hand to hand-grip was the same thing.

I had no idea where Ry had gotten the weapon or how he learned to control it. I didn't understand why he gave it to me.

I'd love to believe what he told me that night: He gave me the gun because he loved me.

But that couldn't have been entirely true, because who gave a gun out of love?

When I pushed the next day, asking the right way—*what made you think of me when you saw this?*—he said I was so much more talented than he was, I deserved the weapon, and the weapon deserved me. And then, the day after that, he admitted he had one too, and we'd go practice with them, just him and me, Upstate, the next time we had the dough.

There was no next time. There wasn't even a day after that. Not for Ry.

Someone caught him in our alley, shredded him, took the tattoos as souvenirs. I found him, still alive, barely. But not alive enough to tell me what happened. Or alive enough to let me know he heard me when, stupid me, I told him I loved him for the first and only time.

***

FAST-FORWARD a decade to the winter that never died. Press coverage that year pegged it as the coldest in two decades, blaming arctic air that should've lived in Canada but, like any other snowbird, decided to move south.

I had my own place by then, two buildings over, tall enough to get the occasional sunset glinting off the nearby roofs. I liked that: the dying sunlight reached the kitchen of my glorious apartment, just about the time (in the winter at least) I was having whatever it was I scrounged for breakfast.

My apartment: three rooms, hard-fought. Actually purchased when the building went condo just before the damn housing crisis. Now I was—as the pundits so euphemistically call it—underwater, and for once, I gave a damn.

Then I'd come to my place, warded and spelled, with the most comfortable furniture I could find (mostly discards on garbage day, dragged up the elevator, refurbished and softened), and reveled in having a safe harbor, somewhere no one else ever breached. Not anyone, including the post-Ry lovers, the so-called friends, the clients and the hangers-on.

Just me and the silence I'd created, a place to refurbish myself after each day's hard knocks and scrapes.

Somehow I stopped being militantly anti-ostentation. I was still anti-ostentation—no one would mistake the interior of this place for anything fancy—but I'd grown up enough to have financial entanglements and to adopt some of the trappings of a good citizen.

Protective coloration, really.

I'd needed it.

Back in the day, me and Ry were a team, and he was the stronger. We'd partner up, go after the shadows, fight till dawn, screw till noon, sleep a little, and start over.

Then he died, and I went full-moon batshit crazy searching for his killers, never sleeping, the edges of the world growing jagged and dark, finding clues where none existed, missing clues that'd probably been there, going, going, going until I ended up face-down in an abandoned subway tunnel and no memory of how I got there.

I had to choose, with my face pressed against the oil and the decades-old piss, whether I'd keep going or whether I'd just let it all end.

And weirdly, it was Ry who saved me. Ry, with his crooked half-smile and his embrace of anything dangerous. Ry, who had a tattoo on his left bicep of a bright yellow smiley face holding a sword in one little gloved hand and a dripping scalp in the other, with the word *Onward* in gothic letters underneath.

That tattoo always made me grin, especially when he flexed it, making the sword move up and down as if the smiley face were marching at a parade.

I saw that tattoo as clearly as if it were in front of me and, instead of regretting the method of its theft, I let out a tiny laugh. That moved the dusty dirt in front of me, and almost made me gag on the stench. Which, for some reason, I also found funny.

I was exhausted and spent, and in some ways, ruined. Completely different than I had been before.

I sat up, then stood up, and staggered my way out of the tunnel, heading back into my life. Which I rebuilt—alone—bit by bit. In the places that had never functioned alone, I built—I trained, I learned, I *became*.

I stayed in the City. Because the City had taken Ry from me. I couldn't get him back: Magic didn't work that way—at least not any kind of magic I chose to participate in. But I could find the missing pieces.

I could find whoever or whatever had killed him.

I could have answers—

Or so I thought. At first. Before I realized that a girl's gotta eat. A girl's gotta live. A girl's gotta move forward.

So I did.

***

AND THEN THE WINTER of our discontent. Valentine's Day wasn't a bright spot for anyone. Yet another storm had arrived the day before, canceling flights, snarling traffic, and delaying the all-important flower deliveries to shops that relied on them. By the time the actual holiday rolled around, the City was enveloped in sleet on top of two feet of snow.

I rented an office near the alley where Ry got attacked. The office wasn't much—third-floor walk-up with a frosted door, frosted windows, and a radiator that clanged to its own tune but at least kept the place warm. I had an actual desk which I got from an office five doors down—a blond wood monstrosity that smelled like old cigarettes, giving the office a slightly musty air, something I actually liked. In keeping with the thirties motif, I kept an open bottle of Scotch in the bottom drawer, although I rarely touched liquor. Any more.

I cribbed an old leather sofa from that same abandoned office, and found two matching desk chairs in the garbage behind my apartment building. The only money I actually spent on furnishing the place was for my chair, which was the most high-tech thing I owned. It had more levers and dials and options than the first (and last) car I ever drove.

The office had no computer or phone or anything remotely resembling office equipment. I don't write reports. I collect funds up front, and don't give paper receipts. If I need more money from my clients, I ask them for more. If they refuse to pay, I refuse to work.

I'm not one of those private detectives who works *pro bono* because the case interests them. I work because I need the money—and if I didn't work, I'd go back down that crazy subway tunnel, and the overwhelming stench of decades-old piss.

It's not even fair to call me a private detective. I use the title sometimes because it's easier than explaining what I do. What Ry and I used to do. What I never stopped doing, after he was gone.

I shove the magic back where it belongs.

Sounds easy, but it's not. And there are only a few of us that can do it.

By now it should be clear: I wasn't sitting alone in my office on Valentine's Day because of the snow. I hated Valentine's Day with a bloody passion. I tried not to. It wasn't the fake holiday's fault I was always so miserable at this time of year.

I usually tried to tell myself that Valentine's Day had peaked for me that night on the roof, with the lantern and the Tiffany box. And sometimes that worked.

But not on the tenth anniversary. Not as I slogged my way through the snow and sleet, watching inane couples in their finery get out of cabs or stumble out of the subway, pretending the day (night) was perfect after all. Maybe it was the combination—wind, snow, Valentines—that caught me.

Or maybe I was finally feeling my age for the first time.

Whatever it was, it convinced me to haul out that open bottle of Scotch the moment I collapsed into my high-tech desk chair. I had had the same open bottle of Scotch for months now, ever since a baby demon with a heart of gold (long story) had slept in my office for two weeks and nursed on the bottle like it was demon-mama's teat. No way was I ever drinking from that bottle again. So I got a new one—after I found baby demon's distraught mama and finally reunited the two of them.

Me, an open bottle of Scotch, sleet tapping the frosted glass like were-wolf claws. I thought I had the night all planned—when the gun appeared out of nowhere.

The gun. You know, the one from the Tiffany's box.

Or so I thought at first.

Well, not entirely true, because you don't think about where a gun came from when it appears right in front of you, business end pointed at your face, trembling as if held by an unsteady hand.

And nothing else.

I set the bottle of Scotch down, then made myself calmly and deliberately screw the cap back on. I would have put the bottle back in the bottom drawer, but the gun's trembling got worse, and I really didn't want to get shot just because I was being a neat freak.

I wondered what kind of bullets were in that thing—silver, holy-water-dipped, flaming hot. Damn near any of them would kill me, since I'm just good old-fashioned flesh and blood. I stared at the wobbling muzzle of that gun, then realized I had some control.

We'd been handfasted after all. The weapon belonged to me and I to it, which was probably why it couldn't go through with the shooting.

I held up my right hand and said in my deepest, most powerful voice, *Come to me.*

The weapon's trembling increased, but it didn't move. My heart moved enough for both of us, trying to pound its way out of my chest.

I tried the command again, and again, the damn gun just shook more.

So, figuring the rule of three, I tried one final time. *Join your handfast partner.*

The gun stopped trembling. And then it whirled as if pursued, and floated away from me. I sat for a moment, stupidly, then realized that the damn gun didn't be-

long to me. It was a different weapon than the one locked in the lockbox I kept in the Tiffany's box.

I got up and stumbled after the gun. It floated down the hallway, then down the stairs, always staying at chest-height, just as if someone were holding it.

It reached the lobby, bumped out the door (I have no idea how it got open), and into the sleet. I followed, coatless, instantly chilled, and nearly slammed into a couple wearing fewer clothes than I was, giggling their drunk way out of a nearby bar. They didn't seem to see the gun, but I couldn't take my gaze off it.

Because it went into the alley, where Ry died. And then it started banging against the brick wall behind a Dumpster, as if it were trying to get into something.

I wished for gloves. And boots. And a coat. I was sliding on ice, and still the alley had the stench of weeks-old garbage. It didn't matter how cold or wet something got, the smells remained.

I tried not to look at the back corner, where Ry bled out. It was covered in a snow pile six feet high anyway. The gun kept banging and scraping, and I finally decided to violate one of the major rules of automated magic.

I got between the gun and the wall. The gun kept hitting the same brick, scraping it white. I grabbed the damn thing, surprised that my fingers fit where the mortar should have been.

So I pulled.

The brick slid out easily, and I slid backwards, nearly falling. I caught myself on the edge of the ice-cold Dumpster.

The gun turned itself sideways, shoving its grip into the open hole. It had stopped trembling.

It balanced on the edge of the brick below for just a moment, then toppled downward.

I jumped back, afraid it would go off by accident.

But it didn't.

It rested on top of the ice as if all the magic had leached out of it. Its color was different too. No longer silver, but a muddy brown instead. I tilted my head, blinked hard, my face wet with sleet.

I wiped my eyes with the back of my hand, smearing the cold rather than getting rid of it.

The gun still looked odd. I figured it actually looked odd—it wasn't my magical sight that had changed; the gun was different.

So I crouched. And looked closer.

And gasped.

Something had wrapped itself around the grip. Brown and mottled. It took a moment for my eyes to make sense of what I saw.

The word *Onward* in Gothic script.

Bile rose in my throat.

I nudged the gun with my foot, then managed to flip the weapon over. The image on this side was a distorted yellow, desiccated and faded.

I swallowed hard, my stomach churning.

Then I stood and made a small flare out of my right fingertip. I used the flare to illuminate the hole in the bricks.

Saw shreds, images. Messed on the top like someone had rifled a drawer, and laid flat below, like carefully folded linen napkins waiting for a fancy dinner.

I lost my not-fancy dinner. And breakfast. And every meal for the past week.

Some investigator.

I'd searched for those patches of skin from the very beginning—all six of Ry's tattoos—knowing his magic lurked in them.

Only, as I braced one hand on the wall, and used the other hand to wipe my mouth, I realized that there were a lot more than six scraps of skin in that wall.

A lot more.

I allowed myself to get sick one final time before hauling out my phone, and calling the only detective at the NYPD who would ever listen to me.

Ryder's older brother.

Dane.

***

HE SHOWED UP ten minutes later, wearing a dress coat over an ill-fitting suit, and a this-better-be-worthwhile attitude. He wore his hair regulation cut, and he didn't have the muscles or the tattoos. Still, there was enough of a family resemblance to give me a start every time I saw him walk toward me. Same height, same build, same general energy.

"Three-hundred dollars up front for dinner," he said. "Includes five courses and champagne. We'd just finished appetizers."

"Special girl?" I asked.

"I'm hoping," he said. "We'll see if she's still there when I get back."

She might be waiting a long time, I thought but didn't say. I just showed him the open hole in the brick.

"What?" he asked impatiently.

"Just look," I said, my voice raspy, throat sore, my breath so foul I tried not to face him.

He grabbed his phone and used it like a flashlight, then backed away when he realized what he was looking at.

"What the hell?" he asked.

He peered into that obscene storage space, then looked at me, his handsome face half in shadow.

"How did you find this?" he asked, as if I had created the horror all on my own.

I poked the toe of my battered Nike against the gun.

He turned the phone's light toward it, saw the desiccated but still visible smiley face, and swallowed hard, then shook his head.

"You're out here without a coat or hat or mittens, and you're telling me you just stumbled on this gun?"

He didn't mention his brother's skin, wrapped around it, or the fact that there was more shredded skin in that opening.

"No, I'm not saying that."

Now that he mentioned how I was dressed, I realized just how cold I was. My teeth started chattering. I shoved my hands in the pocket of my jeans, not that it did much good.

"I asked you how you found this?" Dane snapped.

"And I showed you," I said.

"It means nothing." His voice went up, echoing between the buildings.

"Only because there are some things you refuse to let me tell you," I said, matching his tone.

He stared at me, breathing hard. I tried to stay calm, but it was difficult, considering how bad I was shivering.

"Magic?" he asked with a sneer he once reserved for Ry, but had transferred to me since Ry's death.

I nodded.

Dane rolled his eyes and shook his head. "You think this crap has been here all along?"

I shrugged one shoulder.

"You want to tell me, without talking about magic, how you came down here?"

I sighed. I could have said no, I supposed, but I didn't. "I followed the gun."

"And whoever was holding it," he said.

"I didn't see who was holding it," I said.

"Convenient," he said, "since it looks like Ry's gun."

It is *Ry's gun,* I wanted to say, but knew better. Because then Dane would ask me how I knew that, and I would point to the layer of skin wrapped around the grip.

"Ry told me he had one," I said. "I never saw it. How do you know it's his?"

Besides the skin, I mean, I added mentally. Of course, Dane didn't hear that.

"Pretty unusual thing, huh?" Dane said. "Ry called it magic. Me, I think it's some kind of toy, since it supposedly invents its own bullets."

I ignored that jibe. "He ever use it in front of you?"

"No, he wanted to take me to the range to practice with it, but he...." Dane let out a sigh. "He died before we could go."

"Who ended up with the gun?" I asked.

"I don't know," Dane said. "I never saw it again."

"So you remember it after *ten* years?" Lying on the ice, with Ry's skin wrapped around it, the gun didn't look *that* distinctive, at least not to me.

"I'd tell you I recognized it by that lovely silver barrel," Dane said, "but I didn't even notice that part at first."

I waited. I was going to make him say it, the bastard.

"I don't think we're going to have to test the DNA on that skin," Dane said quietly.

I nodded.

"But we might have to on the rest of this stuff in here." Dane peered at that hole. "Why would the gun turn up now?"

It had been exactly ten years since I got my gun. But I had no idea if Dane knew I had one too, and I wasn't about to tell him.

"The anniversary's coming up," I said.

"Yeah, like I can forget that," Dane said dryly. He sighed again. "I'm going to call this in. You need to go inside before you freeze solid."

"What about the gun?" I asked. "Do you think it should go into evidence?"

He looked at me. He knew what I was thinking. Hell, all of New York would have known what I was thinking. The City had seen a lot of news lately about weapons stolen out of the NYPD's evidence storage.

"You want to pick it up?" he asked.

Of course I didn't. Neither did he. But he had opened the door, and he was the magic-denier, not me. I reached around him, and with shaking fingers, sorted through the Dumpster until I found a box that wasn't too junked up. It was a shoebox with some stains along the bottom, but it didn't smell that bad, so I grabbed it.

I was going to scoop up the gun with the box lid, but I stopped halfway. I didn't want to mess up that grip. (That tattoo.) So I glanced at Dane. He was watching me closely.

I slid the lid underneath the box, then held the box in my left hand. I turned my right palm upward. Then I concentrated on the gun and hooked it mentally to my right hand. Slowly I raised my hand, and the gun rose too.

Once the gun was a foot off the ground, I crouched, slid the box underneath it, and turned my palm down. The gun bounced into the box, and I slapped the lid on it.

Dane watched me, face gray in the half light. His gaze met mine, but he didn't say anything. I knew, if asked, he would say only that I slid the box under the gun and scooped it up.

I offered him the box.

He shook his head. "You keep it."

"There could be evidence here," I said, taunting him.

He shook his head. "We'll have more than enough. Now, go inside."

He didn't have to tell me twice. I scurried to my building, feeling as if I would never get warm again.

***

SO RY had handfasted to the gun, just like I had.

I carried it up the stairs to my office, noting that the box did have an odor, but I wasn't sure if the odor came from the Dumpster or that tattooed slice of skin. I didn't want to think about that either.

Instead, I locked the entire box inside my office safe. Then I went to the ladies room down the hall ostensibly to run warm water on my hands but, in reality, to get whatever was on that box off my skin.

I shivered and shivered, even after I warmed up. The shivering didn't just come from the cold.

After I'd cleaned up, I grabbed my heavy down coat, my unattractive knit cap, and my gloves. I slipped everything on, locked the office, and headed home.

I needed to know if my own gun was still there.

When I reached the street, the cold returned with a vengeance. It was as if I hadn't gone inside to get warm at all.

A crime scene unit had the alley blocked off. Dane appeared to have left, and some unis guarded it all. They stared at me as if I were the bad guy. I pivoted, went the other way, and headed to my place.

At least the sleet had stopped, but the sidewalk was slippery. The restaurants along the way—this place was so gentrified now—were filled with well-dressed couples pretending to be happy. And maybe they were over their—what had Dane said? $300 meals? I preferred the take-out sushi eaten with custom-made chopsticks on a roof so cold it made this evening seem like the Bahamas in summer.

I still missed Ry, the bastard. I liked to think I had moved on, but I hadn't. Not inside. Not where it counted.

I took an elevator to my apartment, and let myself in. The apartment was warm, homey, perfect, just like it had been since I bought it. I closed the door and locked it, then checked the wards just in case.

They were fine.

I peeled off my gloves and tossed them on an occasional table. Then I went into my bedroom and opened the closet.

There, on the top shelf, was the Tiffany's box. I pulled it down, and gingerly untied the ribbon. I tugged the lid off and looked inside. The lockbox was still there. I opened it too, and stared at the gun, gleaming in the light.

It looked no different than it had every other time I had looked at it. It was a shame I had never used it, a shame that it hid here in the dark, as if it were at fault for Ry's death.

I ran my fingers across its cool surface. It glowed faintly, in recognition. I wished I knew how to use it. I wished Ry had told me where he had gotten it, why he had chosen a Tiffany's box to keep it in, what it all meant.

I closed the lockbox, then closed the Tiffany's box, and retied the ribbon, like I'd done dozens of times over the years. I put the gun on the top shelf of my closet, then closed that door. If only it were that easy to put the gun out of my mind as well.

Something had caused the second gun to come to me. Something had powered it. Something—or someone.

I wouldn't know what until I knew more about the guns themselves.

I grabbed my cell to call Dane. Then decided I wasn't going to speak to him on the phone.

I would go to him, wherever that was.

I took my gloves off the occasional table and let myself out of the apartment, using the edges of my magic to track Dane.

It wasn't hard.

He was at the precinct, at his desk—which, I was certain—was not where he wanted to be.

***

THE LIMESTONE FAÇADE of the three-story precinct building looked dirty against the sleet-shiny snow. Ry used to call it the Home of the Enemy, but he didn't really mean it. He was always mad at Dane for refusing to acknowledge the magic or the work Ry and I were doing.

The rivalry between them didn't mask the love they had for each other, though, and I knew Dane had been as torn up over Ry's death as I was.

I let myself inside, the smell of fear and sweat enveloping me. I took the steps up to the detective unit, and slipped inside.

Nighttime made little difference. There were always detectives poring over files, tapping on ancient computers, or talking tiredly into the phones.

Dane was sitting at his desk toward the back, hands pressed against his cheeks, staring down at some paperwork in front of him. His suit coat was hanging over the back of his chair, and his long dress coat was hanging on a peg on the wall.

I walked over to him and hovered, waiting for him to acknowledge me.

"At least fifteen different skin types," he said. "And they're just estimating. Who does that?"

He sounded tired. I guess the possibly special woman hadn't waited for him after all.

"Not who," I said. "*What* does that?"

"Yeah, some kinda animal," he said more to himself than to me. Because we both knew that he was deliberately misunderstanding me.

It was a good question, though. Demons shredded skin, but they used the unbelievable pain from the process to increase their own power. There were lots of creatures from all sides of the magical divide that consumed skin, mostly as food, and a handful that took the magic from tattoos.

But nothing native to New York. Because all of the native creatures destroyed the skin when they did what they did.

I knew of nothing that took tattoos like trophies.

"Was everything—" I couldn't bring myself to say skin fragments. "—tattooed?"

"Yeah," he said quietly. "Mean something to you?"

I shook my head, but he wasn't looking up. Maybe he took my silence as an acknowledgement.

"Do you know where Ry got the gun?" I asked.

Dane finally raised his head. He seemed to have aged years in the past few hours. He seemed surprised by the question.

"There were two," he said. "They belonged to my parents. I figured he had given one to you."

My cheeks heated. I had never told Dane about the gun. I hadn't told anyone.

Dane was frowning. "He was going to—you know—ask you to marry him. He was all goofy about it. He even found a Tiffany's box, because engagement rings come in Tiffany boxes. He thought you'd get it."

I thought we didn't believe in marriage. I thought marriage was so…middle class, so ostentatious.

I had missed the point.

Why me? I had asked Ry.

Because I love you, he had said, so sure, so certain.

And then, at my confusion, he had shrugged, said he was cold, and we'd better hurry. Still, we handfasted me to the gun. *My* gun. And his matched.

Like wedding rings.

Son of a bitch.

"Did your parents have wedding rings?" I asked.

"Oh, yeah," Dane said, "but my folks were pretty traditional. They wanted the guns to go to me and Ry, like we were supposed to split up the rings."

Dane leaned back, closed his eyes for a minute, shook his head, then added, "I was the only sane one. The only one who didn't see little sparklies in the universe or dark things crawling out of corners. My folks were so disappointed…"

Then he rocked forward and opened his eyes.

"I thought you knew," he said again, but I wasn't sure if he was talking about the guns or his parents or all of it.

I shrugged, pretending at a nonchalance I didn't feel. "What were the guns for?"

"Monster hunting," he said sarcastically.

I nodded, not going there.

"Thanks," I said, and threaded my way through the desks.

"Hey," he said. "You need help?"

Not your kind of help, I nearly said. Instead, I shook my head. "You guys are doing it all."

And as I walked out, I realized that was true. After I had come to my senses, I left the investigation in the hands of the police.

Even when I had known that whatever killed Ry hadn't been human—at least, by my definition. Maybe by Dane's.

But not by mine.

***

THE GUNS HAD HISTORY, and I needed to find it. I could look in moldy books or try to find something accurate online. Or I could ask the guns themselves.

I didn't want to ask the one with Ry's tattoo wrapped around its grip. I wasn't sure who or what would answer me.

And I didn't want to find out.

So I walked back to my apartment, and got my gun down a second time.

Everyone describes silver as cold, but it's not. Especially when it's been indoors, and the endless winter continued outside. The gun was warm against my hand, the silver never needing polish.

I wrapped my hand around it, saw—

Ry, grinning as he watched me open the box...

I made that image disappear, saw—

Something huge and scaly, looming over a pair of sleeping boys, then a bright white light zinging out of the muzzle, and the huge, scaly thing exploding into a thousand little pieces...

I shook my head, smiled a little, saw

—

Hands with two matching rings, clasped, each around the grip of a different gun. "With my heart, I hold you," a male voice so like Ry's said. "With my soul, I touch you..."

It was a handfasting ceremony, only of a kind I'd never heard of. With the guns in the middle.

Marriage, the old-fashioned way.

I rubbed my eyes with my thumb and forefinger. Then frowned, thought of an experiment, and decided to try it.

I set the gun on top of the box.

Then I went into my kitchen, and thought, *Join your handfast partner* at the gun itself.

After five minutes, it wobbled its way toward me, muzzle pointed at my heart, trembling like Ry's gun had.

Find your box, I thought, and the gun wobbled its way out the door. I followed it, as it returned to the very place it had started.

I picked the box up and wrapped my arms around it.

Anniversaries had power.

I had thought the gun came to me at the anniversary of Ry's death.

The gun had come to me at the anniversary of our love—the marriage he had tried to give me, ten long years ago.

***

WITH MY GUN in my shoulder holster, I went back to the office.

I doubted I would ever get warm, even though I was wearing my coat, thick gloves, and my hat. I was cradled in the heart of a long, cold winter, and I might as well embrace it.

Ry's gun was inside the safe, the remains of my favorite tattoo still attached to the grip.

First, I put my gun on the desk. Then, gingerly, I picked up Ry's.

He laughed.

I took my hand off the grip, shaking. Then touched it again.

I don't care how dark things get, he said. *We'll always have each other.*

As if he hadn't left. As if he were still here.

I set the guns beside each other, and they started to glow. If they were real guns—real as in the way Dane defined guns—I would be fleeing now, expecting some kind of weird explosion.

But I was curiously unafraid.

The guns glowed and locked to each other. The tattoo grew into an entire man.

Ryder.

See-through, but there.

"I missed you," he said.

I didn't care if he was real or not. "I missed you too."

"I wasn't sure you'd understand," he said. "We never finished the ceremony."

"I know," I said.

He nodded, reached toward me, his hand going through my face. I felt nothing, not even a rush of wind.

And oh, how I wanted to.

"What happened?" I asked, because I had to, because I had a sense time was short.

"Demons," he said, and his image flickered.

He glanced at the guns. The glow was fading.

"No," I said.

"I love you," he said.

"I love you too," I said. "Stay."

"I wish." His voice was faint. "Balance the scales…"

And then he was gone.

Again.

The son of a bitch.

***

I FELT IT—the batshit crazy. It was coming back, or maybe it had never left. I could go after everything, clean up everything, fight everything—and be consumed.

Or I could stand up.

Fight.

Figure it out.

The guns didn't glow any more. The tattoo was gone.

I touched Ry's gun. It was cool. So was mine.

Balance the scales.

Demons—and skin.

I let out a breath, grabbed both guns, and headed to the alley below.

***

NO CRIME SCENE TAPE. No footprints in the snow. No tire marks where the crime scene unit had parked their van.

The brick was back in place.

I walked to it, touched it, felt edges, still there. The hiding place, still there.

Son of a bitch.

"Finally," he said, his voice echoing between the buildings.

I turned. He looked bigger, eyes glowing ever so slightly red, Ry's face covering his imperfectly, five tattoos glowing on his scaly skin.

Saw—in my mind's eye—two boys, sleeping, a demon hovering over them,

exploding in the dark, and scales raining down—on the oldest boy, the one closest to the door.

"Your parents took your magic away from you," I said.

"They thought they could," Dane said, his voice deeper, more echoey. "They took the wrong magic."

They took the good magic, leaving the scales.

Balance them, Ry had told me.

"You killed him," I said.

Dane didn't answer me, but the tattoos glowed. The death hadn't been intentional. I knew that, or Dane wouldn't have crumbled like he had. They had had a fight—over the guns?

"What do the guns have to do with it?" I asked.

"One of them is mine," he said.

"Why didn't you take Ry's after he died?" I asked.

"I couldn't find it. But you found it. Thank you," he said. "Now, give it to me."

I had no other weapons. I hadn't expected to fight demons tonight. I wasn't really in the fighting and slaying business any more. Just the investigating, resolving business.

I pulled Ry's gun out of my pocket. My hand trembled as I gave the gun to Dane.

He took it, looking surprised at the ease.

"I never realized you were this logical," he said.

"You never knew me," I said. Which was fair: I never knew him either.

And I had dismissed Ry. Ry, who had called Dane "The Enemy" right from the start.

Dane grinned. "I like you, you know."

I nodded, as if I cared. He looked down at the gun, and weighed it in his hand, as if it were something precious.

Which it was.

Join your handfast partner, I whispered.

The gun in Dane's hand trembled. He held it tightly. The tattoos on him—Ry's remaining tattoos—glowed.

Then peeled off, one by one, each fastening itself around the gun.

For a moment, there were two men before me, one thinner, less substantial, the other glowing red, the gun between them.

My gun had found my hand as well—and I didn't remember grabbing it. Then I realized it had heard the same command, thought the command was its.

I knew what kind of bullets demons took, but I wasn't sure I wanted to shoot Dane—not with Ry fighting him for the gun.

They struggled, the ice melting beneath their feet, the heat of Dane's evil warming the entire alley. The gun remained between them and then—

Something popped as if a bubble had burst.

Ry staggered backwards, substantial, bleeding (bleeding!!!), and falling, holding his gun.

Dane, dripping scales, reached for the gun and without thinking, I imagined white light—bullets—heading toward him.

They did, shooting out of my gun and hitting his torso.

I reached down, grabbed Ry, pulled him backwards with me, away from the white-and-red glowing demon-man in the center of that alley. We made it behind a stupid snowplow-created pile of snow when Dane exploded, bits raining everywhere.

Except on us.

Balance the scales.

Not just the scales of justice. The scales of a demon, returning where they belonged.

I wrapped my arms around a bleeding, warm, *living* man.

"Ry," I said.

"Took you long enough," he muttered.

"You didn't explain—"

"No excuses," he said, and then he passed out.

***

I HAD NO STORY for the ambulance attendants. I had no story for the cops. I pled ignorance, lost memory, frostbite…I don't know. Those lies are gone, along with any trace of Dane.

Ry thinks Dane died that night ten years ago, and somehow his demon self managed to get to Ry, so that Ry's power would keep them alive.

But I think—the magic suggests it— that Dane died a lot longer ago than that. Maybe the night of the demon attack, the ones the gun stopped.

Because demons can create hallucinations, images, visions, like the crime scene. How easy for one boy to die and feed a dying demon, keeping it alive, just barely, waiting for the right opportunity to grow into something stronger.

From the moment I met him, Ry said he distrusted Dane. I thought that strange for brothers. But it wasn't. It was the man reacting to something he barely remembered from his own childhood.

Ry doesn't agree.

But it doesn't matter.

Because we've done purges. We've saged the entire alley. We've warded it and cleansed it. We invited old friends to do the same.

Dane's gone.

And Ry's here.

And it's no hallucination or vision.

The most romantic gift anyone's ever given me was a gun. And a handfast.

And a future.

Together.

At last.

SINS OF THE BLOOD

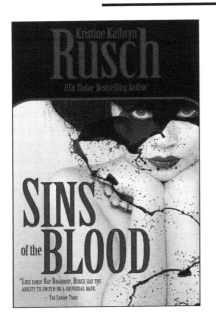

I first realized Robert T. Jeschonek existed when he sent me a story for Star Trek: Strange New Worlds *that I was editing. I read the story, put it down, couldn't believe I had read the thing, picked it up, read it again, then walked it from my office next door to our home and gave it to Kris to read. She couldn't believe it either. "Whatever You Do Don't Read This Story" was a* Star Trek *story where the story itself was the viewpoint character. And it worked. In a new writer contest.*

That story got second in the contest that year only because it would bother the main fans. But he came back the next year with a story that broke every rule of the contest and yet worked and he won the contest that year with a story "The Million Year Mission." From that point forward I have been a Robert T. Jeschonek major fan.

Since those early days, Bob has gone on to write a lot of novels, published his mind-bending short fiction everywhere, and even did some work for DC Comics. I hope to have lots of stories from Bob in upcoming issues because he writes "Pulphouse" stories at his very core.

A Little Song, A Little Dance, A Little Apocalypse Down Your Pants
Robert T. Jeschonek

I COME BACK FROM THE DEAD suddenly, the way I always do, with a great heaving gasp as air and light and consciousness rush into me all at once.

"Easy now, Jody Lee." Binky the Bring-Back Bot says the same thing every time he resurrects me, the same damn thing. "Slow, even breaths, dear. In through the nose, out through the mouth."

Meanwhile, I'm twisting and flopping around naked in what I call the Humpty-Dumptynator—a rectangular glass box half-full of slimy blue goo and squirming anti-maggots. (They *give* life instead of *feeding* on it.) No matter how many times I've been through this—and believe me, there've been *thousands*—I still wake up with the same shock and nausea, spazzing out like this is my first freaking life restoration.

While at the same time, I know I've gotta get over it but fast, as Binky reminds me.

"Snap out of it, honey." The silver-skinned bastard jabs my left bicep with a hypo needle in the tip of his index finger, shooting me full of something that takes the edge off. "Remember, you've got another show tonight." He shoots me with a pale green light from his right eye, which is also soothing. "You have to die again in *three hours* if you want to get *paid*."

***

ONCE I GET cleaned up, I go for a walk, trying to blow the stink off. My long black hair's tied in a ponytail, and I'm wearing a Selfie Suit, which looks like whatever I want depending on who's looking. A hot guy might see me in a little red dress, a not-so-hottie might see me in overalls...and I myself just see a casual black pantsuit.

I can't hold back a yawn as I walk through Tesseractus Prime 'cause it's just another pan-galactic mega-casino in just another multidimensional hotel-cathedral-singularity. It's the same old thing, the same old crowd, in the same old place.

And by that, I mean it's a looney tune wonderland to the zillionth power.

A unicorn centaur in a diaper gallops past, fleeing a flock of mocking blackbirds trying to bomb his horn with poop. A guy with an accordion-shaped body bounces by, burping filthy limericks every time his midsection crumples. A priest, a rabbi, and Hitler walk into the nearest bar, saying something about buying a dog a drink...and then they all turn into poodles.

Welcome to humanity circa 100,000 A.D., when science that might as well be magic makes all things possible. Everyone can be as wacky as they wanna be, in every imaginable way. The universe is one big joke...but nobody's laughing anymore.

And that's where *I* come in.

***

"I HAVE NEVER been more miserable in my life." Standing onstage in the massive theater at the hotel-casino-cathedral, I gaze out at the crowd arrayed before me. It's a panoply of every silly, crazy, bizarre, surreal, and just plain *insane* character you can imagine...and everyone's laughing their heads off (some *literally,* if the heads aren't attached very well). "I mean it. I wish I were dead."

For a long moment, the roar of laughter and applause drowns me out. I stand there and let it flow around me, watching as the horde of ridiculous figures howls in hilarity.

A glowing purple clown in the front row blasts a bicycle horn and stomps his huge red shoes (which are also laughing). Beside him, a gorilla in a pinstriped suit hops up and down, making with the monkey shrieks and whipping banana peels and poo at the stage.

In other words, I'm *killing*. Again. Because I'm the best. I know what makes 'em laugh.

When the roaring dies down, I start talking again. "Seriously, I'm at the end of my rope." That gets a few titters from the crowd. "The more you people laugh, the more I long for oblivion." Cue a slew of scattered guffaws.

Then, a thing that looks like a giant pretzel with eyes instead of grains of salt zips up to the stage and flies around me a dozen times, laughing like a maniac. The audience follows suit with a roar that sounds ten times louder than before.

"Enough of this mortal coil!" The spotlight follows me as I stomp across the stage toward a long table covered by a red velvet shroud. "It is time to end my suffering!"

Everyone cheers and claps and howls with laughter as I pull the shroud from the table, revealing a selection of swords and knives. People shout out suggestions; some even teleport up beside me to point at the weapon of their choice. I shoo them all away and pick up the samurai sword.

"This is the end for me." I kneel on the stage and hold the sword out away from me, pointing the tip at my belly. "I go now to the big comedy show in the sky."

Hands shaking, I falter, and the crowd urges me on. I continue to hesitate, building suspense; it's all part of the act.

"I have the courage to do it at last!" I nod forcefully. "Death, I fear not thy sting!"

Then, before I can slide the sword through my stomach, there's a deafening boom from somewhere off stage. A cannonball blows through my midriff from side to side, cutting a swath where the sword was supposed to cut.

The top half of my body plops down to close the gap. For a moment, as the crowd gives me a standing ovation, I kneel there, my top and bottom halves disconnected but adjacent.

Then, the top half drops over backward, and the darkness of death swirls over me. I feel my mind sliding into the abyss like leftovers sliding from a plate into a trash receptacle.

And then I'm gone, into the great and fathomless unknown. Just like I am every time I do this—two shows a day, six days a week, 52 weeks a year.

***

THREE AND A HALF hours later, I'm staring at a bowl of thin broth in one of the 100,001 ever-changing restaurants in Tesseractus Prime. The broth keeps telling me to eat it, *literally*—it's *conscious cuisine* with a mind of its own—but I can't force it down. Binky the Bring-Back Bot put me back together just fine

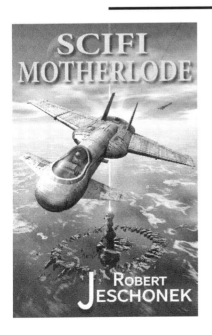

SCIFI MOTHERLODE

after the cannonball, but my stomach still remembers being blown apart just a little too well.

"Excuse me?" Just then, a horse's ass—an *actual* horse's ass, minus the horse—clops over to my table. "Have you seen a *setup* come this way? I seem to have lost mine."

Great, just what I need. Another lost punchline looking for the rest of his joke. "Can't help you, buddy." I stir my bowl of broth as if I'm actually going to eat it.

The broth gets all worked up and starts to yap. "Oh yes, oh *please* put me inside you, dear famous Jo Jawdropper! Eat me right *up*, you vixen!"

The tail on the horse's ass switches excitedly. I can see there's an eyeball staring back at me from its bunghole. "Ohmigod! I can't believe this! I'm talking to *Jo Jawdropper!*"

I never thought I could hate my stage name any more than I already do...but hearing it spoken in the squeaky whine of a horse's ass really does the trick. "Check, please!"

"No check yet!" screams the broth. "You've gotta *slurp me up* first!"

Just as I'm starting to freak out a little, someone clears his throat behind me. "Get lost, ass." His voice is as deep as the croak of a down-dirty drunk just before he turns himself sober so he can start drinking all over again. "*Amscray!*"

Turning, I'm surprised for two reasons: one, he's shorter than I imagined because of that voice, all of five-foot-five; and two, I recognize him, from his black leather jacket to his bald head to his bushy red mustache. I used to *work* with him, back in the day.

"Now git!" He stomps over and gives one of the horse's ass's butt cheeks a powerful slap. "Don't *make* me *kick* you!"

"*Kiss* my you-know-what," snaps the ass, and then he clops off through the restaurant.

"What an ass," says the guy. "Probably doesn't know *himself* from a *hole* in the ground."

"Well, well." I smile and hold out my hand. "If it isn't *The 'Stache*."

The 'Stache (that's his stage name; he never told me his real name) gives my hand a hearty shake. "Long time no smell, JoJo m'dear."

"Thanks for the save," I tell him. "I guess that makes you my hero." Impulsively, I pull him into a big, grateful hug. It's been *such* a lousy day.

Meanwhile, the broth keeps yapping. "Slurp me up! Put me inside you! *Lick my bowl clean!*"

"Shaddup," snaps The 'Stache. "Or else!"

"Or else what?" says the broth.

"You know the one about the fly in the soup?" says The 'Stache. "Well, I'm gonna *show* you the one about the *soup* that *flies*. Across the *room*."

With that, the broth finally shuts up.

***

THE 'STACHE and I catch up while taking a late night stroll on Schrödinger's Catwalk—a promenade that might or might not occupy infinite locations and realities at any given moment.

Fountains of rainbow light cascade all around us, casting colorful glows on our faces. Within the light, I glimpse an ever-changing parade of images, flickering movies of people and events from all eras and alternate worlds.

For an instant, I think I catch a glimpse of The 'Stache and me in the old days, working the comedy circuit together...

but then it's gone, or maybe it was never there at all.

"I was out of the biz for a while," says The 'Stache. "Didja know that?"

"You quit *show biz*? *For real?*"

He grins, flashing gold incisors through his overabundant mustache. "For *ten years* real, Double-J."

"What was it like?"

"Not being on the road all the time, you mean? Not struggling to squeeze laughs out of a bunch of humorless fruitcakes every day of my pathetic life?" The 'Stache looks ahead of us and chuckles. "Why don't we ask *him*?"

"Ask me what?" It's an alternate version of The 'Stache with zebra stripes and elephant ears, loping toward us—one of the side effects of Schrödinger's Catwalk. You never know when you're gonna cross paths with another you from a parallel universe.

"Hey! Did I miss show biz when I gave it up for ten years?" says The 'Stache I came in with.

"You gave it up for *ten years*?" Other 'Stache punches original 'Stache in the shoulder on his way past. "What a maroon!"

Original 'Stache laughs and jerks a thumb at his doppelgänger as he walks off and vanishes. "That guy is such a *prick*, isn't he?"

"You're back in the game, aren't you?" I ask him. "That's why you're here, right? You're doing standup again."

"Maybe I'm just here to see *you*," says The 'Stache.

"So what made you do it? What made you want to get back onstage after ten years away?"

"Because I'm gonna be the greatest comic who ever lived," says The 'Stache. "And I'm gonna make it happen in a one-

night-only performance, tomorrow night." He smiles and takes my hand. "You want in, JoJo? For old times' shake?"

"Sure." I say it with a smirk, waiting for the punchline. "How can I possibly say no?"

The 'Stache stops walking and faces me. "Dead serious here, partner. This ain't a *bit*."

"Izzat so?" Notice I haven't stopped smirking. "So how do you propose becoming the greatest ever in just one night?"

"I've done it before, haven't I?" The 'Stache winks and squeezes my hand.

"*Ten* years off the circuit is like a *hundred* years in *comedian time*." I pull my hand free and shake my head. "You're gonna have to sell your soul to Maxwell's Demon just to make a *comeback*, let alone become the *greatest*."

"Kiss my brain!" The 'Stache laughs and jabs a finger between his eyes.

"Huh?"

"Kiss it!" The 'Stache keeps jabbing. "Because it *knows*, darlin' JoJo. It has a *plan* that will set the worlds on *fire*."

Just then, someone taps me on the shoulder. Turning, I see an alternate me made of rippling green palm fronds. It hurts to look at her flashing gold bouffant hairdo, and she's chewing some kind of squealing gum or bite-sized creature, I can't see which.

"He's right, honey mustard," says Palm Frond Me. "Big Daddy here's got the goods."

"Hear that?" The 'Stache unveils his broadest grin yet. "If you can't trust your salad-based alternate self, who *can* you trust?"

I could say I don't want anything to do with Delusional Dudley Doofus here... but that would be a bald-assed lie. Truth

184

is, he's got me curious; *anything* to break the boredom of my daily lives and deaths.

Not to mention, he and I used to be a *thing* once upon a once-upon. Maybe that's in the back of my mind a little, too.

Also *other* places, like ten feet away, where alt versions of me and The 'Stache just appeared *in flagrante delicto.* In the middle of the act, in other words, and I don't mean comedy.

So what does *my* 'Stache do? Gives 'em a standing-O, of course. "Yeah! Wooo! Bravo!" He whistles and claps for all he's worth.

It's been sooo long since I did what *they're* doing, I applaud, too. My alt-self, who's on top, laughs and shoots me a big thumbs-up.

Good thing I'm not the type who might get a funny idea from seeing something like that.

***

SO LET'S JUST SAY I get a funny idea after all, and the rest is history. And by history, I mean super-nasty sex.

So *sue* me. It's the first time in I don't know *how* long (literally) that I've done anything other than eat, sleep, kill myself, or rise from the dead. Breaking out of a rut is a good thing (or is that rutting till you break?)

Don't bother me about guilt and regret. This isn't our first time at the rodeo. Forget about illusions, too.

Not that *all* the mystery is gone. There's still a burning question hanging over us.

"Got any coffee?"

Not *that* one, though it's the first thing I ask him in the morning.

"So what's this plan of yours?" *That's* the one.

"You mean the plan where I ravish you?" says The 'Stache as he tickles my tummy. "Check and double-check."

Did I just *giggle*? I *never* giggle. "The *other* plan."

"You mean the one with the fifty porcupines, the nudist camp, and the case of bubble gum?"

Did I just giggle again? "The one about becoming the greatest comic who ever lived."

"Oh, *that* one." The 'Stache rolls over and kisses me. "It's a secret."

"A secret?"

"But who knows?" The 'Stache shrugs. "Maybe we can scare up an exclusive preview if you can pencil me in this morning."

"Hey, wait!" I laugh as he makes a grab for me. "What're you doing?"

"Sorry." He doesn't stop. "*I* thought we meant *pencil* me *in...*"

***

"I KNOW, RIGHT?" The 'Stache gives my shoulders a squeeze. "Kinda small, isn't it?"

"Yeah." I'm standing on the field of Hypercube Center, the biggest sports stadium in all of Tesseractus Prime. It's breathtakingly vast, stretching off for miles in all directions. "A real intimate venue."

"My thoughts exactly." The 'Stache gives me a peck on the cheek and undrapes his arm from my shoulders. He walks a few steps away and lets loose a loud whoop that echoes through the stadium. "I want everyone to feel like I'm close enough to reach out and touch."

"Then mission accomplished." Part of me keeps thinking he's pulling my leg, even after I saw his name on the marquee out in front of the place. How he got booked in a venue this big after so long away from the biz beats the hell out of me.

"I'll be a hot ticket, with so few seats to fill," says The 'Stache. "What're we lookin' at? Five thousand, max?"

"If that," I say, though of course we both know it's more like five *million*. "Guaranteed sell-out, I'd say."

"No need to beef up *this* bill." The 'Stache grins. "Though I *might* make room for *you*, if you need the work."

"Lemme think about it."

"I can always use an opening act." He shrugs. "Just sayin'."

"Very generous of you. Thanks loads."

"Fair warning, though. This'll be old school all the way." The 'Stache turns and gazes across the miles-long field. "Just a spotlight, a glass of water, and a microphone." He spreads his arms wide and looks up into the distant heights. "Plus a ginormous mother-lovin' communications array beaming to the fringes of the known freakin' universe in every possible signal and frequency."

Shading my eyes against the glare of the stadium lights, I can just make it out—a spindly silver grid hovering high above, punctuated with upturned disks and spiny antennae. How I completely missed it until now, I don't know; maybe it's got one of those Inexhaustible Apathy Filters that dims external stimuli to the brain based on natural human aversions to Getting Involved.

Whatever the reason, one thing's clear. "That thing's *huge*."

"It's all customized." The 'Stache proudly plants his hands on his hips. "I designed it myself and personally supervised the construction."

"You did?"

"I'm a cosmological engineer, Double-J," says The 'Stache. "I didn't spend those ten years away from show biz just workin' on my memoirs and keepin' it real, y'know."

"But how'd you pay for it? How'd you get permission to install it here?" I sweep an arm around to take in the field and seats. "How'd you get booked here *at all*, for that matter?"

"I made boatloads of money in cosmo-engineering." The 'Stache grins and nods. "Big projects mean big bucks. I worked on everything from Starhenge to the Great Space Roller Coaster, with plenty of hyperdrive bypasses in between." He waves for me to join him. "With the cash I made from my work and investments, I just *bought* the damn stadium and booked myself! Then I gave myself permission to install the array."

I walk over to stand next to him, looking up at the sprawling grid in the sky. "So what's it for? Streaming a pay-per-view special to the cosmos? Beaming a feed to distant primitive cultures so they'll come to worship you as a god?"

"It's something bigger and better than you can imagine." He puts his arm around me again.

Looking down, I slide him a frown. "Seems like a lot of trouble to go to. What's the punchline?"

"Wait and see," says The 'Stache.

"C'mon, tell me."

He shakes his head. "A punchline ain't worth much without the element of surprise, is it?"

I pop an elbow in his side. "What if full disclosure is a condition of my being on the bill?"

"Then I guess you'll miss out on being a headliner at the event of the millennium." Why the bleep is he still grinning? "No skin off *my* chin, Gunga Din."

Is this the part where I'm supposed to sigh and give in? Because dammit, that's exactly what I do. My curiosity couldn't *be* more piqued; my gut instinct is kicking the crap out of all my intuitions, taking their lunch money, and spending it on magic beans.

And yes, *Mom*, my *heart* might have something to do with it, too.

"All right," I tell him. "Good thing I happen to have the day off."

***

THAT EVENING, Hypercube Center is filled to capacity and then some. Every seat in the stands is occupied, and every square inch of standing room on the field is packed. Even the sky is swimming with wall-to-wall spectators; everyone who can sprout wings or rotors or jets or antigravity nards is drifting overhead, angling for the best view in the house.

The only open space within that immensity is the stage itself. As The 'Stache promised, it's a bare bones affair, just a plain black square with a mike stand in the middle and a pitcher of ice water with two glasses on a skinny pedestal table nearby. Old school all the way.

Which begs the question: What's The 'Stache cookin' up? (And the corollary: What's he smokin'?) Without the ingredients of modern comedy—samurai swords, knives, guns, cannons, elaborate Rube Goldberg suicide machines—how the fun does he propose to get any laughs?

"Just go with it," he tells me when I ask him that very question. "Trust ol' Baba Looey here, he won't let you down."

I don't believe him for a second, but I feel better when he folds me in his arms for a pre-show hug. Even better when he stands on tiptoe to give me a long, loving kiss. Am I really that chickified that a little mush can drown out the voices of reason in my head?

Yes, apparently. The voices of reason are screaming for me to make like a banana and get the flock out of Dodge. But the next thing I know...

...I'm standing at the mike onstage, introducing The 'Stache.

Yay me, I get a standing-O all my own, just for being there. It takes a while for the applause to die down enough for me to be heard.

At which point, I put everything I have into singing The 'Stache's praises. I really pour it on, telling the crowd what a great comedian and unique talent he is—what an influence he's had on my career and those of so many others. I tell 'em how lucky they are that he's returned to the stage, what a privilege it is to be there to introduce him to the universe again. I tell 'em how great he is in bed, and how I'm probably mostly doing this because we're romantically involved, so don't blame me if he sucks, bites, and blows. (I skip that last part, but the mind readers out there might catch a whiff.)

Then I start applauding. "Ladies, gentlemen, invertebrates, intangibles, incomprehensibles, unmentionables, and all other lifeforms, artforms, and colorforms, I present to you the once and future comedy genius known far, wide, and in-between as *The 'Stache!*"

The crowd roars with deafening cheers and applause. I've done a great job warming them up; now it's up to him to close the deal.

The 'Stache bursts out from behind an Apathy Curtain that kept him invisible until now. Waving and grinning at the crowd like a beauty pageant contestant, he marches up and takes my place at the mike. Then he winks at me and gestures at a mark on the floor, a glowing red X ten feet behind the mike where he wants me to wait.

As I take my position and the crowd settles down, he starts talking.

"What is comedy?" That's how he starts. "It's what makes you laugh. And that changes through time as *humanity* changes."

The 'Stache spreads his arms wide to encompass the crowd around him—the millions of people who are listening in dumbstruck silence. He sounds more eloquent than usual, as if he's channeling his inner Einstein instead of his typical Wisenheimer. "Humans have evolved to a level where technology enables them to do so many things...things that would have been considered *magic* to their ancestors thousands—even *hundreds*—of years ago.

"And these human beings of today, so changed now from what they once were, have a very different definition of comedy. Since almost anything is possible to them, even commonplace...and every bizarre situation that might once have been the basis of a *joke* is now the basis of *reality*...they no longer laugh at what they once did."

At that moment, the crowd *shifts*. I can see and feel and hear it from the stage. The people in the stands and on the field and in the air have waited through what's amounted to a lecture so far, but they've passed the tipping point. It's just a matter of time until they turn ugly.

The question is, does The 'Stache know it's coming? And does he have something planned to head it off?

If he does, he gives no sign of it. "So what does it take to make humans laugh in this modern day and age?" He counts out the answers on the fingers of his right hand. "Cruelty. Shock. Atrocity.

"This is what their sense of humor has become. Laughing at someone mutilating or killing themselves." He shoots a glance in my direction.

Suddenly, a loud male heckler shouts from the audience. "What the Fermi are you *talkin'* about, 'they'?"

The 'Stache ignores the heckler and keeps talking. "But here's the irony...the *ultimate* irony, that *none* of them can see. In the course of their evolution to a *less* funny species, humans have stumbled upon the biggest *joke* of all time."

Again, the heckler calls out from the crowd. "What's with the 'them' and 'they'?"

A second heckler joins in. "*We're* human, and we're right *in front* of you."

The 'Stache ignores them. "It goes like this. It took billions of years for the universe to evolve...for the planet Earth to evolve in such a way that the conditions were optimal for sentient life to develop...and for that sentient life, *humanity*, to evolve to its current, highly advanced state. It has taken that long for human beings to reach a level of technological advancement that makes them masters of their own bodies and minds and the physical laws of the universe itself.

"Have they used this mastery to transcend their limitations and set out in search of greater knowledge? To probe the hidden mysteries of existence itself?"

Another heckler interrupts. "Why does he keep calling us 'they'?"

"What has humanity done?" continues The 'Stache. "They've used their *mastery* to turn themselves into a trillion variations on the same self-referential silliness...the same images of clowns and celebrities and fictional characters they've been recycling for the past ten millennia. They've got the power to become *gods*, and they're still pissing around in the same damn *kiddie pool*, laughing at the suffering of their fellow men and women.

"In this way, humanity itself has become the greatest *joke* in the history of the *universe!* The kind of joke that *my* audience will appreciate!*"

By now, the crowd is restless to the point of open rebellion. I smell danger in the air like smoke from a fire.

There's a murmur through the crowd, a susurration of thousands of disaffected voices...but the shout of the first heckler still manages to punch through above them all. "For the last time, why do you keep calling us 'they'? We *are* humanity. We *are* your audience."

A dark smile curls its way across The 'Stache's face. "What the eff gave you *that* idea?"

The murmur of the crowd drops away as all ears lock onto his next words.

"I'm not *talking* to *you* people." The 'Stache points upward. "I'm talking to *them*."

"The airbornes?" asks the heckler. "The flying-room-only people?"

"Not even close." The 'Stache raises his arms overhead and spreads them wide. "I *should've* said I'm talking to *it*. The *universe*."

Just then, I remember the communications array he installed above the stadium, the one that's "beaming to the fringes of the known freakin' universe in every possible signal and frequency." I figured it would be streaming his show to people on distant worlds and vessels...but maybe I was thinking too small.

"*That's* who this whole show was *meant* for," says The 'Stache. "*You people* are just here to prove my *point*."

"You're full'a *shazbot*," shouts the heckler. "The *universe* isn't sentient!"

"Sure it is!" says The 'Stache. "And I just told it the funniest joke it's ever heard!"

Suddenly, a deafening blast of thunder crashes through the stadium, and everyone falls silent. The airborne audience scatters like cockroaches from a kitchen light, and everyone in the stands and on the ground looks up.

"Hear that?" The 'Stache hikes a thumb toward the sky. "I'd say *somebody's* getting the joke!"

There's another blast of thunder, and another—each progressively louder than the one before. The stars in the sky dance and swirl like gold dust in a prospector's pan, flashing in unnatural rhythms.

Down below, the ground rumbles and shakes. That sets the earthbound crowd in motion, as everyone stampedes toward the exits. Millions of screams rise together, exploding through the miles-long/miles-wide stadium in a tsunami of cascading terror.

Not that The 'Stache looks the slightest bit worried. His face is calm as he turns and gestures for me to join him.

I wonder if I ought to be fleeing for the exits instead, but I run to his side anyway. "What's *happening*? What *is* this?"

The ground shakes harder than ever, and the thunderous blasts keep coming. Every light in the stadium blows out at the same time, showering the crowd with sizzling shards of glass.

The 'Stache wraps his arms around me. "I'm *killing*, that's what!" He grins up at the reeling stars in the sky. "They freakin' *love* me!"

The booming thunder becomes a continuous roar. The stars spin faster and faster, and the ground splits apart. Thousands of fleeing audience members tumble into the widening crevices.

The 'Stache tightens his grip on me. "Don't worry, Double-J!" He has to shout for me to hear him over the cacophony. "You and I have nothing to worry about! We'll be fine!"

A powerful wind rushes past us, a hurricane wind—only it's not trying to blow us away. It's *sucking* everything upward, pulling people and pieces of stadium into the sky with inexorable, furious force.

"How can you *say* that?" My voice is a terrified shriek.

"Because!" says The 'Stache. "I haven't done an *encore* yet!"

Just as he says it, the wind hauls us off our feet. We both go tumbling toward the stars, still locked in our embrace as if that will save us somehow.

***

AT SOME POINT after we leave the ground, I lose consciousness—which is probably a blessing, given the circumstances.

Then, I awaken in The 'Stache's arms. His eyes are locked on mine, and his smile is gentle.

"Hey there, sleepyhead." He kisses me softly on the cheek. "Rise and shine."

As awareness returns more fully, I realize our surroundings are calm. There seems to be no trace of the apocalyptic mayhem that engulfed Tesseractus Prime.

"Wait." I push away from him and look around. It's only then that I see where we are: in a transparent bubble, floating through uninterrupted white space.

"What is this?" My voice quivers when I say it.

The 'Stache runs his hand along the surface of the bubble, which flexes and stretches under his fingertips. "Nothing... yet."

I feel panic twisting inside me, straining to burst free. "What're you talking about? What just *happened*?"

"Pretty sure the *universe* just *laughed*," says The 'Stache.

"What do you *mean*, it *laughed*?"

"What do you think all the *noise* and *shaky-shaky* were about?" The 'Stache's eyes glitter as he grins.

Things still aren't making sense to me. The white space, the bubble...our *lives*, which somehow still exist. "But where *is* everything?"

"Out there somewhere." He waves dismissively at the milky void. "Compressed into a super-dense, super-heated ball of energy. The seed of a *new* universe, in other words."

"Wait, what?" Am I losing my mind here? Did he just tell me..."The universe *ended*?"

He waggles his hand and squints. "More like *reset*. It suddenly contracted..." He jams his hands together. "Now there's a *pause*, like a *breath*. And soon..." He makes a whooshing sound as he pulls his hands apart. "It'll *reboot*."

"Like a *big bang*, you mean?"

He touches the tip of his nose. "Exactamundo. There'll be a shiny new universe in place of the old one. Happens once every 14 billion years or so."

"And what about us?" When I press my hand against the bubble, it feels like a warm rubber balloon. "Why didn't *we* get mashed up with the rest of the old universe?"

"Funny you should ask." The 'Stache takes my hand. "It's been talking to me..."

"The universe."

"Yup. Apparently, it likes my work so much, it wants me to help set up the next version of itself. I mean the next *joke*."

My head is spinning. I'd think he's lost his mind if we weren't floating in a transparent bubble through some kind of white void after witnessing a cosmic apocalypse.

"So that's it then?" A hysterical giggle escapes my lips. "*Our* universe—the one we *knew*, our *home*—is just *gone?*"

"Gone forever." The 'Stache nods.

Again, a crazy giggle escapes me. "*Forever?* Everything we know is gone *forever?*"

"Yeah, and wouldn't ya know it?" The 'Stache laughs and shakes his head. "*Now* I'm hungry for *Chinese* all of a sudden!"

I think about it, chewing a fingernail. More giggles slip out.

"What is it?" asks The 'Stache. "What's so funny?"

I laugh a little harder now. "All those times I killed myself for comedy...and now here I am, a last survivor while everyone else is dead."

The 'Stache nods. "It's ironic, all right."

I keep laughing. "And you know what *really* cracks me up? I can't figure out whether the joke's on *them*, the people who are *gone*...or on *me*."

"Then everything's as it should be, Double-J. Remember the Groucho Marx Effect from physics: *A universe simple enough to be understood is too simple to produce a mind capable of understanding it.*

"Or as Groucho himself put it..." The 'Stache flicks an invisible cigar and waggles his eyebrows. "'I wouldn't want to belong to any club that would have me as a member!'"

Acknowledgements

Thank you to the following wonderful people who supported the 2017 Pulphouse Fiction Magazine Kickstarter Subscription Drive.

Steve Perry
Woelf Dietrich
Martin Greening
Nancy Sweetland
Paula Meengs
Tasha Turner
Dan 'Grimmund' Long
Linda Banche
Ken Hattaway
Justin Burnett
Andreas Flögel
Amadan
Jessica Doyle
B.J. Baye
John Devenny
Vera Soroka
Cathy Green
Willard A. Stone
Paul McNamee
Keith Garrett
Dayle Dermatis
Mark Kuhn
Ron Vitale
Diana Deverell
Sean Mead
Diane Sayer
Skevos Mavros
Jaq Greenspon
Simo Muinonen
Rick Lawler
C. Kirk
Blythe Ayne
Lillian Csernica
Sam Turner
Jeff Metzner
Joy Oestreicher
John Rogers
Richard Boulter
Tanith Korravai
Vito Michienzi
John M. Portley
Lauren Gemmell
Andy
Kev Partner
Angela Penrose
Geoff Palmer

Steve Jenkins
Christian Wood
Lynette Aspey
Denise Baker Gaskins
Amy Browning
Darragh Metzger
Wulf Moon
Lianne
Sharan Volin
Brian D Lambert
Marianne Villanueva
Linda Bruno
Tony Hernandez
John Ordover
Debb & O'Neil De Noux
Chuck Gatlin
Kate Pavelle
Chuck Emerson
Eric Kent Edstrom
Keith Beals
Risa Scranton
Kathryn Goldman
Walter Hawn
Lois Malby Olmstead
Mary Haldeman
Sam McDonald
Danny Evarts
Doug Red
Lisa Silverthorne
Caryl Giles
Darren Eggett
Erik T Johnson
Ann Kellett
D.V. Berkom
Nancy Johnson
Christina
Donald Mark
Anne J
Cassidy Percoco
Jason Zippay
Andrew Bain
Lee French
Richard Parks
M. Mahar
Jamie DeBree
A.J. Abrao

Valerie Brook
Michael A. Burstein
Mary Jo Rabe
Jim Gotaas
Anders M. Ytterdahl
Tony
David Macpherson
M. L. Buchman
Ryan M. Williams
Thomas Bull
Meyari McFarland
Maralee Nelder
Pierre L'Allier
AJ Lemke
Doug Houseman
C Kobayashi
Leah
John Lorentz & Ruth Sachter
Stephanie Lucas
Kristyn Willson
Piet Wenings
David Macfarlane
David Bruns
Rob Menaul
AnnieB
Katherine Crispin
Kai
Sara Litt
Kathryn Hodghead
Charles Pearson
Lisa Owen
Kate MacLeod
J Stuart Pratt
Greg Gorden
Robert Clemens
FredH
Gary Piserchio
Dawn Watson
Marnilo C
Terry gene, novelist
Rob Voss
Luigi Ballabio
Gregory Lovell
Allan Kaster
J.V. Ackermann
Rebecca M. Senese

Acknowledgements

Thank you to the following wonderful people who supported the 2017 Pulphouse Fiction Magazine Kickstarter Subscription Drive.

J.R. Murdock
Steven Rief
Bill
AM Scott
Brent Bissell
J & M Lowry
Rick Lohmeyer
James Husum
Debbie Nulf
A.R. Henle
John Haines
Kate Rooney
Jane Reeves Newell
Travis Heermann
Gregory Wade Stitz
Anonymous Reader
W.A. Brown
James Beach
Melissa H. Taylor
Joshua Maher
Sarah C
J. E. Hopkins
Gary Jonas
Marcelle Dubé
Joanna Penn
Rob Slater
David Hendrickson
kathryn mccloskey
Camille Lofters
Kenneth Norris
Stuart Jaffe
Len Chang
Anthony St. Clair
Marie Laura
Keith West
Stephen Couch
Catalyst Games
Joseph Wrzos
Lynda Foley
Steven H Silver
Bonnie S Warford
R.F. Kacy
Karen Shannon
Michael Harbour
Scott Tefoe
Christel Adina Loar

Christine Connell
John Winkelman
Leigh Saunders
donald crossman
Rob Vagle
Mark Leslie
Jeff Soesbe
Eugenia Parrish
Sean Roach
Justin Johnson
Robert McCarter
Lana Ayers
Werner Meyer
Ray Vukcevich
Christina York
Patrick
Damien Filer
Harvey Stanbrough
Paula Whitehouse
Annie Reed
Felicia Fredlund
coraa
Chris Abela
Sheila Watson
Chong Go Sunim
Laura Ware
Angie Simon
Linda
Linda Maye Adams
Carolyn Rowland
John Payne
Robert Battle
Lena Goldfinch
Kari Kilgore
Emily Williams
Matt Herron
Johnny Pedersen
Terry Mixon
Fran Friel
Todd Goetz
Al Harris
Joy Johnson
Bonnie Koenig
Lyndon Perry
Michael Nisivoccia
Michael La Ronn

Ashley Pollard
Steve R
Christine
Louisa Swann
Sharon Rowse
I.G. Frederick
Michael Kowal
Teri Babcock
Ken Talley
Jennifer Brinn
Mary Kennedy
Gerard Ackerman
Stefon Mears
Simon Horvat
Fred A. Aiken
Joshua Cooper
Andrew Hatchell
Sabrina Chase
Alexandra Brandt
Ranveig Wallace
Trent Walters
Daphne Riordan
Celine Malgen
Chrissy Wissler
Johanna Rothman
Danica Oakley
Amy Laurens
Mary Fishler-Fisk
Katrina Tipton
Mark Grant
Sharon Reamer
James Wisher
Christina Martin
Derek Miller
Michael and Nitu Gulati-Pauly
David Brown
Tracy May Adair
Turner L.
Lisa Satterlund
Sandra Hofsommer

Minions at Work 2.0 - "4th Wall Broken"
J. Steven York

Hi! Minion No. 1 here, taking a break from our busy shooting schedule here at Minions at Work Studios. I just wanted to give you a behind-the-scenes look at all the detail and hard work that goes into shooting these web-comics!

These comics are a real labor of love, done by one person, hand-crafted just for you, our audience!

That's one person and a lot of action figures, of course, of which I'm proud to be on---

Are you frickin' talking to yourself again?

Hey! I'm totally talking to my peeps here!

I'M your "peeps." You seeing lights again? Movie cameras?

Uh-- Yes.

You know how many times you've been hit on the head from behind and knocked unconscious, total?

4,237. That I can remember, anyway.

My frickin' point exactly!

I hope you know you're not frickin' real, right?

- END -

Printed in Great Britain
by Amazon

61470623R00111